Dear Mystery

As you know ... ... the mystery connoisse ... ...uzzlers. Amateur sleuths, private investigators, cozies, and police procedurals all have a home at DEAD LETTER.

An often-overlooked mystery genre is the historical, where the life and customs of previous centuries are detailed and examined through the eyes of an intrepid investigator. With *A Time for the Death of a King*, Ann Dukthas (a pen name for the critically acclaimed novelist P. C. Doherty) launches a truly unique historical series. Nicholas Segalla is a scholarly sleuth who travels back in time to investigate the great unsolved mysteries of history. In *A Time for the Death of a King*, Segalla unravels the four-century-old Mary Queen of Scots mystery. Was she a murderess?

Also be on the lookout for Dukthas's second Segalla mystery, *The Prince Lost to Time* in hardcover from St. Martin's Press in November 1995. In *The Prince...*, Segalla investigates the mysterious death of the son of Louis XVI and Marie Antoinette.

Keep your eye out for DEAD LETTER—and build yourself a library of paperback mysteries to die for.

Yours in crime,

Shawn Coyne
Senior Editor
St. Martin's DEAD LETTER Paperback Mysteries

Titles now available from St. Martin's
Dead Letter Mysteries

THE LADY CHAPEL by Candace M. Robb
THE BALLAD OF ROCKY RUIZ by Manuel Ramos
NINE LIVES TO MURDER by Marian Babson
THE BRIDLED GROOM by J. S. Borthwick
THE FAMOUS DAR MURDER MYSTERY
by Graham Landrum
COYOTE WIND by Peter Bowen
COLD LIGHT by John Harvey
NO ONE DIES IN BRANSON by Kathryn Buckstaff
THE SCOLD'S BRIDLE by Minette Walters
A TIME FOR THE DEATH OF A KING by Ann Dukthas

Upcoming Titles from St. Martin's
Dead Letter Mysteries

THE SEVENTH SACRAMENT by James Bradberry
THE MAIN LINE IS MURDER by Donna Huston Murray
KNOTS AND CROSSES by Ian Rankin
CUTTER by Laura Crum
MURDER IN THE EXECUTIVE MANSION by Elliot
Roosevelt
THE GOOD DAUGHTER by Wendi Lee
FALCONER'S CRUSADE by Ian Morson

On Sunday, 2 February 1567, as a heavy sea mist floated up the Firth of Forth, Mary, Queen of Scots, brought her husband, Henry Darnley, along the twisting paths to the Old Provost's House at Kirk o'Field outside Edinburgh. Staring up into the sky behind her, Mary shivered as she glimpsed the great black raven, its wings beating slowly against the breeze.

"That bird of ill omen," she whispered in French, "has followed us all day."

Although only in her twenty-fifth year, Mary was growing accustomed to looking into the darkness of the human heart, where grievances were nursed and murder was planned. To distract herself, the Queen began to hum the tune of a madrigal: above her, the raven, as if in answer, opened its yellow, cruel beak and cawed its baleful song.

A Time for the Death of a King

Ann Dukthas

St. Martin's Paperbacks

A TIME FOR THE DEATH OF A KING

Copyright © 1994 by Ann Dukthas.

Library of Congress Catalog Card Number: 94-32243

ISBN: 0-312-95613-4

Printed in the United States of America

St. Martin's Press hardcover edition/December 1994
St. Martin's Paperbacks edition/October 1995

10 9 8 7 6 5 4 3 2 1

*To Charles Spicer, senior editor at
St. Martin's Press, another ardent Marian.*

Historical Note

In 1567:

In France, Catherine de' Medici rules the kingdom: her first son, Francis II, has died and his beautiful wife, Mary, has returned to Scotland. Catherine watches Mary, seeing her as a pawn against either Elizabeth of England or Philip II of Spain. Catherine's advisers, the powerful Guise family, also hope Mary will remember that her mother, the wife of James V of Scotland, was a member of the Guise clan. Mary's real interests in France are handled by her aged and saintly envoy, Archbishop Beaton.

In Scotland, Mary is married to the dissolute Henry Darnley: they have a child, the baby James, and they have also faced a succession of crises culminating in Darnley's jealous murder of Mary's secretary, David Rizzio (1566). Mary, however, is keen to forgive and forget: she wishes Darnley to return to her so that she can better nurse him through the pox, which has nearly killed him. Mary also must watch the great nobles: the Lords of the Congregation, led by her illegitimate half brother, James Stuart, Earl of Moray, along with Douglas of Morton and Maitland of Lethington. Only the border lord, James Hepburn, Earl of Bothwell, can really be trusted.

In England, Elizabeth studies events in Scotland, aided by her three confidants: Robert Dudley, Earl of Leicester, William Cecil and Francis Walsingham. Elizabeth is fascinated by the crisis between Mary and Darnley: she recalls that she and

Dudley would have been married if his wife had not died in such mysterious circumstances some six years earlier at Cumnor Place. Walsingham, her master spy, also remembers this as he watches the crisis in Scotland. He broods and sends letters through Marshal Drury, governor of the English fortress of Berwick on the Scottish border; Walsingham's principal secret agent in Scotland, the Raven Master, is about to act . . .

Introduction: Dublin 1992

A nn was ill at ease as she took her seat in the elegant restaurant that stood in a side street off Merrion Square in Dublin: true, Dr. Nicholas Segalla acted the perfect host. He was, dressed in his dark blue woollen suit, the personification of courtesy and good taste. Ann noted that Segalla's shirt and tie were of pure silk and his cufflinks and matching tie pin looked to be solid gold. Segalla's hands were perfectly manicured, his sallow face closely shaved; not a hair on his head was out of place. Nevertheless, his stare unnerved her: his dark, seemingly soulless eyes studied her as she ordered her drink, even though he kept up a mundane, empty chatter, the news of the day: the busy roads, the traffic congestion in Dublin, the decor of the hotel. Only once did Ann catch something out of place. They were discussing Oxford when she was sure Segalla murmured, "Yes, yes, Oxford has changed since I was there last." This was followed by a lopsided smile, as if he were savouring a secret joke. By the end of the first course, Ann had had enough. She put down her spoon and dabbed at her lips with a napkin. "Dr. Segalla, why have you invited me here?"

"I thoroughly enjoyed your lecture at Oxford on Darnley's murder at Kirk o'Field."

"Are you a historian?" Ann asked.

Segalla pushed his own plate away.

"In a way, yes."

"You have been to Oxford before?" Ann insisted.

"Yes." Again the polite reply, though slower this time.

"And when were you there last?" she asked.

"Really there?"

Ann raised her eyebrows. "Yes, that's what I asked."

"Oh, in the winter of 1561, when Edmund Campion gave the oration at the funeral of Amy Robsart, wife of Robert Dudley, Earl of Leicester. She fell down the stairs at Cumnor Place and broke her neck." His words came out in a rush.

"You—you are joking!" she stammered.

"Oh, no, I'm not." Segalla indicated the gold chancery ring on his left hand. "I worked in the chancery of Archbishop Beaton in Paris. That's where I obtained this."

Ann kept her face impassive, yet she felt a tremor of fear and excitement. The circle of diners around her seemed to recede; the chatter of the waiters in the far corner and the soft melodies of the harpist faded like the sound of a radio being turned down. Here she was, sitting at a table with this enigmatic, beautifully dressed stranger who wore a chancery ring on his left hand and claimed to have been alive 430 years ago. She watched his eyes for some glimmer of amusement.

Segalla, however, gazed calmly back. Ann blinked, folded her napkin carefully and laid it on the table.

"Dr. Segalla, you are joking? You are teasing me?"

"No, I am not."

"Then, sir"—she pushed back her chair—"you must think I am witless."

Segalla smiled. "Witless, Ann? It's many years since someone used such a word."

Ann pushed her chair farther back and made to rise again. "Dr. Segalla, I thank you, but I really must go."

Segalla, the perfect gentleman, also got to his feet. "Miss Dukthas, please." He spread his hands. "I will not keep you long; then you can go. After all, I did send the car. I have ordered the meal. I mean you no harm and you are in no danger." He grasped Ann's wrist. "Ann, please, just a little of your time."

Ann nodded and sat down while Segalla tactfully shooed away the enquiring waiter.

"I was in Oxford in 1561," Segalla repeated. "But more, importantly, and of more interest to you, I was at Kirk o'Field in Edinburgh on tenth February 1567."

As Ann made to rise again, Segalla leaned across the table and grasped her fingers. His grip was firm but warm. Ann saw the pleading in his eyes.

"You are in no danger," he said again.

She stared coolly back and wondered whether he was telling the truth. On arriving at the restaurant she had glimpsed his eighteenth-century walking stick, and she knew enough about antiques to recognise the hidden sword.

"Dr. Segalla," she murmured. "I thank you for your hospitality." She took her hand away. "I do not believe you are mad, but if my fellow writers were here, or if I told them what you'd said, they'd either roar with laughter or send for a doctor."

"Being gon from the place where I had left my harte, it may be easily judged what my countenance was."

Ann stared open-mouthed. Segalla had just quoted, in sixteenth-century English, from the Second of the Casket Letters, those documents which, allegedly, proved that Mary Queen of Scots was an adulterous murderess.

"I am not," Segalla whispered, "what I appear. I cannot explain, but I will prove my claims."

Segalla didn't seem to relish Ann's astonishment. He put his hand in his jacket pocket, brought out a small bag of coins and spilled them on the table. The coins looked almost new, polished and glittering in the candlelight. Segalla simply pushed them towards her: a shilling from the reign of Edward III, a French écu, a Spanish doubloon.

"You could have bought those," Ann quietly commented.

"Yes, yes," Segalla said. "But I didn't buy this!"

3

He put his hand inside his jacket and drew out a transparent plastic wallet. He moved his wine glass away and held it up.

Ann stared at the drawing of a mermaid sitting on an oar, a crown on her wavy locks. "Where did you get that?" she exclaimed. "It looks original!"

"Oh, paintings like this appeared all over Edinburgh in February 1567," Segalla answered. "You know what it is?"

Ann leaned over and pointed at the mermaid. "In the seventeenth century the word 'mermaid' was the slang term for prostitute. The hare was part of James Hepburn, Earl of Bothwell's, coat of arms. After the murder of Darnley in February 1567, such placards appeared all over Edinburgh alleging that Mary and Bothwell had killed Darnley because of the Queen's infatuation with her rough border lord."

She almost snatched the plastic wallet from Segalla's hand.

"There are a few of these left, mostly in record offices in Scotland or England, but this is an original," he said.

She stared at the savage caricature of Queen Mary. The mermaid's features were quite clearly hers: a sensuous pose intended to whip up feelings of revulsion amongst the good burgesses of Edinburgh.

"It is genuine," she repeated.

"Oh yes," Segalla said. "Mary's enemies in Scotland could have taught our modern spy agencies many a trick when it comes to the destruction of their enemies."

Ann moved to give it back. Segalla shook his head.

"No, keep it." He smiled. "It's a present. Now, we have talked enough. Let us have dinner."

"No, no," Ann said, asserting herself. "What would happen, Dr. Segalla, if I reported this to a physician? Or raised it in a more public forum?"

"Then I would deny everything you have said and disappear," Segalla said. "You would lose the opportunity of a lifetime as well as cast doubt on your own judgement and scholarship. I am confident you won't."

"Why?"

"Because you are Ann Dukthas, writer and lecturer on historical mysteries. I know and respect your integrity."

"You were with Mary in Edinburgh, or so you claim?" Ann asked, incredulity in her voice. "Where else? Where do you come from? If you have such power, what is its source?"

"I cannot answer that, at least not yet; just trust me." He sipped from his wine glass. "Now." He leaned across the table. "You gave a splendid lecture at Oxford on the murder of Darnley, but it posed as many questions as it provided answers." He smiled. "Drink your wine, and please, give me a résumé of what you said."

Ann stared back. Should she go? she wondered. She had advertised for any historian in the United Kingdom and Eire who could throw light on the murder of Henry Darnley, husband of Mary Queen of Scots, at Kirk o'Field just outside Edinburgh early in the morning of Monday, 10 February 1567. Segalla was the only one to reply. He had not only rung her but booked this restaurant and ordered a car to collect her. She smiled to herself; the least she could do was be civil.

"At first the problem looked quite simple," Ann began. "We have the historical event, both its cause and effects, but when we study the mystery . . ." She shrugged. "To put it bluntly, no two historians can agree. Mary Queen of Scots," she continued, looking down at the table, "was born in 1542 and executed in 1587. Her father was James V of Scotland, her mother the French princess Mary of Guise. James was defeated at Solway Moss by Henry VIII's generals and died shortly afterwards. Henry wanted to marry his son, Edward, to the infant Mary, but the Scots wouldn't have this. During the regency of her mother, Mary was sent to France as the prospective bride of the Dauphin, Francis. She was raised at the French court under the guardianship of her mother's powerful relations, the Guises. In 1558, Mary married the Dauphin, who, a year later, became Francis II of France."

Ann tapped the table. "Consequently, by the time she was seventeen, Mary was Queen of France and Queen of Scotland, and in England, the Catholic faction regarded her as their rightful monarch, dismissing Elizabeth, daughter of Anne Boleyn, as illegitimate."

Segalla filled her glass and gestured to the waiters to serve the main course. "Continue."

"In December 1560, Mary of Guise, Regent of Scotland, died. Six months later Francis II perished of a rotting ear. The following year, the nineteen-year-old, widowed Mary returned to Scotland. She faced a country torn apart by the Reformation and had to confront opposition led by the Lords of the Congregation." She paused. "But you should know them."

Segalla grinned. "They were led by the Calvinist John Knox, a religious fanatic. He couldn't stand Catholics and he couldn't tolerate women."

"I have met a few Knoxes in my life," Ann said. "And the rest?"

"Three main luminaries," Segalla said. "James Stuart, Earl of Moray, Mary's illegitimate half brother, a real snake in the grass. George Douglas, Earl of Morton. You'll find many Mortons in the files of Amnesty International. Cruel and vindictive, Morton liked hanging women, even as they carried their babes in their arms."

"And?"

"Maitland of Lethington: cunning, the sort of man who wouldn't recognise the truth if it jumped up and bit him on the nose."

Ann felt herself relaxing as she did in debating any great historical mystery, especially this one. She always felt a kinship with this long-dead queen. Mary had returned from the luxury of the French court to face an array of men who made modern gangsters look like babies gurgling in their cradles.

"But Mary held her own?" she said.

"Oh yes, she was brilliant," Segalla said warmly. "She danced rings round them until her one fatal mistake."

"Henry Stuart, Lord Darnley?"

"Precisely. A grandson of Henry VIII, Darnley also had a claim to the English crown. He was tall, brilliantly good-looking, sophisticated, a drunkard, weak-willed and vicious to boot." Segalla studied Ann. "Do continue," he said.

"Darnley was an empty vessel," Ann said. "To be sure, Mary did her best, but Darnley displayed a streak of vicious paranoia. Mary had become pregnant early in her marriage, and when she realized what kind of man her husband was, began to rely heavily on an Italian, David Rizzio, her secretary. In 1566, Henry Darnley sided with the great nobles, and Rizzio was hacked to death in Mary's presence at Holyrood Palace. The rebels fled. Mary kept her nerve and her head. Eventually the Lords were pardoned, including Darnley, who had fallen ill of either smallpox or syphilis, I'm not too sure which."

"Possibly both," Segalla muttered.

"Whatever. Mary attempted a reconciliation. She went to Glasgow and brought the sickly Darnley to recuperate at a house on the outskirts of Edinburgh called Kirk o'Field. They arrived there on first February, 1567. Mary stayed with Darnley, sometimes sleeping in a chamber beneath his: on Sunday, ninth February, she returned to a masque at Holyrood Palace, then retired to bed. There, at two in the morning of Monday, tenth February, a massive explosion, sounding like thirty cannon firing, woke the city. Kirk o'Field had been blown up, and in an orchard forty yards from the house, they found Darnley's corpse and that of his squire, Taylor, with no marks or bruises." Ann sipped her wine. "From this mystery flowed a broad river of tragedy. Mary was blamed for the murder. She allied herself to a powerful nobleman, a born rogue, James Hepburn, Earl of Bothwell, who was accused as her accomplice. Mary was hounded out of Edinburgh. The Lords

7

of the Congregation, led by her half brother, Moray, rebelled. Mary fled to England, where she was kept a prisoner for nineteen years until her execution at Fortheringay Castle."

"You have seen this?" Segalla handed her a photocopy of a drawing Ann recognised as being kept in the Public Record Office in Chancery Lane, London. She nodded and placed it on the table before her.

"Yes," she whispered. "But that tells us nothing."

"If you study it carefully," Segalla said, "it will tell the truth."

Ann shook her head. "Nothing makes sense. Darnley was left at Kirk o'Field with five or six servants. Two, Nelson and Symonds, scrambled out of the ruins; the rest were killed." She drummed her fingers on the table. "I can't understand it. How was Darnley taken out into the open? Why kill him there and then blow the house up?"

"Perhaps he panicked?" Segalla asked teasingly.

"But the other servants who were with him slept on. Why didn't Darnley try and save them? And how can you kill someone without leaving a mark on his corpse?"

"Where was Bothwell?" Segalla asked.

"At Holyrood."

"And the Great Lords?"

"Moray was in Fife, Morton miles away at St. Andrews, as was Lethington. The real problem," Ann continued, "is that we have a great deal of evidence that puts the blame squarely on Mary and Bothwell. The only drawback is, all this evidence was wrung from tortured men who were later hanged for being involved in Darnley's assassination." She grinned wryly. "The murder at Kirk o'Field is not just a mystery but one which people have deliberately gone out of their way to create by fabricating an entire corpus of evidence: confessions, letters, documents. Perhaps some mysteries should remain so and this is one."

Segalla pointed to the photocopy lying on the table. "Believe me," he said, "that's the only piece of the truth you have."

Ann looked down at the detailed sketch, supposedly the work of an English agent in Edinburgh. It had apparently been drawn on the morning of tenth February and depicted the ruins of Kirk o'Field after the explosion. On the left, the Old Provost's House where Darnley had been sleeping was a pile of ruins, as Mary herself had written to Archbishop Beaton in Paris. "Not one stone left upon the other." On the other side of the page was an orchard: here the artist had sketched the bodies of Darnley and his squire Taylor, still dressed in their night robes, lying beneath the trees. Beside them was a chair, a furred robe, a dagger and what looked like a pile of rope.

"It tells us what happened," Ann said. "But not how."

"I once thought that," Segalla said. "And how wrong I was."

Ann became so discomfited at Segalla's cool stare that she continued with her meal, eating quickly without thinking. Yet she felt so excited, she had lost all appetite. She put down her knife and fork.

"I feel rather silly." She laughed. "Like a schoolgirl babbling."

Segalla shook his head and gestured at her plate.

'No, no," Ann said. "I have eaten enough. I really feel I must go." She played with a napkin to hide her confusion. "Dr. Segalla, you have posed me a mystery yet done little to solve the one I am studying."

Segalla sat back in his chair. "Far from it, Ann. I admired your lecture. You set forth Darnley's murder, then and now, in a correct and truthful way. You make no attempt to fashion bricks out of straw."

"In other words, I confessed to meeting a brick wall."

"Yes, you did, and that's a good place to begin. Every book written on Darnley's murder claims to have a solution. Yet every book overlooks those facts which mitigate against its conclusion. You're different. You give a lucid account of the problem and go no further." He threw his napkin on the table. "Now you are sitting here wondering if you are having a meal with a madman, and for that I don't blame you. Do you want coffee?"

Ann shook her head, aware that this mysterious stranger was about to show his hand.

"I will let you go." Segalla smiled. "But tomorrow morning at ten o'clock, two packages will arrive at your house by special courier." He tossed a card on the table. "When they do, ring that number. I want you to study the contents of both these packages. The first will contain some pictures, the second the manuscript of a novel. If you wish, you may destroy both and regard this meeting as a terrible mistake. I leave it to you."

"So you trust me?"

Segalla grinned. "Without reservation."

A short while later Ann, still in a daze, left the restaurant and caught a cab back to her flat. She tried not to reflect on her meeting with Segalla and spent the rest of the evening reading a biography of Lord Bothwell to keep herself distracted. She slept fitfully that night but the next morning found it difficult to control her excitement as ten o'clock approached. True to his word, Segalla's courier arrived. Inside the parcel, Ann found two manila envelopes, both sealed with red wax bearing the imprint of Segalla's ring. She was tempted to tear both open and examine the contents, but now that the parcels had arrived, she was determined to keep to her agreement. She took the card Segalla had given her, rang the number and found it was one of Dublin's principal hotels. The receptionist put her through to Segalla's room: at the end of the telephone his voice sounded soft and warm.

"The—the packages have arrived," Ann stammered.

"Good," Segalla said. "Now, open the less bulky one."

Ann obeyed and shook the contents out onto the table.

"They are picture postcards," Segalla explained. "There's a number on the back; please place them in numerical order."

Ann, feeling as if she were playing some strange, sophisticated game, obeyed. "They are all copies of famous paintings," she said.

"There should be seven in all," Segalla said. "Describe them to me."

"The first is a fifteenth-century painting of a group of singers. The second is a painting by Titian entitled *The Young Englishman*. Next comes Holbein the Younger's *Portrait of Thomas More and His Family:* Boulet's portrait of *Two Lovers*. Rembrandt's *Members of the Clothmaker's Guild*. A copy of Renoir's *A Box at the Opera* and, finally, a photograph of Lenin and his staff taken in October 1918."

Segalla must have heard her puzzlement.

"You have a magnifying glass?" he asked.

Ann said she had and went and fetched it.

"Now," Segalla said urgently. "Take each one in turn."

Ann obeyed. At first she couldn't believe it. "Oh Lord, save us!"

"What's the matter, Miss Dukthas?" the voice on the telephone whispered.

"There's the same man in each painting," she exclaimed. "It is you! Oh, the hairstyle's changed. In one painting you have a beard, in another you are clean-shaven." She had to steady herself against the table. "Why?" she breathed. "Why have you told me this?"

"I like you, Ann," Segalla said. "You are a searcher for the truth and . . ."

"And what?"

"You remind me of someone I once knew. Ah well." Segalla's voice became brisk. "So, are you going to ring your doctor friend? Your newspaper?"

"No."

"Of course not," Segalla said. "Then open the second envelope. Read the manuscript. Find the truth. We shall meet again." And he hung up.

———————

Prologue

Murder's red masque was about to unfold: it had been prophesied by omens and signs that had spread through Scotland like a ghostly mist. The prophets and seers reported these portents, birds dashed to the ground: storms erupted and heavy winds ripped down the spires and turrets of churches. Two moons shone. Three suns appeared. A long line of living dead, so one visionary reported, had been seen pouring along the high road, their faces livid and dark, their eyes like withered flowers. At night the fields around Kirk o'Field outside Edinburgh glistened in the moonlight as if covered in blood. At midnight, so it was said, innumerable regiments of devils and hordes of dark demons swarmed above Holyrood Palace, their wings outspread. The walls of Kirk o'Field, that quadrangle of buildings which lay to the south of Cowgate outside Edinburgh, were bathed in a ghostly winter light. Inside, the servants of the Crown prepared for the arrival of their King and Queen. They, too, had heard the rumours. Murder was prophesied and evil was about to take place. Had not John Irvinge of Livingstone on his deathbed suddenly risen, long-faced, stark with terror, one bony finger pointed to the cobwebbed rafters?

"The King is about to die!" Irvinge had screeched. "The King is about to die!"—before falling back unconscious.

In the January of 1567, Murder was becoming a common visitor to Scotland's harsh, wild land, where people lived close to the earth and the beasts that fed upon it. The common people believed in the magical influence of the sun and plan-

13

ets, in the magic of their pagan past, in devilish imps and monsters as well as the crucifixion of their Saviour. A wild, savage country where war often blazed from sea to sea and the gold-red bracken was littered with the rotting dead. Now winter had come to Scotland. A harsh coldness, more of the spirit than the body. It turned the russet heather to a black, soggy mess and touched the evil humours of the human soul.

The paltry roads and common trackways of Scotland had become mud-clogged, but they were still busy. Dark-cowled riders galloped under a stark, cold moon, taking messages hither and thither, for complex designs were plotted. Mary, Queen of Scotland, she of the auburn hair, golden complexion and dazzling eyes, with her French ruffs and lace-fringed skirts, was attempting to make peace with her estranged husband, Henry Darnley. He had hidden his putrefaction behind the walls of Glasgow Palace; some said it was the smallpox, others that Darnley had syphilis. Whatever the physicians muttered, Darnley was truly rotting: his lustrous hair had fallen out, his beautiful woman's face was covered in black, erupting pimples, while his body sweated evil vapours. Nevertheless, Mary, daughter of James V, by the Grace of God Queen of Scotland and, some whispered, of England, wanted peace with her once handsome husband, Darnley. Some said she was only being cunning. Did she not hide her Catholic faith beneath a pretence as she tried to make peace with the Lords of the Congregation, those zealots of reform led by her bastard half brother, James Stuart, Earl of Moray, and that viper in the grass Maitland of Lethington?

The crones whispered how Scotland had never been at peace. James IV, Mary's grandfather, and all the flower of the field, his earls and barons, had been swept aside fifty years earlier at the great disaster of Flodden. Twenty or so years later, James V, Mary's father, was defeated by his own uncle, King Henry VIII of England's general, the Earl of Hertford: James had slunk away to his castle by the sea. When he had heard that his wife, Mary of Guise, had given birth to a daughter, the King had whispered about the founding and ending of his own Stuart dynasty.

"It began with a lass, aye, and it will end with a lass!"

And, turning his face to the wall James had died of a broken heart. Was this prophecy, the ancient ones whispered, about to be fulfilled? Mary had come back from France when her first husband, the youthful Francis II, had died of a suppurating ear. Mary, eager for a new husband, had wrapped her arms around young Darnley, sent for her delectation by her cousin, Elizabeth of England. Yet this marriage, which many thought had been planned in heaven, turned to a hatred forged in hell. Darnley, dissolute, disenchanted and eager for power, had made Mary pregnant and immediately plotted against her. Henry Lennox Darnley, King of Scotland, the "tall boy," long-legged, with as pretty a face as the most beautiful woman, fell victim himself to jealousy.

On Saturday, 9 March 1566, Mary held a small supper party in her own apartments in the Palace of Holyrood. Darnley, she thought, was sulking elsewhere. Beside the Queen was her favourite secretary, the man Darnley envied, the Italian David Rizzio, in his nightgown of damask over a satin doublet and hose of russet velvet. Suddenly Darnley appeared in the room, fresh from some harlot's bed, his voice thick, his face flushed with drink. He glared in hatred at his rival Rizzio as others came up the stairs behind him. Lord Patrick Ruthven, a reputed warlock, was dressed in armour with a steel cap on his head, eyes burning in a pallid face. Hell already had Ruthven in its grasp: he was a dying man and the only breeze that fanned his flame of life was an unabiding hatred for David Rizzio.

"Let it please Your Majesty," Ruthven screeched. "That yonder man Davy come forth from your privy chamber where he has been too overlong!"

Mary resisted, but Ruthven and others, Darnley amongst

them, pushed into the room. Rizzio began to scream. He clutched the Queen's skirts, yelling for justice and for the Queen to save him. Mary did her best, but her belly was big with child, and Ruthven and the others threatened her with dagger and pistol. Rizzio was not so fortunate. He was hacked with fifty wounds. His blood-streaming corpse, dragged from the chamber, was thrown downstairs like meat from a butcher's slab, cut and slashed into collops.

Rizzio died, but Mary fled. She fell ill. She gave birth to a boy, James, and thrust the child into the arms of her estranged husband. Then Mary plotted. The murderers of Rizzio had to flee as Mary fell ill again. The Angel of Death almost wrapped his feathery wings round her, but Mary recovered and all Scotland held its breath. Would the Queen go to war? Mary schemed, as did Elizabeth of England with black-haired, black-hearted Francis of Walsingham in their privy chambers at Whitehall. The French, too, watched: sharp-faced, Catherine de' Medici, ruler of France, sat in her chamber at Blois and questioned her astrologers as to what Mary might do.

In the end Mary surprised them all. She showed mercy to Rizzio's murderers, and when her husband fell ill, the fruits of some fetid coupling, the Queen travelled across Scotland to meet him. She sent her estranged husband fair messages. She coaxed and teased him; Darnley responded, and Scotland sighed with relief. The Queen was being merciful: no eye for an eye, or tooth for a tooth. Mary hired Darnley the softest horse-drawn litter to carry him from Glasgow to the Old Provost's House near the ruined Kirk of St. Mary's in the Fields outside Edinburgh. He was to be fed the best food and physic. She also promised that as soon as the contagion passed, they would once again be husband and wife, King and Queen.

On Sunday, 2 February 1567, as a heavy sea mist floated up the Firth of Forth, Mary, Queen of Scots, brought her husband, Henry Darnley along the twisting paths to the Old

Provost's House at Kirk o'Field outside Edinburgh. Despite the chilling breeze, the procession was a glorious one. Darnley, wrapped in furs, lay in an oak-carved litter slung on the broad backs of the brown-berried palfreys specially hired for the occasion. Scotland's King-Consort was only too glad to hide his rotting face behind the litter's gold-fringed purple curtains. He found it hard to bear the laughter and cries of the Queen and her court, which rose above the clop of hooves and the jingling harness of the horses.

Two royal heralds, dressed in their brilliant tabards, preceded the procession. Behind them and out along the flanks of the royal column were the heavily armed mosstroopers, retainers of the Earl of Bothwell, brought in to reinforce the company of royal archers under their captain, John Stewart of Traquair. Mary herself rode alongside the litter, her auburn hair hidden beneath a jaunty cap adorned with a swan's feather. Sitting on her silver-grey mare with its polished harness, and dressed in a dark blue riding dress and matching cloak fringed at the hem and pockets with gold lace, Mary looked like some fairy princess moving back to her magical castle. Now and again, the Queen would draw in the reins and look down at the litter before going back to converse with her Great Lords, particularly James Hepburn, Earl of Bothwell, his face hard and grim under a velvet bonnet. Beside him, the Earl of Moray was still rather taciturn, for he was only freshly returned to the Queen's favour and grace. On the other side of the litter walked Darnley's personal servants, his faithful squire Taylor and the softly spoken Thomas Nelson, who carried wineskin and goblet, ever ready to slake his master's raging thirst.

A joyous procession, but Mary broke off her conversation with Bothwell and, staring up into the sky behind her, shivered as she glimpsed the great black raven, its wings beating slowly against the breeze.

"That bird of ill omen," she whispered in French, "has followed us all the day."

She forced a smile and went back to her conversation. She caught the eye of her half brother and, once again, wondered whether all would be well or shadows from the past would swoop down upon her. Although only in her twenty-fifth year, Mary was growing accustomed to looking into the darkness of the human heart, where grievances were nursed and murder was planned. To distract herself, the Queen began to hum the tune of a madrigal: above her, the raven, as if in answer, opened its yellow, cruel beak and cawed its baleful song.

Chapter 1

Nicholas Segalla, priest of the Society of Jesus, spent, as he always did, the vigil of his birthday praying in the Lady Chapel of the Church of St. Denis on the outskirts of Paris. He knelt at his prie-dieu and stared up at the marble face of the Virgin, illuminated by a corona of light from the iron ring of candles below her. Segalla crossed himself, sat back in his chair and stared across the gloomy sanctuary. He had just celebrated evening Mass. The citizens, merchants and burgesses of Paris, those who bothered to attend, had now left to hurry along the narrow, smelly alleyways to the safety of their own homes. The door at the back of the church had been left open to the cold night air. Segalla caught the faint sounds of the city's hostelries and taverns. He shivered and crossed himself again. A man of the open countryside, Segalla had, despite his studies at the Sorbonne, never really felt at home in Paris. Sometimes at night, just before he fell asleep in his little chamber high in the Louvre Palace, Segalla would daydream about the green fields, lush, dark copses and bubbling streams of his ancient birthplace.

A woman's scream made him flinch, and he recalled the stories of a garrulous inquisitor. How, in the suburbs of Paris, the power of the Dark Seigneur reigned supreme: about warlocks who could summon up crowned demons astride blood-red crocodiles. These same magicians, so Segalla had been told, dug up corpses and fashioned concoctions, brewed in human skulls, boiling worms mixed with dead men's flesh. And how, in a secret vault, somewhere beneath Paris, a sinister Magus lay buried in a seven-sided vault lit with lamps that would never be extinguished until Satan, the Great Beast, returned. Segalla's sombre face broke into a smile and he scratched his head with its close-cropped hair. His superiors in the Jesuit order were forever warning him against his vivid imagination. Segalla often wondered who was responsible for this. His father? That blunt, rather grumpy veteran soldier? Or his sylphlike mother? Segalla recalled her: dark eyes in a white face framed by flowing black hair. She would, so long ago, sit by his bed when he was a child and whisper stories about the fairies and demons of the woods. Segalla looked up at the statue and grinned.

"It was Mother's fault," he whispered. "Oh Lord, she was a great storyteller!"

He blinked and stared into the candle flame. His mother was gone, dead so long ago, following her husband into the cold, hard soil beneath the ancient stones. Segalla, a man of mystery, had then drifted through the years like a will-o-the-wisp: secretarius to this great merchant, clerk to that noble lord. Yet the passage of the centuries had worked their influence. Segalla could find no satisfaction in the reformed faith of England. The Catholic influences of his long sojourn were ever with him, so he fled abroad, first to the English seminary at Douai, then on to the Jesuit College in Rome. Now he was a priest of the Roman Church, a member of the hated Jesuit order. If he returned to England, he'd find nothing except the hunt, cruel capture and a dreadful death on the end of a noose at Tyburn. Segalla had volunteered to return, but his Jesuit masters shook their heads: those sombre-visaged men had sent him to be clerk and chaplain to the Scottish envoy in Paris, Archbishop James Beaton. So, instead of moving in disguise amongst the Catholics of England, Segalla lived amongst the great nobles of France; those popinjays, dressed in their yards of shot red and yellow taffeta, gold damask suits, jerkins edged with silver and white Florentine serge stockings. At Beaton's insistence Segalla took on yet another guise to blend in with this background. At times he'd wear a bonnet of silver thread and black silk, an ermine-edged gown and silver-fringed gloves of dog- and deerskin. He'd learnt to dance in rooms lit by crystal mirrors where the walls were draped with thick silk tapestries. Or discuss politics in opulent chambers where brass chests stood half open, stuffed with pearls, rings and precious coins.

Segalla sighed noisily and moved in his chair: Archbishop Beaton, despite his long, saintly face, rheumy eyes and flowing beard, was a man who combined the cunning of the serpent with the innocence of the dove. Segalla had served him three years, and Beaton was always reminding him:

"Don't dress like a crow, Nicholas! Dress in finery and fripperies like the rest. Move amongst the French court. You know English, French, Spanish, Italian and Latin. You can listen to what people say."

"And be your spy, my lord?"

Beaton had scratched his bald pate and stared at Segalla from under lowering brows. "A spy, Nicholas? Why, sir, you are a Jesuit priest. You have taken an oath of allegiance to the Church, to serve it with all your strength, with all your mind, all your heart and all your soul. Write my letters, say your Masses, pray your rosary, but be my eyes and ears at the French court. See which way the river flows. What rumours hang in the breeze." Beaton's face had become sober. "I am Mary of Scotland's Ambassador in France. She is a fawn surrounded by wolves. Whatever her religion, I have sworn to protect her interests, and you, as my chaplain, are duty bound by God and your superiors to protect mine."

Back in the present, Segalla stirred as he caught a fragrant perfume. He whirled. A woman, cowled and hooded, stood silently behind him. Segalla rose quickly to his feet.

"Madame, I did not hear you. You wish to pray?"

A musical laugh answered his question. "I do not wish to

pray, Father Segalla," the woman replied in a lilting English accent. "But I do wish to see you!" An elegant hand appeared from the voluminous sleeve of her gown and pulled the hood back.

Segalla nervously folded his arms and controlled the panic surging within him. Paris was full of potential assailants: perhaps some nobleman resented his gadding about the court on Beaton's business. The woman walked closer, into the pool of candlelight, and Segalla relaxed. She moved easily, softly, and her face was both frank and tender. Segalla tried to speak, but he felt tongue-tied as he always did, slightly embarrassed and shy in the presence of an attractive woman. And the stranger, despite her sudden appearance and mysterious ways, was striking: soft, auburn hair, petite face, not beautiful in the classic sense like the old King's mistress, Diane de Poitiers, or other beauties of the court. She was small, round-faced with a retroussé nose, a laughing mouth and merry eyes beneath finely drawn brows.

"Madame, you—you know me?" he stammered.

"Madame certainly does," she said. "You are Father Nicholas Segalla, of indeterminate extraction: a member of the Jesuit order, chaplain to Archbishop Beaton as well as his clerk and secretarius. Now you are dressed in the dark robes of your order, but tomorrow you may be at court, floating in gaudy clothes like the other butterflies." She cocked her head. "You are quiet and studious, with an interest in clocks which only bores someone like me, but"—she laughed—"they say you are English and so must be eccentric." She leaned forward and touched the rosary wrapped round Segalla's fingers. "Though you'd best not return to England. Walsingham's spies might trap you, and Master Topcliffe, the Queen's torturer, would, with fire and iron, subject you to the most cruel torments."

"You know a great deal about me, Madame."

"Of course." She laughed again. "I am to be your wife!"

"Who are you?" Segalla snapped. "Is this some form of prank? Some courtier's joke?"

The woman's face became serious. "This is no joke. I, too, am employed by His Grace, Archbishop Beaton. My name is Janette Lindsay. His Grace told me you would be celebrating evening Mass here, well away from the court." She stared round the church. "I can understand why. It is quiet here, but soon, sir, you will enter more troubled waters. We are to Scotland, you and I, on the Archbishop's behalf. He wants to see us now." She looked over her shoulder. "Thomas!" she called.

A tall, thickset man came from behind a pillar and walked down the transept of the church. He bowed at the woman and grinned at Segalla.

"Thomas Vartlett," he announced, sheepishly scratching his black, curly head and trying to comb his unruly moustache and beard into some semblance of order.

Segalla stared at him. Vartlett walked with the swagger of a fighting man, but he was dressed like a petty court fop in his exquisite jerkin with hanging, scalloped sleeves, tight green hose and high-heeled boots of red leather from Cordova. Vartlett's gloves and leather belt were adorned with little silver bells and trinkets: his thick, fleshy fingers glittered with tawdry jewels. One ring, gold with a silvery pearl, hung from an earlobe. A veritable roaring-boy, Segalla thought, with his laughing eyes and rich red mouth. A courtier, a hanger-on, but still a fighting man with a stabbing dirk pushed into its sheath over a rather protuberant codpiece, whilst from his belt swung a needle-pointed rapier. Vartlett stepped forward, eyes narrowed.

"Sir?" he asked. "Do you know me? You stare at me long."

Segalla's hand went beneath his robe to the long Italian

stiletto hidden there. He had been at court too long not to recognise the fighting man's belligerent attitude at any insult, intended or not.

"Oh, for heaven's sake!" Janette seized Vartlett's arm. "Don't play your games now, Thomas." She gestured at Segalla. "He is a Jesuit, a priest, not some fighting man."

Vartlett grinned, shrugged and gave a mocking bow. "Father, I was only testing you." He ran his tongue round his lips. "I mean no quarrel. After all, we will get to know each other very well."

"What is all this?" Segalla demanded. "You, Madame, are here and I know you not. You, sir, swagger into this church armed with sword and dirk."

"I have told you," the woman said. "We are off to Scotland. Beaton's envoys to Queen Mary's court. You will be Monsieur Segalla. I shall be your lady wife, whilst Thomas here is to be our servant."

"As ever and always," Vartlett said sarcastically.

"And why has His Grace not discussed this with me?" Nicholas asked angrily.

Janette walked forward slowly, rather languorously, her body swaying. "Oh, don't be so pompous, so cold, Father. And use the sharp brain God has given you. How can we mean harm? You were sitting with your back to us. As for Beaton? Well, His Grace does not have to reveal his mind and heart to you every second of the day. The business is urgent. We are his messengers. Come." She beckoned. "Our escort awaits! To stop you worrying further"—she opened her hand to display Beaton's purple wax seal—"His Grace gave me this as his token."

A bell high in the church tower began to toll. Segalla looked at his two visitors, shrugged and genuflected towards the high altar before following them out of the church. At the doorway Vartlett went before them. Janette, however, caught Segalla by the arm.

24

"You are a man of God, Nicholas," she whispered. "But when Vartlett was teasing you, your hand went for the stiletto beneath your cloak."

Segalla nodded. Janette tossed her head and laughed. "Good!" she said, her eyes dancing with devilment. "We may not be husband and wife, but I still may enjoy this."

Boatmen in dark garb and black masks were waiting on the freezing quayside to take them down to where Beaton was waiting. On either side of the Seine, Paris now slept. A silver hunter's moon slipped between the clouds to glint and shimmer on the black water of the river. The boatmen pulled away. Segalla's companions were now quiet, huddled in their cloaks against the coiling mist. Nothing broke the silence except for the creak of the oars and the breathing of the boatmen. They swung midstream, following the far bank down past the river gallows and the ghastly green faces of the corpses that dangled there. These showed up all the more gruesome by the flickering torchlights that spluttered around the scaffold: a harsh warning to other river pirates of what the future might hold for them.

The boat slipped past handsome timbered houses, lit by the glow of fires from the heaps of refuse burning in the city and under the narrow arches of the Grand Pont. Above this, the wheeling scavenger kites fought over the putrefying heads of the traitors spiked there. The galleys and barges docked along the different quaysides were also busy unloading fruit, meat, flour and cloth as well as live apes, peacocks, silks and spices from the Indies. At last they pulled in towards the bank and disembarked. Vartlett led them through the narrow, squalid alleyways, turning and twisting until even Segalla, who knew Paris well, began to wonder where they were going. At last they entered a great open square, illuminated by huge braziers burning in every corner. They crossed and went under the archway leading into the great Hôtel de Guise. In the courtyard, all was music and light, full of grooms, servants and members of the royal guard.

"Beaton's here," Janette whispered. "Queen Catherine is holding one of her masques."

Captains of the household wearing the royal livery stopped them. Janette produced letters and warrants; then they were led along a maze of wainscoted galleries. They passed through black-and-white tiled antechambers, into the great *salle* where the Court were watching a masque about the Merovingians, those long-haired kings of France who ruled the country long before the Valois were ever heard of. Segalla and his companions stood just within the door. They watched as a great ship constructed specially for the masque was wheeled in. Ivory sails billowed, and on deck stood a fairy pavilion with its front removed to display gold-covered couches and silver-topped tables. In the prow of the ship sat a hoary-headed man on a throne of sable fur, and all about him stood beautiful maids garbed in white silk with circlets of gold round their long red hair. Segalla watched, fascinated. He was always astonished at the wealth and skill lavished upon such spectacles. He jumped as the elderly Beaton appeared behind him and grasped him by the arm.

"Come, come!" Beaton whispered. "All of you!"

They followed him out of the hall, down a gallery and into a warm, stuffy chamber. The windows were shuttered and covered in drapes. A fire burnt in the hearth, and chafing dishes full of glowing charcoal stood round the room. Beaton sat at an oval table, indicating with one vein-streaked hand for Segalla and his companions to do likewise. He pushed a silver high-sided tray containing goblets and a jug of wine towards Vartlett.

"Thomas," he said. "If you could do the honours?" Beaton smiled at Janette. "And don't worry, that wine is from my own cask. It cannot be tainted."

The cups were filled and distributed. Nicholas sat and sipped as he listened to the faint music coming from the *salle:* the melodious sounds of the tambour, rebec, lyre and viol. He drank again and hid his smile. Beaton was right to be fearful of poison, for Catherine de' Medici was as much Queen of Poison as she was Queen Mother of France. Beneath all the finery, the cloth-of-gold depicting red and gold salamanders, the classical statues and the silver brocade, lurked the hidden violence of France's Queen Mother. Catherine would brook no opposition, and many of her opponents seemed to suffer some mishap at table. Beaton also sat listening to the music. The woman, Janette Lindsay, stared into her goblet of wine, whilst Vartlett seemed more interested in the silver bells sewn on his glove.

Beaton shifted his gaze. "May your birthday be pleasant, Nicholas."

Segalla smiled and plucked the rosary beads from his pouch; its crucifix, inlaid with mother-of-pearl, dazzled in the candlelight.

"Your Grace, I thank you for your gift, though I understand you have other surprises?"

Segalla did not turn as Janette laughed. Beaton chuckled. He scratched his high-boned cheeks and ran his fingers through the tendrils of his grey beard before clutching the gold pectoral cross resting against his tunic of scarlet brocade.

"How long have you served me, Nicholas?"

"Three years, Your Grace."

Beaton rocked himself gently in the chair and stared up at the timbered ceiling. "Do you know," he said, "this is the only chamber in this benighted palace free of any spy-holes or secret passages." He clasped his hands together and leaned across the table. "Nicholas, you are a good priest. You say your Mass. You pray your rosary. You say the divine office. A good Jesuit: a man in the world but not of this world. You do not politic, but you listen to those who do. You read your books, you go for your walks and, in your chamber, study your fine array of clocks."

Segalla, embarrassed, looked away.

"Do you miss England?" Beaton asked abruptly. "Or do you really come from there, Nicholas?" The Archbishop peered at Nicholas. "You're a good priest but a man of mystery. Sometimes I am sure we've met before, years ago, when I was a student, but that can't be, can it?"

"Tricks of the mind," Segalla said slowly. "I must remind you of someone else."

"And your family?"

The Jesuit smiled: so many questions, always the same, and how could he answer them? He noticed Janette watching him curiously. "They all died in England," he said flatly. "When I was a child. The plague came. If I went back there it would only be for my faith, Your Grace."

Beaton studied him. "Be careful, Nicholas. Be wary of that sin we priests so often commit. We are so busy loving everybody we have no time for anyone."

Segalla accepted the gentle rebuke because he could find no reply.

"I want you to go to Scotland!" Beaton continued sharply.

"Why?" Segalla asked.

"For the Church, for the Faith and for a Catholic monarch."

"Your mistress, Mary of Scotland?"

"Yes," Beaton said. "My mistress, Queen Mary of Scotland, to whom, Nicholas, you owe no allegiance." He smiled faintly. "But, before you ask, your Father General in Rome approves of this."

"Why me?" Segalla asked.

"Because I trust you. Because, Nicholas, you can move among people and yet remain hidden. You are good at listening but keep a still tongue in your head. The Queen needs, and will implicitly trust, a good priest. Only she will know your true identity."

"They'll kill me," Segalla said curtly. "If they find out, the Lords of the Congregation will hang me as a papist or bundle me into a cart and send me south for Walsingham's men."

Beaton smiled and shook his head. "They won't do that, will they, Janette?"

"No," the woman replied, though this time her voice was devoid of teasing or merriment. "I'll travel with you, Father," she continued. "Monsieur Nicholas Segalla, French clerk, diplomat, envoy, and his wife, Janette, together with their trusted servant, Thomas Vartlett."

"And who will believe that?" Segalla asked.

"Why?" Janette exclaimed, turning in her chair to face him. "His Grace will send letters saying that we are such. No Romish priest can have a wife." She laughed. "Let alone a Jesuit."

"Why?" Segalla retorted. "Why not by myself? Why this masquerade?"

"Because they will suspect," Beaton snapped. "People believe in what they see. You can act the part, and so can Janette."

"Madame." Segalla turned. "I mean no offence. You come as my wife?"

"In name only!" she said tartly. "Such details, Father, have yet to be discussed."

Segalla blushed with embarrassment. Beaton began to chortle; the expression on Vartlett's face showed he was thoroughly enjoying himself.

Beaton tapped his cup on the table. "No games," he whispered. "What is today's feast? St. Thomas Aquinas, the twenty-eighth of January. You are to be in Scotland soon. Nicholas, this is not some madcap scheme. Janette Lindsay is, as you may know, half French. Her father was an archer in the Scottish guard here in Paris. An officer of rank whom I dearly respected." Beaton smiled shyly. "Janette was sent to a convent school outside Lille, whence she absconded to join a troupe of strolling players." He held up his hand. "Now, hush, woman. Don't start protesting. I know you well as a firebrand." He wagged his finger at her. "A fact your father learnt to his cost. Janette is special, Nicholas. She knows the Scottish tongue. She has been to Edinburgh. Her father was known to Queen Mary. She knows . . ." Beaton pursed his lips and stared into the darkness. "She knows the webs her countrymen can weave. She and Vartlett have done good service for me before. Above all, Janette is an actress. Aren't you, Janette?"

The woman must have caught the disbelief in Segalla's eyes. She rose to her feet, winked at Beaton, then swept out of the chamber.

"What's the matter?" Segalla asked.

Beaton just waved his fingers. "In a while, in a while, Nicholas. Now, Master Vartlett, here, is also Scottish. A former soldier in the royal archers." Beaton ran a finger round his lips. "Some say Thomas left Scotland because of his allegiance to the old Faith. Others claim he's a rogue, an accomplished thief, a cunning man, a counterfeit, a braggart, a street-brawling boy." Beaton picked up his cup. "But I say," the Archbishop continued softly, "that Vartlett has a heart and soul. He may take my gold and silver but he'll keep faith, or so I think."

"And if he doesn't?" Segalla said.

Vartlett's face didn't change a whit. Old Beaton leaned across the table and touched the manservant's hand.

"Thomas has been paid good silver," he whispered. "Moreover, if Thomas betrays us where can he go? Back to Scotland? Or is he Scottish? Or from the northern counties, where there's a price on his head?"

The smile faded from Vartlett's face. "I am your man," he

said in a voice that grated. "And I have as much to lose as you, Father. Those who travel with Catholic priests tend to suffer the same penalties."

"I did not intend offence," Segalla said. "Thomas, you know my meaning." He spread his hands placatingly. "England and Scotland crawl with government men, agents looking for quick profits, and I would have a price on my head."

The easygoing mercenary shrugged. Segalla realised he would have to make the man his friend: Vartlett was right to say that he, too, would have a lot to lose. Segalla sipped from his cup and quietly cursed: here was cunning old Beaton at his games again. The wily Archbishop already had him half agreeing to go to Scotland before he'd even asked the reason why. A sound from the door made him whirl round. A bent crone, her cane tapping on the floor, hobbled into the room. Segalla pushed his chair back in alarm.

"Madame," he exclaimed. "You are in the wrong room."

Beaton and Vartleett stayed stock-still. The old woman, with her greying hair and face hidden in a hood, simply staggered towards him.

"Qu'est-ce que c'est?" she whined in a guttural patois.

Beaton chuckled. Segalla looked back at the Archbishop, who sat drumming his fingers gently on the table, then in astonishment at the crone, who had now straightened up. She tossed the old cloak to the floor and began to shake the white dust from her hair.

"I was," Janette Lindsay declared defiantly, "the best in my troupe of actors!"

Segalla sat down. He had seen the mountebanks in the squares of Paris perform such tricks, changing shape and guise, but never so quickly or so convincingly. Janette, wiping the dust from her face, took her seat and glanced up at Segalla. Now she was dabbing her eyes with a little *mouchoir*.

"And yet you don't believe me!" Janette's voice and face,

the whole posture of her body, had changed, now she expertly acted a spoilt, refined lady trying to get her own way with tears.

"I—I—" Segalla stammered. He sat down, not knowing whether to laugh or simply apologise.

The *mouchoir* disappeared, as did the tears. Janette leaned forward, her face hard, eyes bright, shoulders back. "Nae. Nae, ye dinna ken, ye stupid ghillie!" Now she was a brazen tavern wench. "Ye hae the mind of a fey bairn, ganning hither and thither!"

Her accent was thick, reminding Segalla of soldiers in the Scottish guard in Paris. She pulled her cloak closer about her, her face becoming relaxed and soft. She clasped her hands across her stomach, glancing at him from under fluttering eyelids.

"But there again, my son." Janette's voice was serene and modulated, slightly singsong as she aped some sanctimonious nun or pious court lady. "You are truly only a child and, as St. Paul says, think as a child."

Segalla laughed as Janette's eyes fluttered even faster; with her movements and posture she parodied those high-born ladies who immersed themselves in good works and made sure everyone knew about it.

"There!" Janette flounced back in the chair and smiled across at Beaton. "In my time I have acted as a boy." She tapped her bosom. "One advantage of being rather flat-chested. I can ape the court dandy, the crone, the benevolent mother, the brazen hussy, and, if you give me time, even the secretive Jesuit!"

Segalla joined in Beaton's and Vartlett's laughter.

The Archbishop rapped the table. "Enough!" he said. "All three of you to Scotland, not through England but the port of Leith in Edinburgh. I will give you warrants and letters and arrange safe passage on a French merchant cog. You are to be my envoys to Her Majesty, Queen Mary of Scotland."

"I have heard rumours," Segalla said. "Is she in danger?"

The Archbishop stared into the corner, watching the rushes on the floor move as mice scurried about. "The real danger," he said, "is Mary herself. She suffers the same temperament as her father, James V: seizures, fits of hysteria, which wrench the stomach, ice her heart and numb her mind. Now, to the world, Mary is every inch a queen. She has ridden against rebels with chain mail under her cloak and pistols at her belt. Nevertheless, her good father's sickness lies just under this eggshell hardness. Mary is a woman who wants to be loved. Her first husband, King Francis, God rest him, was withered root." The Archbishop lowered his voice. "They say his testicles were undescended. I doubt if their marriage was ever consummated."

"Darnley's a handsome beau," Janette put in.

"Fair without," Beaton replied. "Rotten within. He was behind Rizzio's murder. Darnley is a lecher with whom no woman, whore or maid, is safe. Now he lies sick with black pustular eruptions and, fearful of death, tries to woo his Queen again."

"And this danger?" Segalla asked.

"The French Ambassador in Scotland, Monsieur Claude Nau," Beaton said, "is absent, but spies say some secret stratagem is being planned."

"Against whom?" Janette asked.

"I don't know."

"By whom?" Segalla asked.

Beaton shook his head. "Again, I don't know." He opened his hands and began to shove coins across the table. "We have Mary, who wishes a rapprochement with Darnley. But is this genuine? Do they plot against each other?" He shrugged. "I have no evidence." He shoved another coin across. "Next are the Lords of the Congregation, led by Mary's half brother, James Stuart, Earl of Moray, a man who would like to be King if he hadn't been born illegitimate. Behind Moray lurk more sinister figures, Douglas, Earl of Morton, and Secretary Maitland of Lethington.''

"And the danger?" Segalla insisted.

"Have you heard of the Châtelard incident?" Beaton asked abruptly.

"Vaguely," Segalla said. "A poet much smitten by Mary's beauty."

Beaton played with the coins on the table. "Yes, he followed her from France to Scotland. The fool hid in her bedroom. Some people claim he tried to rape Mary: Châtelard paid for his lèse-majesté on a scaffold at St. Andrews.''

Segalla studied Beaton's face. "What has that got to do with the Queen now?"

"What if," Beaton said slowly, "there was another Châtelard? But this time a man Mary respected, even liked?''

"Such as?" Segalla asked.

"Well, the gossips mention James Hepburn, Earl of Bothwell, a professional soldier, an adventurer." Beaton heaped the coins together. "He once served in Paris as an officer in the Scottish guard." Beaton clinked the coins. "A man of power and violence, Bothwell now sits close to the Queen." He sighed. "The Queen cannot afford any scandal!''

"But if the Queen is seeking a rapprochement with Darnley, why the danger?" Segalla asked. "Why this urgency?"

"Ah!" Beaton sighed. "I have a spy at the English court. Nothing much, tittle-tattle: he claims Walsingham has a man close to the Scottish Queen, an agent provocateur. No one knows his name, though he is given the title the Raven Master, God knows why! However, if Cecil and Walsingham of England are closely involved in Scottish affairs, some great danger threatens Mary. You are to warn her of this and counsel prudence.''

"And the Raven Master?" Segalla asked.

"Search out his plots. Try to discover who he is. Once you do—" Beaton's voice fell to a whisper and he gestured to

Janette and Vartlett to withdraw. The Archbishop paused. "Let Vartlett clip this raven's wings!" he said at last. "But Nicholas." Beaton's vein-streaked hand gripped Segalla's wrist. "As the Gospel says, I am sending you as a lamb amongst wolves. Do not trust anyone: in the end, you will know what I mean."

Chapter 2

As Segalla and his companions prepared to leave France from the port of Saint-Omer, a black-draped barge, rowed by masked boatmen, made its way along the Thames to the Tower. The guards, seated round the man in the middle of the barge, never talked or glanced to the left or right; their captain stood eagle-like in the prow, behind the fluttering red, blue and gold banner of Elizabeth of England. At last the captain stirred as he glimpsed the turrets and battlements of the Tower high above the swirling mantle of mist.

"Make ready to pull in!" he ordered.

The oarsmen obeyed, and the barge swept to the left to berth beside steps leading up to the quayside which stretched under the grim, grey mass of the Tower. More guards carrying torches appeared; words were whispered and secret passes shown. The man in the barge at last stirred and, helped by two of the royal archers, came up the steps and through the barbican gateway of the Tower. They marched along its narrow passageways, across the ice-frosted green towards the moonlit chapel of St. Peter ad Vincula. The captain of the guard pushed the door open: his master, Sir Francis Walsingham, scholar of King's College, graduate of the Inns of Court, Member of Parliament, soon to be husband of Ursula Wolsey and Elizabeth of England's most skillful of spies, swept through the door and up the small nave of the church. His hooded, black-cowled henchmen and guards marched behind, their spurred boots ringing hollow on the cold paving stones. Walsingham allowed himself a grim smile, aware that they were walking across the tombs of many of England's noblest executed traitors. The church was cold, but Walsingham did not flinch: the deep furrows round his mouth and hooded eyes betrayed nothing. His henchmen were too wary to chatter. Oh, Sir Francis could be charming, soft-spoken, but they regarded him as forbidding as the figure of death. Sometimes he would smile like the fondest of uncles, but on other occasions he would turn away, his thin upper lip curling like that of a dog. Sir Francis strode into the sanctuary of the church and sat down on the high-backed, thronelike chair specially placed before the stone altar. His henchmen gathered round him.

"Bring them in," Walsingham ordered.

The captain of his guard raised one gauntleted hand and snapped his fingers. Two figures walked slowly into the church, one pushing the other before him. They reached the sanctuary, and the prisoner, John Bowler, lately tried before the Queen's Commissioners of Oyer and Terminer for treason, slumped to his knees and clasped his hands, his eyes watering with fear.

"Sir Francis, mercy!" he begged.

"Sir Francis does not grant mercy," Walsingham answered slowly. "Only Her Majesty, God bless her, can grant such grace." He stretched out one foot and tapped the man gently on the chest. "You, John, are a disappointment. I gave you a task and you failed."

"It was not my fault," the man wailed, scratching his head, trying to smooth the streaks of greasy hair covering his balding pate.

Walsingham's dark brows furrowed. "Not your fault, Master Bowler? Would you lie in the house of God?" He tapped his silver-topped cane on the floor. "Beneath here, Master Bowler, lie traitors; their souls gone to God, their bodies rot here. Only God knows where their heads are." Walsingham's lip curled as if he found this amusing. He stared at the man standing next to Bowler. "Master Topcliffe, you have been chattering to our good friend here?"

"Of course, Your Grace." The Queen's master torturer lisped. His thin, skull-like face broke into a lopsided grin. "And, if it please Your Grace, I believe Master Bowler tells the truth. It was not his fault. The messages you sent to Scotland did not arrive. According to the evidence I have gathered, Master Bowler was attacked on a road outside Berwick and the messages stolen."

"By whom?" Walsingham snapped.

"By footpads," Topcliffe said. "Bowler's money and whatever arms he carried were also filched."

"You are certain of this?" Walsingham snapped. "Not by the Queen of Scots' men? Perhaps her good friend, the Earl of Bothwell?" Walsingham fingered his close-cropped beard. "He has mosstroopers along the border."

"Impossible!" Topcliffe replied. "They would have killed Bowler."

Walsingham nodded, rocking himself gently in the chair, and hid his fury at the stupidity of the messenger who crouched before him.

By the Queen's stomach and heart, he thought, what can I do? The news from Scotland was serious: talk of a rapprochement between Mary Stuart and that stupid poltroon of a husband. Walsingham stared into the darkness. Darnley was Mary's weakness. Walsingham had plotted and prayed that Mary would destroy him and so plunge Scotland into civil war.

"The news is grave?" Topcliffe asked, then bit his lip at the look of anger in Walsingham's eyes.

"Do not presume to read my thoughts, Master Topcliffe." Walsingham looked over his shoulder to where Culpepper, his principal clerk, stood behind him.

"What do you think, Master Culpepper?"

The small, grey-faced man shrugged. "Your Grace, the messages Bowler were carrying probably now lie rotting in some peat bog. Even if they were taken and laid before the Scottish Queen, she could not break their cipher. And if she did, she would still not understand the coded message."

"So, what choices do we have?" Walsingham asked.

"Very few, Sir Francis. If the Scottish Queen and her husband, Henry Darnley, become like two turtledoves, what then? They already have a son. Mary will continue to win the hearts of her subjects. She has the support of all the great nobles, except, of course, of her half brother, James Stuart, Earl of Moray. Douglas of Morton may be fickle, but the rest, Argyll, Huntly and particularly Bothwell, are for her."

Culpepper leaned closer to whisper in Walsingham's ear. "Both Darnley and Mary are papists. Both Mary and Darnley are well thought of not only in Scotland and France but even in our own Parliament, recently sitting at Westminster. They will always pose a danger to our Queen. Sir Francis, you must tell the Raven Master to act!"

Walsingham stared down at his black leather gauntlets. Culpepper was only repeating the same advice he had given Cecil and the Queen: Mary of Scotland's magnanimity had surprised them all.

"But Darnley was behind the murder of Rizzio?" William Cecil, secretary of the council, had exclaimed. "Surely she will want his head?"

"No," Walsingham had replied. "Mary now sends Darnley gifts and sweet love letters."

"Sir Francis?" Culpepper interrupted his master's reverie.

"What is happening in Scotland now?" Walsingham asked.

"The Queen has moved Darnley by litter to Kirk o'Field, just beyond the city walls, south of Edinburgh."

"Why there?" Walsingham asked. He waved his fingers. "I know, I know, you've told me. Just refresh my memory."

"It is close to Holyrood. But free of the stench and fetid smells of the city. It lies in its own quadrangle with fields and gardens—"

"Who recommended it?" Walsingham interrupted.

"The Queen herself." Culpepper smiled. "At the advice of her half brother, the Earl of Moray."

Walsingham chuckled. "Of course. Now I remember. The house lies near the ruins of Blackfriars monastery, yes? It was once used as a hospital for those suffering some contagious infection?"

"Precisely, Sir Francis."

"And Darnley has agreed?"

"The Queen wished to take him to Craigmillar Castle, but Darnley, fearful of his life and safety, refused to go there."

"Ah yes," Walsingham said as if talking to himself. "And when the Queen came to Kirk o'Field, she went to the Duke of Hamilton's house nearby. The Duke being in France, the place lies empty."

Walsingham paused as if listening to the sounds of the Tower. He was glad he had come to this straight and narrow place with no spy squints in the wall, secret passageways or anyone lurking behind an arras or some wainscoting. He glared down at Bowler. The fool still had his purposes. Walsingham stroked his moustache with one finger.

"You will take a letter, Bowler," he said. "To my man in Edinburgh. Leave it at the Kirkall tavern, which stands in an alleyway just off the Canon Gate. Take lodgings there. Don't hold the letter yourself. Give that to the landlord. Only when it's collected will the Raven Master arrange to meet you." Walsingham snapped his fingers. "Now, Master Topcliffe, take your guest to the soldier's quarters. Give him strong meats, good drink and a change of clothing. Tomorrow, Master Bowler, you will receive your warrants and letters. You will take a cog from the Thames and are to be in Edinburgh within ten days."

Bowler leapt to his feet, bowing and scraping. Topcliffe led him out of St. Peter ad Vincula. Walsingham waited until the door had closed behind them before slowly walking down the nave, beckoning to Culpepper to follow. He passed before an arrow-slit window that looked out over the execution block on Tower Green. In the moonlight it looked even more ghostly, and Walsingham had to hide a shiver.

"Sir Francis?" Culpepper came up softly beside him like a shadow.

"Draw up a letter for the Raven Master," Walsingham whispered. "Tonight, bring it to my private chambers. Tell the Raven Master to act. He is not to worry. He will find the wherewithal when he sees his opportunity. Queen Mary is not to be injured, though it is time Darnley joined his ancestors."

"And Segalla, Your Grace?"

"Ah yes, Segalla." Walsingham stared out across the White Tower. Who was he? Where did he come from? Walsingham scratched his chin. His spies in Paris had gleaned scraps of information about Master Segalla, but they didn't make sense. One source claimed he had been born in Yorkshire of an English father and a French mother.

"We have made enquiries at York." Culpepper spoke up as if he could read his master's thoughts. "Segalla has no family there."

"So what else do they say about him?"

"Segalla was in England for a few years. He studied here and worked there but then he returned to Europe. He travelled around before being drawn into Beaton's circle in Paris."

"So, what's the mystery?"

"There's no mystery, Master, except Monsieur Segalla never seems to grow old."

Walsingham turned in surprise. "But that's impossible!"

"Sir Francis, I only report what I have been told."

Walsingham pulled a face. "Tell the Raven Master to

41

watch Segalla. Send the man's description on to Drury at Berwick and the other English garrisons on the Scottish march. If he dares to cross into England, I assure you, Master Culpepper, Segalla will be our guest here in the Tower."

Culpepper made to turn away.

"Sirrah, I have not finished!" Walsingham rasped. Then he smiled and, seizing Culpepper by the shoulder, drew him so close the scrivener could smell his foul breath. "Who owns the house at Kirk o'Field?"

"Sir James Balfour."

"One of Moray's men?"

Culpepper nodded.

"Send a letter to Moray," Walsingham whispered. "Say that his good friends should hide some gunpowder at Kirk o'Field, a large barrel, primed and ready."

"And the rest, Your Grace?"

Walsingham shrugged. "Nothing. The Raven Master will know what to do. Oh—" Walsingham turned back to the window. "Tell the Raven Master Bowler is no longer needed!"

Segalla was dreaming of Rosencrantz, the carrier of the rose cross, who now lay buried in his secret vault, lit with lamps that never went out. Rosencrantz, leader of the Caballa, who'd constantly hunted him for his secrets. Segalla was standing in that strange vault, staring at the paintings on the wall of dark lords, crowned demons riding crocodiles, with blood-red kestrels on their wrists. Segalla stirred restlessly. The smell in the vault was fetid. Some dreadful concoction, brewed in a human skull, of boiling worms mixed with dead men's flesh.

"Monsieur Segalla."

Nicholas opened his eyes. Vartlett was grinning down at him. Segalla blinked and stared round. He was in no vault, but in the fetid hold of a ship, and the stink came from the slops along its unwashed planks. Segalla sat up.

"What is it?" He shivered at the cold and pulled his cloak closer around him.

Vartlett grinned. "We are in the Fourth. Aiming like an arrow for the Port of Leith. We will be in Edinburgh by midday."

Segalla smiled, his nightmares forgotten. "I'll be glad," he whispered. "Happy to be free of this stinking, rotten ship."

Vartlett helped his self-styled master to his feet. "How's your stomach?" the manservant asked.

"Sour and dry as an old rag!" Segalla snapped. "God forgive me, but I hate the sea. How long did the voyage take?"

Vartlett squinted through the gloom and gripped one of the beams to steady himself. Above them, Segalla could hear the patter of bare feet on the deck and the shouts and cries of the sailors as they reefed the sails. Again the ship lurched.

"What's the date?" Vartlett asked.

"Seventh February."

"Then it's been nine days," Vartlett said. "And we have hardly seen you."

Segalla followed him through the gloom, up soaking steps and onto the deck. At the top of the ladder he braced himself against the cold, biting wind. Nevertheless, it was a welcome relief after being tossed like a ball, and fed rancid, weevil-infested meat and wine that tasted like vinegar.

"You are well, Monsieur Segalla?"

Segalla looked at the cheery, squat tub of a captain, who stood, one hand gripping a halyard. Segalla forced a smile.

"Captain Revignon, don't take this personally," he said, gingerly walking along the deck. "You may love your ship, but I pray to stand on terra firma."

"Your wife has enjoyed the voyage." The captain gestured to where Janette stood at the ship's rail.

Segalla hid his surprise with a curse. He must remember, he

and Janette were man and wife. He thanked the captain and staggered across the heaving, slippery deck to Janette, who held the ship's rail and stared out into the shifting mist.

"Good morning, husband." Janette's auburn hair flew free in the biting wind. She turned, her cheeks pink and her eyes sparkling. "You are no sailor, husband," she continued mockingly. "Why, if it hadn't been for the good captain, his crew and Vartlett, I would"—her voice cooed—"have been ever so lonely."

Segalla pinched her on the arm. "You are a minx and a hussy," he whispered. "I wager you enjoyed every second of their attention."

Janette stared out across the grey sullen sea. Segalla glanced up at the lowering clouds and wished he were back in France. Not in Paris, but the golden south, amongst sweet-smelling cypresses, green vineyards and rolling, flower-filled meadows.

"If I could only have the sun on my back," he said.

"You'll be in Scotland soon." Janette nudged him, and, as if in response to her eagerness, the mist shifted. Segalla glimpsed the rooftops and spires of Leith port.

"How long is it since you've been here?" he asked.

"Years."

"Don't be disappointed," he said. "Scotland has always been a killing ground, and this present time is no different." He breathed in deeply, savouring the tangy salt air. "The English no longer pour over the border to burn the heather and sack the towns. Norwegian pirates no longer wade ashore with sword and axe. And those bitter clan fights which ended in severed limbs and rotting heads are a thing of the past." He braced himself against the rail. "This time the battle is more vicious." He glanced at Janette. "Who will rule this kingdom?"

"You speak as if you have been here before." Janette took a step closer and Segalla caught her musky perfume. He stared at her sensuous lips, perfect white teeth, the soft glow on the smooth skin of her face.

"Wife," he teased, "I have been many places."

Janette smiled. "Yes, so I've heard."

"What?" Segalla asked sharply, realising Vartlett was moving closer.

Janette looked away toward the port. "I have heard stories. About a Monsieur Segalla seen here and there."

"That's the nature of Jesuit priests."

"Oh yes. But is it the nature of Jesuit priests to live hundreds of years?"

Segalla smiled. "What nonsense is this?"

"No nonsense. Just stories. Even Beaton is beginning to wonder about them. In the diaries of Louis XII, King of France some fifty years ago, Beaton discovered entries about a Monsieur Segalla."

Nicholas looked away. "An ancestor," he said tersely.

Janette pointed to the shoreline. "Out beyond the city," she said, "there are ancient standing stones. My father took me to see one. It carried strange carvings: a goose with a backward-turning neck. Huge stags with lowered heads and splendid loins. Curling serpents, bars of lightning, charging wolves and a sharp-tusked boar at bay. Were you there when they were carved, Nicholas?"

Segalla stared back. "Oh yes," he said. "I and the Queen of the Fairies!"

Janette laughed and the conversation ended as the ship suddenly turned and the crew scrambled about preparing to bring their vessel into dock.

An hour later, Segalla and his companions disembarked on the quayside, their baggage piled high around them. For a while Segalla had to sit in a dingy, black-beamed alehouse eating bread and sipping watered wine. His two companions did not seem to notice. Janette was pleased to be back in Scotland, eagerly listening to the rough dialects and watching the rest of the customers. Vartlett, too, was happy: he was hungry for the sights and openly relieved to be free of the cramped conditions of their voyage. At last Segalla pronounced himself ready, and they hired a carter to take them along the rutted country track into Edinburgh. Before they had left Saint-Omer, Beaton had given them careful directions, and the carter took them along the narrow wynds to the Crucible tavern, a spacious hostel in an alleyway near the Tolbooth. Grooms took their baggage, and the tavern master, inspecting them from head to toe, came out wiping his dirty fingers on a greasy apron. He saw the finery of their apparel, smiled ingratiatingly and led them up a wooden staircase to the tavern's most spacious chambers. Janette played the role of a spoilt wife. Now and again she'd lapse into French as she insisted on a chamber to herself. The tavern master hastened to comply, ushering her into a low-ceilinged room, one with a narrow casement window and a steel-bound chest at the foot of a four-poster bed. The tavern master assured her the mattress was of down and the sheets changed at least once a month. Nicholas was given a chamber alongside, and at the end of the gallery, up three or four more stairs, a small garret was reserved for Vartlett.

Once he was alone, Nicholas threw himself down on the bed, stretched and looked up at the grass-stained tester. He still felt queasy and sore after his jogging ride from the port. He heard a tap on the door but chose to ignore it and drifted into a deep sleep. Once again, in his dreams, he stood in a seven-vaulted chamber, though this time it had a window looking out onto an island where a massive funeral pyre roared to the starlit skies. He was woken hours later, after darkness had fallen, by a hammering on the door. He grabbed his dagger and, still half asleep, staggered across the chamber.

"Who is it?" he croaked, his lips and mouth dry as a timber.

"Ta femme," came the lisping reply. *"Oh, Monsieur, ouvre la porte, s'il te plaît."*

Segalla smiled and threw the door open. Janette, fresh as a daisy, with Vartlett behind her smirking from ear to ear, stood in the darkened gallery. A tapster carried in a tray with a jug of wine, three cups and a plate of bread and various cheeses. Segalla took this off him as he invited his "wife" and manservant in.

"Slept like a child, you did," Vartlett declared. "I came at least twice to waken you."

Segalla sat on the edge of the bed and rubbed his face.

"Better than my chamber," Vartlett commented, kicking at the rushes on the floor. "These appear to have been changed since Christmas; the ones in my room were old when I was a boy, whilst the sheets on my bed fair hop with fleas."

Segalla glared up at him. "Master Vartlett, I am tired, hungry, unshaven and unwashed."

"Yes." Janette smiled, sitting down next to him. "But today is Saturday, eighth February, beloved husband, and there's business to be done."

Vartlett served each of them wine, placing the platter of bread and cheese on the bed. He then pulled up the chamber's one and only stool and sat down opposite them. "I have been out listening to the gossip," he began.

"The city fairly seethes with intrigue, like a beehive on the hum. All the Great Lords are here with their retinues. There's a dark atmosphere, just like the weather before a thunderstorm. People chatter that something is about to happen, but no one knows what."

"And the court?"

"As I have said, divided between Kirk o'Field and Holyrood. Tomorrow is Carnival Day. The last Sunday before Lent. There will be celebrations and bonfires throughout the city. The gossips say the Queen will be at Holyrood for the wedding of one of her ladies-in-waiting."

"And Darnley?"

"The gossips claim he is nearly better. When he has recovered, he will join the Queen at Holyrood, where the infant James is being nursed."

"And the Queen's feelings for her husband?"

Vartlett looked enquiringly at Janette.

"Sometimes," she said slowly, "I forget my father was Scottish, but this afternoon, when moving round the city, I felt I was home. I could understand the dialect." She smiled and shook her head, breaking free from her reverie. "The alehouse gossips say all will be well between the Queen and Darnley: they will begin life again as man and wife. But whether that is allowed, is another matter."

"Why?" Segalla asked.

"What do you think, Monsieur Segalla?"

Segalla stared into the wine cup and recalled his meeting with Beaton. "The Scottish nobility are not used to being ruled by a queen," he said. "It is twenty-five years since Mary's father died. The Great Lords do not like bridles round their necks and would prefer to canter free and untrammelled, without any royal ruler on their backs."

He put his goblet on the floor and stood up. "But how can they act?" he said. "To rebel against Darnley is to rebel against the Queen, and that's treason. They would forfeit life and limb." He stared down at Janette. "There is one other matter," he added slowly.

"The Raven Master?"

"Aye, the Raven Master, though God knows who he is."

"There are many English in Edinburgh?"

"Enough," he said. Janette smiled back. "Merchants, traders, seamen, clerks. You must not forget that, on the surface at least, there is supposed to be amity between the two kingdoms."

Segalla moved across the chamber and stared out into the night. "So, the Raven Master could be any one of these?"

"Oh, yes," Janette said. "Or someone very close to Mary. Most of the great Scottish lords, with the exception of James Hepburn, Earl of Bothwell, secretly receive English gold. I wonder . . ."

"What?" Segalla asked.

"Why the title Raven Master?"

Segalla smiled to himself. "Sir Francis Walsingham often goes to the Tower. He sits there and plots, free of any court spy or secret agent of a foreign power. He likes to sit in one of the chambers overlooking the execution block. Now, in the Tower are ravens, with black plumes and glossy feathers, birds of prey that feast on the severed heads of traitors." Segalla toyed with the ancient ring on his finger. "Walsingham is allowed to keep his own privy purse, from which he makes payments to his spies, both in England and elsewhere. A great deal of silver is spent on the Raven Master. In theory, the fellow's responsibility is to look after the ravens in the Tower." Segalla looked round and smiled grimly at his companions. "In practice, the money goes to Walsingham's most skillful agent. The post of the Raven Master is a sinecure, hence the title: there's an ancient legend that if the ravens at the Tower disappear, the fortress will be taken and the kingdom fall. As long as the Raven Master is there, the kingdom is safe. Walsingham has had at least two or three Raven Masters. God knows who this one is." Segalla paused. "What o'clock is it?" he asked.

"Between seven and eight in the evening," Vartlett said.

The Jesuit smiled. "I must say my Mass."

"Here?" Janette asked.

"Yes, here. Canon Law says that, provided I have bread and wine, Mass can be celebrated."

"Then do so by yourself." Vartlett looked apologetically at

Segalla. "Don't take offence, sir. I have no religion." He tapped his dagger. "Except this and my wits."

Janette also excused herself. After they had gone Segalla went down to order a cup of the best wine and some plain white manchet bread. The tapster looked stangely at him, but Segalla smiled.

"I have yet to recover from the sea voyage," he explained.

The man just shrugged, muttering about the strange ways of foreigners.

Segalla returned to his chamber and took from his saddle-bag his missal and a small crucifix. He set these on the table and, with the sounds of the taproom ringing below him, celebrated his strange and lonely Mass. Afterwards he went down to the taproom for some heartier fare. Then he returned upstairs, unaware that a hooded figure had been sitting in a shadowy corner of the taproom, watching him intently.

Chapter 3

The next morning Segalla roused both Janette and Vartlett.

"How did you find the city?" he asked as they assembled in the taproom to break their fast.

Janette smiled, though she looked rather pale. Segalla glanced sharply at Vartlett and with a slight tinge of jealousy wondered whether the two were lovers. But as a priest he was bound to celibacy.

Vartlett pointed at Segalla's elegant dark blue quilted jerkin: it had puffed-out sleeves, slashed with mauve silk, with a white linen collar peeping above it. "You look the elegant courtier."

Segalla brushed crumbs from his murrey-coloured hose and stretched out his foot so that Vartlett could admire his high-heeled leather riding boots. "When in Rome, Vartlett, do as the Romans do."

Segalla looked admiringly at Janette Lindsay's gold samite dress and delicate white ruff. Her auburn hair was covered by a linen veil fringed with small precious stones. Segalla leaned forward.

"We look the part," he whispered. "The elegant Frenchman and his wife about to present their credentials at court!"

"But where do we go?" Vartlett asked. "Holyrood or Kirk o'Field?"

"Let's visit the palace first," Janette said.

They finished their meal, collected the horses Vartlett had hired from a local stable and rode out into the busy streets and wynds of Edinburgh. Segalla stopped and reined in: he found the noise and smell, even on that freezing cold morning, a welcome relief from the silent rocking of the ship that had brought them from France. Some passersby stopped to stare open-mouthed at these wealthy, well-attired strangers: the elegant man in his long woollen cloak, and Janette, fresh as a morning star in her colourful dress and fur-lined robe.

"The palace will know we are here before we arrive," she whispered.

"Then act the part, good wife." Segalla smiled. "Let's ride through the city. Our lives could depend on our knowledge of its streets and gates."

"Ever cautious, eh, Monsieur?" Vartlett called out.

"Come, come, Vartlett," Segalla replied in French, urging his horse forward. "Have you not done the same when you visit any strange city? Survey it carefully so you know its entrances and exits?"

Segalla led them on. At times he regretted his decision, because on that Saturday morning the crowds were out, and with the weather cold but fine, Edinburgh was as busy as an ant heap. The air was thick with the clatter from the stalls and full of the sour odour of the middens. Scavenging dogs chased cats away, whilst everyone was wary of the fat-bellied hogs that lumbered through the streets and narrow alleyways looking for scraps. At first Segalla found it difficult to gain his bearings: Beaton had told him that almost forty thousand souls lived within Edinburgh's walls.

"They must live packed cheek to jowl," Segalla said, studying the square sea-stone houses, fronted by wooden galleries and roofed with grey slate or red tiles.

Janette leaned towards him. "Thatched roofs are forbidden here," she explained. "Unlike Paris or London, the sensible burgesses have a great fear of fire."

They rode on and entered the High Street, which ran the length of the city, from the castle high on the crag to the city

52

gates. The street was completely paved and, despite the wandering animals and heaps of refuse, easy to traverse. Segalla led his party between the stalls where fish, cloth and other produce were being busily sold and up Canon Gate. They passed the houses of nobles with their gleaming white plaster, black-beamed fronts, glazed windows and strange decorations on their intricate stone gables and cornices. Curious, Segalla turned off the High Street and forced his way along the narrow alleyways. He reined in and looked back at Janette.

"If we ever have to run for our lives, this city will be a death trap."

Segalla glanced at the midden heaps, tar barrels and stacks of leather-bound peat, which, Janette explained, the Scots used for burning. The squalor and dirt were indescribable; Segalla, used to the filth of many a city, had to pinch his nostrils. He looked farther down the alleyway, noticing the many narrow stone and wooden arches that spanned these narrow runnels to link the houses on either side. He turned his horse back and entered the High Street. Here the houses were protected by small crumbling dykes and had their own gardens, where a little corn or cabbage was grown and bee steppes stood under the outstretched branches of an apple or pear tree. Slowly Segalla memorised the city. He noticed that each trade had different quarters: in the Shambles, the butchers with their bloody flesher's knives; the goldsmiths near the Mint; the linen merchants in the Lawn Market; the noisy glaziers and tinsmiths along Canon Gate. Each booth was separate, and Janette explained that every trader, by law, had pike and lantern ready in case of unrest.

Segalla had difficulty hearing her: the shouting and noise assaulted his ears whilst he observed, with some alarm, the swaggering soldiers dressed in boiled leather jackets, battered chain mail or the plaids of their different clans and houses. Now and again he glimpsed royal archers dressed in their shabby gold livery with the insignia of the Red Lion Rampant of Scotland. Segalla recalled Vartlett's words: the city was tense as a summer's day before a thunderstorm. As they entered the Trond, the central marketplace under the towering spires of St. Giles Cathedral, Segalla reined in and beckoned Janette and Vartlett closer.

"If things go wrong," he said in French, "we must leave the city by foot: horses would be useless. Master Vartlett, I would be grateful if, at your earliest convenience, you'd go back to the Leith road and have three horses stabled there."

"Would that be the safest way?" Janette asked, her pretty face showing alarm.

"Monsieur Segalla is right," Vartlett said. "In the city we would be trapped. On the wild moorland beyond we could soon become lost, and God knows what we might stumble into. If we rode south, the English would be waiting for us. The best escape would be by sea."

"Could it come to that?" Janette asked.

"Yes, it could," Segalla replied. "Mary has been back in Scotland five years. There have been at least three armed revolts, and when that happens, it's *chacun pour soi.*"

He looked round at the thronged marketplace, where bailiffs and pursuivants also carried out the Queen's justice: the great stocks were full, each malefactor wearing a yellow cap, whilst on the far side of the square a lofty, three-branched scaffold stretched up to the iron-grey sky. On a platform beneath the gibbet, a town crier, having blown a huge brass horn, declared that Peter Turnbull, known as the Monk, was to be regarded as an outlaw. Next to him, the city executioners were piling the severed limbs of a traitor into a huge battered vat to be pickled and salted before burial in the dung heaps outside the city walls. In a shabby box before the platform lay the naked corpse of a man with a scrawled notice on his chest. His balding head was thrown back, his throat one bloody gash from ear to ear. THE CORPSE OF JOHN BOWLER,

ENGLISHMAN, the notice proclaimed. FOULLY SLAIN BY PERSON OR PERSONS UNKNOWN.

Segalla wondered who Bowler was but was distracted at their horse's unease. He led his companions down the High Street towards the yellow-bricked walls of Holyrood Palace. At its gates, royal halberdiers stopped them, asking for warrants and letters whilst leering at Janette. Segalla produced the documents Beaton had given him in Paris. A captain of the guard, his face hidden by a steel visor, led them along the gravel paths towards the royal quarters in the northwest corner of the palace. Segalla scarcely had time to view the place, its crenellated walls, cone-top towers and great jutting bay windows filled with glass.

"Is the Queen here?" Segalla asked.

"Och no," the captain said. "Her Majesty the Queen is gone to Kirk o'Field, but you can wait."

Segalla was about to protest when two men came out of a small postern door, almost as if they had been expecting him. The first man had narrow eyes and blond hair with a friendly face. He looked like a typical farm boy as he ambled slowly towards Segalla and his party.

"I heard an English voice." The man's face broke into a grin and he put down the fardelol he was carrying. "Thomas Nelson of Pontefract in South Yorkshire: valet, servant." His grin widened. "And sometimes confidant of Henry Darnley, King-Consort of Scotland."

Segalla leaned down, shook his hand and made his own introductions. The Englishman pointed over his shoulder at his companion. "My lord's groom, Symonds."

The fellow shuffled forward. He had a thin, white face, black hair that was beginning to turn grey at the temples. Symonds was small in stature, with bleak-looking eyes and a slack mouth. His head and face did not match his body: he had a powerful chest and long dangling arms, which gave him a simian appearance. The captain of the guard, eager to be free of these strangers, quietly slipped away. Nelson picked up his fardelol.

"I know we might not look it," he declared, his face becoming serious. "But I speak the truth. We are the King's retainers." He turned and whispered to Symonds, then looked back at Segalla. He indicated his white ruff, his long-sleeved, dark red doublet and black hose. "We should be wearing the King's livery, but we scarce have time to sleep, never mind change our clothes!" He pressed his boot into the gravel and made it crunch. "If you wish"—he gestured airily—"we are going to Kirk o'Field. You are from the French court, envoys from Archbishop . . . ?"

"Archbishop Beaton," Segalla said.

Nelson's face became alive with interest. "Then Her Grace the Queen will be eager to see you."

Symonds brought their horses round. Nelson tied his bundle to the saddle horn and vaulted into the saddle, whilst Symonds almost crawled into his.

"So, no one is here?" Janette asked, pushing her horse alongside Segalla's.

"No." Nelson said. "All the lords, except Morton, who is at St. Andrews, are in Edinburgh." He led them out of the palace along side streets, through the city gates and into the frozen countryside.

"And what news of the Queen?" Segalla asked.

"Things fare well," Nelson said. "Her Grace has given my lord gifts: a new bed made of violet velvet enriched with cloth-of-gold and decorated with curtains of damask and pillows of scarlet and velvet. He has the best Holland linen sheets."

Segalla caught the sarcasm in Nelson's voice.

"And what is the King's illness?" Janette asked.

Nelson looked slyly at her. "Some people say it is the *petite vérole,* smallpox." He let his words hang in the air.

Segalla looked away, remembering Beaton's words in Paris.

"It's probably *roneole,* syphilis," the old Archbishop had whispered. "Darnley would have intercourse with a mountain goat provided it wore a petticoat."

"Why is everyone at Kirk o'Field? I mean," Segalla added hastily, "The King is there, but . . ."

"Well, tomorrow is Carnival Sunday," Nelson explained. "Feasting and celebration before Lent begins: the Queen says farewell to Moretta the Ambassador from Savoy and then attends the marriage banquet of one of her ladies-in-waiting. A time of festivities. Dancing and revelry until the early hours."

"Will the King attend?" Segalla asked.

Nelson's face became somber. "I doubt it. The doctors have treated him. He has had his bath and purged himself, and on Monday he leaves with the Queen for Seton. We, those of the King's retinue, will miss all the feasting. But look." They came to a brow of a small hill and Nelson pointed to the buildings below. "We have reached Kirk o'Field. You can ask Her Grace yourselves."

Segalla looked down at the quadrangle below him. They had approached Kirk o'Field through a circuitous route, leaving the city by one of the small postern gates in the southeastern corner of its walls. The building of Kirk o'Field sprawled out under an icy blue sky. The hard hoarfrost of the previous evening still glinted on its rooftops, gables and window ledges as if covering the King's residence in a fine sheen of silver.

"An ill-fated place," Segalla murmured, then silently cursed himself for betraying such knowledge.

"Why, sir, have you been here before?"

Segalla glanced at Janette, who was staring at him curiously. "No, but I have learnt about the place. Didn't Henry VI, who was later murdered in the Tower, stay here, as did other Lancastrian lords who fled from Edward IV? And the Pretender, the Fleming Perkin Warbeck, who claimed to be one of the Princes in the Tower? Didn't he also shelter at Kirk o'Field for a while?" Segalla shook his head. "No, this is the first time I have been here." He pointed to his left. "What are those ruins?"

"St. Mary's in the Fields," Nelson replied. "Pillaged by the Reformers."

Segalla looked at the gaunt shell of St. Mary's. Its walls and towers were still standing, but they were nothing more than a blackened shell; the windows, joists, lead piping and roof tiles had long been removed. Around the church lay the scattered, forlorn tomb slabs of its long-dead parishioners.

"And the great house beyond it?"

"The Duke of Hamilton's house; it used to be the old hospital," Nelson said. "Before the break with Rome, the entire area was a sanctuary for those suffering from malign infection or pestilence." He pointed to the east. "These are the ruins of Blackfriars monastery. The King's quarters lie in that quadrangle of buildings." He pushed his tired-looking nag forward. "Let me explain further. The wall which runs along the outside of Kirk o'Field is the one built after the great defeat at Flodden. The small alleyway alongside it is nicknamed Thieves Row." He smiled at Segalla's puzzled look. "No, sir, footpads don't lurk there." Nelson seemed pleased to air his knowledge in front of his betters. "It's called Thieves Row because the church once had the right of sanctuary: outlaws and wolvesheads used to hasten there to claim this right."

"You were talking about the King's lodgings," Vartlett said with annoyance.

"Yes, the long building built alongside the Flodden Wall is known as the *salle* or long hall. The dwelling at the far end of it, you can see its gallery resting on the Flodden Wall, is where my lord is staying."

"And the other buildings?" Janette asked.

"Well, on the other side of the long hall is the New Provost's House, to distinguish it from where my master stays. The rest of the square, both to the north and east, are simply cottages."

"Why didn't my lord Darnley stay in one of these?" Vartlett asked.

Nelson shrugged. "Why should he rest and recuperate there? No, the Old Provost's House provides my lord Darnley with regal chambers overlooking fields and gardens."

Segalla sighed in agreement, his breath hanging heavy as smoke on the freezing air. As they made their way down the hill, Segalla studied the Old Provost's House, where Darnley was staying. It was a substantially built manse: two stories high, it had a gallery held up by wooden struts; its large window, overlooking Thieves Row and the orchard beyond, was large and filled with glass.

A pleasant enough sight in summer, Segalla reflected, but now the grass was frozen hard and the orchard's apple and pear trees stood black and stark, stripped by a cruel winter of all leaves and fruit. They rode into the quadrangle, packed with loud-mouthed retainers, grooms and stableboys. Some of these hurried across, curious about the well-dressed visitors. Segalla winked at Janette.

"Remember, my dear," he whispered in French. "In the eyes of Archbishop Beaton, if not God, we are man and wife."

Janette grasped his hand and blinked prettily. *"Mon cher, toujours, toujours."*

"Always?" Segalla teased, but Janette just winked back.

Nelson saw to their horses' stabling and came back, still carrying his bundle. "Come on." He urged. "Let's not stand on idle ceremony."

They entered through a rear door into the long hall or *salle:* it had whitewashed walls and a low, black-timbered ceiling. Nelson led them up a spiral staircase: on the first storey was a small gallery, which apparently led to a chamber, now sealed by a heavy, metal-studded door.

59

"The Queen stays there," Nelson whispered. "Sometimes she comes back and spends the night with His Grace her husband."

"But they do not share the same chamber?" Janette asked, pausing to catch her breath; the stairs were steep.

"Tomorrow is the last day of his isolation," Nelson said, shoving the bundle at the taciturn Symonds. "As I've said, on Monday he and the Queen will be man and wife and ride to Seton."

He took them farther up the stairs, pushing aside a half-opened door that hung on hooks and into a small antechamber. Here royal archers sprawled, stretching their frozen fingers towards small, metal-capped braziers or playing dice. A burly, blond man partly covered in armour came over. He had a neatly cut moustache above a pointed beard, cold blue eyes and a seamed face, which lit with pleasure as he glimpsed Janette's appealing figure.

"I'm John Steward of Traquair," he announced. "Captain of Her Majesty's bodyguard." He glanced at the warrants Segalla handed across. Traquair studied the French writing and seals, then hastily handed them back. "You'd best come with me."

He led them into the chamber proper: it was stuffy and hot. To the right the room jutted out where the gallery had been built and filled in with wooden plaster and a large glass window. This was the gallery, Segalla recalled, that stood on timber struts just above the old Flodden Wall. Across the room was another large window, which must look out over the garden and ruins of Blackfriars. Segalla stared round as the captain of the guard pushed his way through the throng of people, who paused in their chatter to stare curiously. Segalla was surprised by the smallness of the room: no more than twenty-four square yards, though opulently furnished. He surveyed the velvet bed curtains, drapes fringed with gold: small tables, chairs and stools of green or violet also covered in velvet and a double-seated chair of state covered with yellow-and-red-striped taffeta. Segalla glanced at the men and women there. Some he recognised from the gossip at the French court as well as Beaton's description. The Four Marys, the Queen's ladies-in-waiting, in dresses with high necks that were trimmed in satin, with matching veils. Next to the canopied hearth stood Lord Moray, with his red beard and a face with the appearance of a fox. The Earl stared coolly at him before returning to his conversation with a large, heavy-set figure who, by his appearance and stance, must be a professional soldier. Segalla also recognised the colors of the Lords Argyll and Huntly. Traquair, who had gone before them, now came back, beckoning Segalla and his companions forward. The area in front of the large four-poster bed was empty. The bed itself had been pulled away from the wall, and Segalla glimpsed a slender, woman with auburn hair sitting between the bed and the wall, a pack of silver-edged playing cards in her hands. The man sprawling on the bed turned to face the newcomers. Segalla and his companions went down on their knees.

"Visitors from France?" The voice was languid and high-pitched.

Segalla stared up under lowered eyelids and tried to remain impassive. Darnley was dressed in cambric shirt, black hose and soft, furred slippers. A red robe edged in ermine was slung across his shoulders; a jewelled bonnet covered his balding head, and the long, thin face was hidden by a velvet mask. Even from where he knelt, Segalla could see the purple pustules on Darnley's cheeks. He noted his petulant expression and the long fingers fretting at the linen sheets.

"You are shocked to see your King like this?"

"Your Grace," Segalla tactfully replied. "We have travelled far to bring you, and Her Majesty the Queen, warm messages from Archbishop Beaton in France as well as his congratulations on the improvement in your health."

Darnley sat up, tossing aside the Book of Hours on his lap as well as the silver cup and ivory-inlaid dice.

"Yes, I have recovered, and on Monday I leave for Seton. Is that not so?" Darnley turned to the woman who still sat in the shadows on the other side of the bed.

Segalla quietly cursed Darnley's arrogance and caught the smirk on the Prince's lips as he looked over their heads at Nelson standing behind them. The rest of the room had fallen quiet, watching this tableau. By all the laws of court equiette, Darnley had no right to interrupt officially accredited envoys to his wife, the Queen. After all, he only bore the Crown Matrimonial. Segalla sensed the tension and watched the woman at the far side of the bed. He did not dare to approach her. Darnley would view that as an insult, for no envoy could greet a monarch without a personal invitation. Darnley swung his legs off the bed and sat on the edge. He stretched out the fingers of his black glove, gently touching Janette under the chin.

"Such a pretty wife, Monsieur."

"Thank you, Your Grace." Segalla gripped his letters and warrants more firmly. He was determined not to hand them over.

"Monsieur Segalla, please, stand up."

Segalla looked up at the Queen. She now stood with her back to the window: the light gleamed on her hair under its fresh lawn cap and glittered on the jewels in her splendid gown of crimson taffeta. She moved closer. Segalla glimpsed the silver belt that hung round her slender waist, bearing a gold perfumed apple and a bejewelled miniature Book of Hours.

"Monsieur Segalla." The Queen's voice had an amused tone. "You are most welcome."

Segalla rose, praying he would not catch his foot or stumble against the King. The Queen, fingering her gold pectoral cross set with diamonds and rubies, smiled at him. Segalla, surprised, just stared back. He was astonished at how tall Mary was, though it was her face which fascinated him: a luminous complexion, generous mouth and large, smiling eyes, that seemed to change from light chestnut to hazel. Segalla recalled Beaton's description of Mary as a fawn. He caught her shy look from under heavy eyelids and realised why. She reminded Segalla of a picture of a fairy princess with her well-marked eyebrows, finely arched forehead and slender, beautiful hands that could never stay still.

"Monsieur," she whispered. "You stare!"

"Your Majesty." Segalla bowed his head. "I was merely thinking how the poet Ronsard was a liar when he described your beauty."

Mary's face became grave, though Segalla caught the mischief in her eyes. "What are you saying, sir?" She seemed to whisper in a way that Janette, standing behind Segalla, could only envy.

"Your Majesty," Segalla murmured. "He did not do you full justice."

Mary's head tilted back and her laugh was throaty and warm. She extended her hand for Segalla to kiss. He grasped it, smooth as silk, and caught a glimpse of emerald and diamond rings, one with a carved image of a beautiful mermaid. He brushed her fingers with his lips and, as courtesy demanded, was about to let go when the Queen suddenly caught the skin of one finger between her nails and squeezed. Segalla glanced up: the Queen's eyes had become watchful and she gestured with her hand to the floor. Segalla understood. Mary did not wish him to speak or present his letters in public but to wait until she gave the order to retire.

Accordingly, Segalla made his introductions. Mary did not stand on ceremony but, grasping Janette's hands, drew her close, called her "kinswoman" and kissed her gently on each

63

cheek. Vartlett knelt before her; Mary gently stroked him on the back of the head, then drew him to his feet whilst pushing silver coins into his hand.

"You have come so far," she said in a low voice. "But this is not the time nor the place."

Once again she caught Segalla's eyes and glanced quickly to where her husband sat like some spoilt boy on the edge of his bed. She leaned over and kissed Darnley on the brow.

"Sweet husband, I must see what the good Archbishop has sent." .

"Can't I come?" Darnley peevishly asked. "Madame, I have been for too long from affairs of state."

"Soon," Mary whispered. "You shall return to those matters." She clapped her hands softly.

A young man in black velvet jerkin, with a white shirt peeping over the top and the tightest pair of hose Segalla had ever seen, seemed to appear from nowhere. He was about eighteen or nineteen summers old. His thin, pockmarked face was oddly sensual under a thick, jet-black mat of unruly hair. The Queen smiled at him.

"Monsieur Segalla, may I introduce the groom of my chamber, Hubert or French Paris, as we like to call him."

"Bothwell's French boy!" Darnley hissed.

The Queen chose to ignore this, though Segalla saw the sneer on Paris's lips. He disregarded the King and gave the Queen a most elegant bow.

"Your Majesty is leaving?"

"Yes, Paris, I am."

The page walked into the centre of the room.

"My lords, ladies!" he cried in a surprisingly strong voice. "Her Majesty the Queen is retiring to her own chambers to receive the envoy of His Eminence Archbishop Beaton!"

The chatter died immediately. Segalla realised all eyes were on him. Mary gripped the front of her dress, raising the hem slightly. Traquair appeared, two halberdiers on either side.

"Monsieur Segalla, you will join us," the Queen whispered. "Your wife"—the Queen emphasized the word—"and your servant will be well looked after here by Paris. We shall have words alone!"

Chapter 4

Preceded by Traquair and the two halberdiers, Mary left the chamber. Segalla whispered his excuses to Janette and followed suit. He went back down the spiral staircase. The captain ushered him into the Queen's chamber, closing the door behind them. For a while Segalla stood self-consciously staring round the room as Mary visibly relaxed, free from the oppressive atmosphere of the upper chamber. She waved her hand elegantly at the thick wall hangings and the few sticks of furniture.

"Not a room for a Queen, eh, Monsieur Segalla?"

She eased herself into a high-backed chair next to a fairly narrow cot covered by a green and yellow cloth. Segalla saw Mary wince with pain as she gripped her right side.

"Your Majesty is unwell?" he asked.

All the hauteur and rigidity seeping from her body, Mary drooped in the chair. She looked worried; she caught her lower lip between her teeth. She put her arms across her stomach, clutching the heavy brocade bodice of her dress. She took a deep breath and smiled at Segalla.

"Her Majesty is very well," she said. "A slight pain in the side." She lifted one arm and rubbed the side of her head. "And I have a pain like a circle of fire, here."

"Your Majesty should relax."

Segalla, who knew a great deal about pharmacopoeia and the effect of physic, recognised that the Queen held her shoulders and neck so stiffly that it was small wonder she suffered such violent pains. "Your Majesty, gently move your neck and your shoulders," he advised.

Mary sighed but followed Segalla's directions, moving her shoulders slightly and twisting her head from left to right. She paused and stared at Segalla.

"Someone should massage my neck," she said.

She continued to watch Segalla even as she moved her head and he understood why Mary had broken so many hearts. She was flirtatious but in a natural, easy way. She maintained her dignity and grace, yet she made him feel her equal, her confidant.

"Are you a physician, Monsieur Segalla, as well as a priest?" She laughed at the surprise on his face. "Oh yes, I know. Archbishop Beaton had already sent a message saying you were coming."

She rose to her feet and walked to a small table, where she filled two jewel-rimmed cups to the brim and brought one to Segalla.

"Burgundy," she said. "Full and rich. If you drink it slowly, Monsieur Segalla, and think of the sun"—her eyes grew misty—"then you are back in France. The vineyards are ripening. The smell of blossom is still heavy in the air and the sun will rise and grow stronger so that you can sit in a garden arbour and hear the drone of the bees as they plunder for honey."

Segalla watched the light in her eyes change. Mary blinked and patted him gently on the hand.

"I thank you for your forbearance, Monsieur." She raised her head slightly as if gesturing at the ceiling. "The King is not in good humour and must be indulged. Come, come, this won't do." She put the wine cup back on the table and, before Segalla could stop her, knelt before him. "Bless me, Father." Mary whispered. "If I had time I would ask you to celebrate Mass. But your blessing will do."

Segalla, surprised, hastily put down his own wine cup and, raising his hand, sketched a benediction above her as he quietly said the words. He then held out his hand and helped Mary to her feet. The Queen rose gracefully but held on to his fingers.

"Do you know, Monsieur Segalla." Her face was now only a few inches from his, her eyes studying him carefully as if she were remembering every hair on his head, the colour of his skin, the texture of his beard and moustache. It was no longer the visage of a coy woman but the face of a young child, innocent and open.

"Your Majesty?"

Mary shook her head. "Madame will do," she said. "Monsieur, I have seen you before. I am sure I have. Were you not in the service of my mother?"

Segalla hid his alarm.

"Have you not been to Scotland before?" Mary asked.

Segalla looked askance. "Madame, I was not in the service of your mother."

"No, no, not here." The Queen said. "When she was a girl in France, before she was betrothed to my father. She came to live in, and later tried to rule, this beautiful but godforsaken country." The Queen picked up her wine cup, cradling it in her hands as if it were some magic orb that could summon up the past. She walked languorously back to Segalla. "Monsieur, I am sure of it! My mother had portraits drawn by the Frenchman Corneille de Lyons. He executed many such paintings at the French court. When my mother left for Scotland, they were put in a chamber, high in the Louvre Palace, in a garret stacked there like lost memories." Mary dipped her finger into the wine cup, then ran it round her dry lips. "When I was betrothed to the Dauphin, I used to go up there and sit for hours looking at Mama's portrait. There was one behind it, much smaller, a man like yourself, with the same head, face and moustache. But, above all, the same eyes, with that lost, haunted look. You have it now, Monsieur Segalla."

He shrugged in embarrassment. "Madame, that is impossible. I am just past my thirty-second summer."

The Queen returned to her chair. "Everything goes in circles." Her eyes were fixed on Segalla. "My mother was raised in France but died in Scotland, her belly and legs swollen with dropsy. Now I do the same: raised in France, have I, Monsieur Segalla, come back to die in Scotland? Is my end my beginning? My beginning my end? So all goes in a circle?" Mary paused as if listening to the faint gossip from the chamber above. "I marry one husband and he dies. I marry another and he, too, dies, at least spiritually." The Queen shook her head suddenly. "Monsieur Segalla, for a queen my manners are appalling." She gestured at a chair behind him. "Pull that over. Let me see the good Archbishop's letters."

He obeyed. Whilst Mary broke the seal and opened the documents, Segalla studied her carefully. He saw a faint streak of grey hair amongst the auburn: lines of worry ran near her mouth; her skin now looked not golden but pallid. Every so often, Mary shifted in pain. All the time, those long, slender fingers would move, tapping the letter, plucking at her dress or smoothing the polished armrest of her chair. Segalla looked round the chamber. A piece of embroidery in rich colours lay on a stool at the far side of the bed: a rebec and viol stood in one corner. Segalla recalled that many considered the Queen an artist, whether playing the virginals, composing a poem or employing the delicate art of embroidery. He looked over his shoulder at the small writing desk, inlaid in mother-of-pearl, now covered in a pile of parchments, ink pots, quills and pumice stones. Bits of sealing wax stained the woollen rugs and the floor beneath. He looked back at the Queen, but she was studying the letters, her brow furrowed. She abruptly glanced up, and Segalla flinched at her stony expression.

"Do you know what's written here, Monsieur Segalla?"

"Madame, they are written in the Archbishop's secret cipher."

Mary smiled, though the bleak look never left her eyes. "I have read so many of the Archbishop's letters. The cipher is no secret any longer."

She rose, gesturing to Segalla to remain seated, and went to the fire burning in the grate. She leaned down and tossed the letters onto the coals, not returning to her chair until the flames had reduced them to whitened ash. She sat back in the chair and stared at a point above Segalla's head.

"Do you know, Monsieur, I did not know whether to hate or love this country. The wild moors, the heather turning golden under the sun. Fresh streams, fertile meadows and teeming woods. The common people wish to live in peace, each man in his own house tending his own garden, but the nobles are different. They love war: setting fire to the thatch, burning the heather or covering the cobblestones of town marketplaces with bloody gore. Have you been out of Edinburgh?"

Segalla shook his head.

"Go along the highways," the Queen said hoarsely. "At every crossroads stands a gibbet bearing fruit: hangings and whippings are common. A cruel, barbaric coven. One of the rebel lords, when captured, dropped dead from fright. Do you know what they did, Monsieur Segalla?"

He gazed back.

"They insisted he still had to face trial by his peers, so his corpse was opened and gutted like that of a pig. It was stuffed with spices, embalmed and then brought south for trial. Can you imagine, Monsieur? An embalmed corpse sitting in a chair before my judges?" Mary rubbed her eyes and stirred in the chair. "Beaton talks of great danger," she said sardonically, leaning forward and playing with the pectoral cross before fussing with the rings on her fingers. "But what danger, Monsieur?"

Segalla placed his wine cup on the floor. "Madame, the dangers are all about you. Your husband will be better soon, but will he remain faithful? That is Beaton's worry."

Mary glanced away. "I don't know," she said softly. She glanced back. "Darnley is a child." He has the body and legs of a beautiful man but the mind and soul of a spoilt boy." She gestured at the writing table. "He sends letters to his dreadful father the Earl of Lennox saying how sweet and loving I am. But . . ."

"But what, Madame?"

"He also sends letters to Philip of Spain asking the Spanish to mass troops in Flanders."

Segalla caught his breath. Mary quickly noted his change in expression.

"Surely, Father," she teased gently, "you, a Jesuit, would welcome this? Catholic troops landing at Leith? The Inquisition ready to root out heresy and so bring Scotland back to its ancient Faith?"

"It would cause bloody civil war."

"Of course!" Mary's eyes blazed. "Of course it would! No woman, Father, is a more true or loyal servant of Holy Mother Church than I. Yet I realise you cannot force religion down men's throats or make windows into their souls."

"And your husband plots this?"

"So rumour has it." Madcap schemes to seize Edinburgh Castle! Whispers about a ship waiting for him in the Clyde off Glasgow! No wonder the Lords plot against him."

"They have said as much, Madame?"

"Oh yes, they first asked me to divorce him, but how can I do that? Eh, Master Segalla? Ask Archbishop Beaton whether Holy Mother Church would annul my marriage? And even if it did, what would happen to my son? Would he be declared illegitimate and lose the crown?" She kicked the rug lying in front of her chair with her elegant, shoe edged in silver. "Darnley might like that." Suddenly her face was tense with fury. "He still casts slurs on my honour. He is the father of my child, yet also the father of the gossip that his own son, James, is the offspring of an unnatural lust between myself and David Rizzio."

Segalla watched the Queen, fascinated by her changes of mood: the regal Queen, the coquette princess, the loving wife, the tolerant spouse, and now the mother filled with anger at a man who would stain her honour and that of her baby.

"There is no other way, Madame?" Segalla asked.

Mary looked down at the ring on her finger. "Last autumn the Great Lords Moray, Argyll, Bothwell and the rest met beneath a yew tree at Whittingham. They swore an oath and made a bond to do away with my husband. They even had the temerity to send a messenger to ask for my approval." Mary's eyes held Segalla's. "By the Mass, Father, I swear, I told them I would have no part in it. And would regard its perpetrators as traitors."

"But they still plot?"

"Yes," she said wearily. "They still plot. They hate Darnley for betraying them. He was with them over Rizzio: now he turns his back. They claim he not only wants the Crown Matrimonial but the Crown Absolute."

"Would it not have been safe to leave him with his kinspeople?" Segalla asked.

Mary shook her head. "No, no. Darnley had fallen ill. People were whispering that it was due to poison sent by me." She gave a half laugh. "Darnley poisoned himself. He's bedded every doxy." She rubbed the side of her face. "They even say he has been in bed," she whispered, "with the Bishop of Orkney! My Lord Darnley has the morals and ways of an alley cat." She looked up, her face defiant. "But he is still my husband, the father of my child. And whilst he is in my care, no lord will raise his hand against him."

"But Madame, Archbishop Beaton warned of some great enterprise against him."

Mary shook her head. "Monsieur Segalla, you are here to advise about such danger. Where could it lie?"

"There are English spies: a man called the Raven Master. Beaton says he is close to you."

Mary stared solemnly at Segalla, then burst out laughing and, leaning over, caught him by the hand.

"Monsieur, I do not mock you." She pointed to the ceiling. "Most of the nobles"—her eyes fell away—"except for James Hepburn, the Earl of Bothwell"—Segalla glimpsed the faint blush on her face—"are in the pay of Elizabeth's spy masters. So, as the psalmist says, 'Nothing is new under the sun.' What danger can there be?" If any man lifts a hand against my husband, he is guilty of treason."

"There is poison, Madame."

The Queen shook her head. "Henry Darnley," she said flatly, "is most careful about what he eats and drinks."

Segalla moved in his chair. "Madame, what happens if the plot is against both of you?"

Mary chewed the corner of her mouth. "Aye," she said wistfully, almost as if she welcomed the thought. "Now that would be an end to all our troubles."

"It is possible," Segalla insisted, staring at the Queen, "that both you and your husband could be the victims, God forbid, of some dreadful plot."

"You are talking about my beloved half brother, James Stuart, and the Earl of Moray?"

"Perhaps." Segalla was surprised at the Queen's bluntness.

Mary smiled. "Beaton may regard me as a fawn surrounded by wolves. Oh, aye! The Archbishop believes I am an innocent, yet I know what he thinks: that Moray will do away with me and Darnley, rule the kingdom through my infant son, and who knows then, eh, Monsieur Segalla, what might happen? How many babies live to manhood?" She shook her head. "I don't think my lord of Moray would be so heartless. Secondly, the other Great Lords would not allow him to reign in peace. Finally, he would be an outcast in Europe: not even my good cousin Elizabeth would stomach the murder of a fellow monarch."

Segalla stared at her: despite her youth and naivete, Mary was shrewd. She had calculated correctly. She was married to Darnley: a rapprochement would not only enhance her status but keep Darnley under close guard. No one would dare strike at him, the Queen's good husband, and who would stoop to the bloody-handed murder of the Lord's anointed?

"But—but there is danger," Segalla stammered. He pointed to the viol standing in the corner on a stool. "A musician, Madame, once told me that music is infinite and the variations on one note can be limitless."

"Come to the point, Monsieur."

Segalla looked sharply at the Queen and recalled Beaton's warnings in Paris. "What happens, Your Majesty, if a more devious plot is devised to destroy your good name?"

Mary reddened again and her eyes fell.

"Madame." Segalla rose and went on one knee before her. "Madame, six years ago, Elizabeth's favourite, Robert Dudley, Earl of Leicester, had a wife. You have heard the story?"

Mary held his gaze and nodded.

"The gossips said," Segalla continued, "that Dudley loved Queen Elizabeth of England, and that she had a great passion for him. Gossips also said"—Segalla steeled himself to continue—"that Dudley planned to divorce his wife and so marry Elizabeth."

"I like all the rest of the world have heard the story." Mary leaned forward and touched Segalla's cheek. "Monsieur, speak from the heart; let me hear your counsel."

"Dudley's wife," Segalla went on, "fell downstairs at her

house in Cumnor Place in Oxfordshire: her neck was broken though the headdress about her head was scarcely disturbed. Some people believe she was killed by Dudley so that he could be free to marry the Queen. Others claim she was killed so that the consequent scandal would prevent that."

Mary moved her head slightly to one side. "Your meaning, Monsieur?"

"If Elizabeth had married Dudley after the mysterious death of his wife, they would have both been branded as murderers. God knows what might have happened."

Mary rose quickly to her feet, weaving her fingers together. She stepped behind Segalla as if to hide her emotions and school her features.

"I have spoken honestly," Segalla said over his shoulder.

"And who is my Dudley?" Mary asked.

"People say James Hepburn, Earl of Bothwell."

He heard the Queen turn and walk towards him. She stroked his hair, touched him gently on the cheek and, stretching out her hand, helped him to his feet. Segalla was surprised to see her amused, clearly trying to stifle a burst of laughter.

"James Hepburn, Earl of Bothwell, is a handsome rogue but not my consort. He is certainly not my paramour. Tell Mother Beaton when you go back to Paris that I need Bothwell. He is wild, passionate, but he does not take bribes and is regarded highly by the troops we can muster and the captains of the few ships I possess." She paused at a knock on the door, her face becoming grave. "Come in."

The door opened and James Stuart, Earl of Moray, entered the room. He caught Segalla's eyes, bowed and then stood with his back to the door, his bonnet in his hand.

"Sweet sister." Moray forced a smile. "You tarry long here."

"Sweet sister is most busy!" Mary retorted. "Affairs of state, dear brother."

Moray bowed. "Madame, I beg permission to leave court."

Mary took a step forward. "Sweet brother, but why? Tomorrow is Carnival Sunday. We must bid farewell to the Ambassador of Savoy. The marriage festivities at Holyrood. Will you not join us?"

"Aye." Moray took a step forward. "Jigging and singing, Madame, whilst my wife lies ill in Fife."

Mary walked towards him, grasping him by the wrist.

"Oh, sweet brother, I'm sorry. Give her my good wishes. Do you need anything?"

Moray held his hand up. "Madame, I shall return as soon as possible." He took a step back, gave the most elegant of bows and, without a word or second glance, strode out of the chamber.

"So," Segalla said. "The Earl of Moray leaves you."

Mary shrugged and looked at him over her shoulder. "Sweet brother has his tantrums. He does not like Henry Darnley."

"Aye, Madame, and he does not like you!"

"You are blunt." Mary went to lean against her writing desk. "Monsieur Segalla, remember, Moray is illegitimate, the child of my father's mistress Margaret Erskine: born of a king but never king." She tapped her fingers on the desk. "But enough of business, Monsieur Segalla; you must join us at Holyrood. You wish lodgings there?"

"Madame, we already have them in the town."

Mary did not reply: she was already striding with her long-legged gait across the room as someone else knocked on the door. Segalla heard gruff tones followed by Mary's exclamation of delight.

"Jamie, you are not leaving us as well?"

The Earl of Bothwell swaggered in. He smiled at Mary and strode across the room to grasp Segalla's hand. Moray had been dressed in sober attire, but after one look at Bothwell,

Segalla had to bite his lip to hide his smile; one wag had described the Earl as an ape in purple, and there was some truth to the witticism. He wore a gold doublet of ribbed silk with puffed shoulders: little golden studs buttoned it up to a narrow laced ruff, which encircled a lean, muscular throat. He had short, straggly chestnut hair, dark eyes with deep sockets; their gaze was never still. The gibe about the ape seemed appropriate when Segalla observed Bothwell's long, protuberant upper lip and square, thick jaw, which even his wild moustache and beard could not hide.

"You stare at me, sir?"

"Monsieur le Comte." Segalla was careful to use the French title. "Your exploits are known even in France."

Behind Bothwell, Mary laughed, clear and merry. The Earl looked suspiciously at her.

"Madame, what have we here, eh? Are you going to tarry with this Frenchman all day?" Bothwell glared across the room, his long arms dangling at his side, his muscular legs, in thin, tight-fitting hose, wide apart, reminding Segalla of a sea captain on the deck of his ship.

"Jamie, you are never content unless you are moving." Mary tapped the earl on his broad chest.

"I canna take no more of that." Bothwell pointed to the ceiling.

"The King will soon be better," Mary said. She extended her hand for Segalla to kiss. "And I am just about to leave. Jamie, you will come with me, eh?"

Segalla kissed the Queen's hand. She squeezed his shoulder gently and glanced quickly at him. Bothwell hastened ahead to open the door, and Segalla followed them out of the room.

He knew the ways of princes. Mary had received him. She had listened to his warnings, but that was the end of the matter. He had not been invited back to the King's presence, so as Archibald Bethon, the Queen's chamberlain, locked the door behind him, Segalla returned downstairs to the long, empty *salle*. Janette and Vartlett were there, deep in conversation with French Paris; beside them was a freckle-faced young man with ginger hair whom Vartlett introduced as Alexander or "Sandy" Durham, porter to the King's privy chamber.

"Life is hectic," Segalla said. "Her Majesty is very busy."

"Aye." Sandy Durham spoke in a lilting lowland accent. "And will become busier when the King has recovered."

Janette ignored the salacious remark; Vartlett just chuckled. He, Durham and Paris were already on a first-name basis. As Segalla, Janette and Vartlett took their leave, returning to the courtyard for their horses, Thomas Nelson caught up with them. Segalla assured him that they would attend the next day's festivities.

Then, punching him playfully on the shoulder, Nelson disappeared back upstairs.

Once they had collected their horses and were riding back towards Netherbow Gate, Janette gave a loud cry of relief.

"Thank God I'm free of there!"

"Why is that?" Segalla pulled his horse alongside hers.

"Oh, on the surface all is amity and peace." She sighed and dabbed her mouth with a kerchief. "But underneath, dark passions swirl. The Lords talk but they do not meet each other's eyes. There's a feeling of . . ." She reined in and looked back at the low-gabled turrets of Kirk o'Field. "Oppression, hatred, tension."

"Don't forget," Segalla said, "it's only a year since the murder of Rizzio. Master Vartlett, how did you find the servants?"

"They are all retainers," Vartlett said slowly. "Not ordinary servants or servitors, more trusted henchmen." He stroked his horse's neck. "Bethon, Paris and Durham are the Queen's men, but Darnley is well protected. He has Nelson, Symonds, a squire called Taylor, who is out buying supplies, and three grooms. Two of whom I have met, Glen and Macaig. All young men and handpicked. They are Darnley's bodyguard."

"But isn't he vulnerable?" Janette asked.

Vartlett shrugged. "Both he and the Queen are, though Mary has her archers, halberdiers and captain of the guard. Bothwell also has his mosstroopers, whilst the city streets and wynds are patrolled by a watch ten to fifteen strong. As long as they stay in Edinburgh, the Queen and her husband are safe. But when they leave?" Vartlett shrugged. "God knows what might happen."

"And the Raven Master?" Segalla asked. "Could he be there?"

"I don't know. I suspect Walsingham has suborned one of the Great Lords. It might yet prove to be Moray and I say this warily, but it could also be Bothwell."

"Why a lord?" Segalla asked.

"If damage is to be done to the King or to the Queen, it must be someone who holds power, has the keys to fortresses and can call up troops."

"And what else?" Segalla caught the hesitation in Vartlett's voice.

"There are the Douglases. The Earl of Morton may be sulking in St. Andrews, but the city is full of his henchmen. They have no love for the Queen, and if they found Darnley out on a lonely moor, he would be singing with the angels within the hour!"

Segalla thanked him and urged his horse on, lost in his own thoughts.

"Nicholas, husband dear?"

Segalla started and glanced across at Janette, who was looking at him strangely. She grinned. They had entered a tavern yard.

"Nicholas, what is the matter?" Janette whispered. She narrowed her eyes. "Are you smitten by the Queen?"

Segalla smiled and dismounted, then helped her down. He was about to lead her into the tavern when the landlord came bustling out.

"Monsieur Segalla, I have a message for you. A poor beggar boy brought it by."

"Well, man, where is it?"

"No, no, it was by word of mouth. The beggar simply said: 'Tell Monsieur Segalla that the raven who flies on high can see everything.'"

Chapter 5

On Sunday, 9 February 1567, darkness fell early across Edinburgh. Earlier that day, the Queen had attended the Ambassador of Savoy's farewell dinner, where there had been junketing and feasting. The Queen and her guests looked splendid in their yards of red and yellow taffeta, gold damask suits, jerkins edged with silver and bonnets embroidered with precious thread and black silk. They had supped and danced in rooms lit by the reflections of candles in crystal mirrors, the walls draped in velvets and silk. After that, the Queen had decided to return to Kirk o'Field. She would sit and talk there to her husband before going to the special banquet at Holyrood she had arranged for Christiana Hogg, one of her maids, who was marrying Bastian Pages, who had often devised subtle masques and clever court games to amuse the Queen. More importantly, he and Christiana had assisted Mary to escape from Holyrood after the murder of Rizzio. Now the Queen was going to reward them at that same palace with feasting, dancing and the bestowal of gifts.

By nine o'clock on that Sunday evening the reception for the Ambassador of Savoy was over. The Queen washed her hands in fragrant rosewater, French Paris standing behind her to attend to her every want. Then Mary gave the signal to return to the Old Provost's House at Kirk o'Field. She and her party, preceded by servants carrying flaring torches, swept up the streets of Edinburgh. Musicians followed, playing softly to mark the Queen's passage. The courtiers grumbled at the little flurries of snow that had fallen, though the skies were now clear and a new moon slipped between the clouds. Under the dark orange torchlight, the snow turned to russet-coloured slush as Mary, laughing and chatting with her companions, processed out of Edinburgh and into the quadrangle of the Old Provost's House.

The silent reception room had been specially arranged with tapestries of black fringed velvet. Only the Queen and her Great Lords, Bothwell, Huntly, Argyll and the rest, entered the King's bedroom through the antechamber where the King's commode stood in majestic isolation under its canopy of yellow shot silk with red and green fringes. The noble guests thronged in: Darnley, now dressed for bed, lay against the bolsters and like the pampered boy he was, received his wife rather sulkily. Now and again he would stare across at the Great Lords, who squatted on red velvet cushions playing dice. Darnley bit his lip in annoyance. Their masks were pushed back on their foreheads; this was Carnival Night, when people hid their identity as an excuse, of course, for furtive kisses and greedy sexual fumblings in the dark. Tomorrow he would be King again and come into his own. He glanced into the dark recesses of the small gallery that jutted out over the town wall. Mary sensed her husband's mood and poured him a goblet of wine, and eventually his spirits lifted. But the Lords were impatient to be free of that sickly chamber and return to the spacious galleries and wide rooms of Holyrood Palace. Soon Mary stood.

"Husband, I must leave."

Darnley, under his black velvet mask, scowled.

"Husband," Mary repeated, "I must go. I have promised Christiana I will be there to throw the stocking and give my personal gift."

Darnley stared up at his Queen, splendid in a dress of white satin fringed with gold; her luminous complexion glowed under the influence of wine and the excitement of the evening.

"Madame, you promised to stay." He scowled.

"Harry." Mary bent down, kissed him on the head and murmured into his ear. "I must go, but tomorrow I will return and we shall both leave for Seton." She slipped a ring off her little finger and thrust it into his hand. "My pledge." She smiled. "I will return."

"Then do so, early." Darnley looked across the chamber to where his henchmen were preparing for bed in the small gallery. "Tomorrow at five!" he shouted. "Have my great horses ready!"

The henchmen bowed.

Mary kissed Darnley again and, preceded by her Great Lords, the captain of her guard following behind, went down the winding staircase to where their horses waited in the great quadrangle. In his chamber Darnley lay back against the silken bolsters and glowered at the doorway.

"Taylor!" he shouted.

His squire was a blond, smooth-shaven fellow who had shared many of Darnley's exploits as well as his bed: after all, he was the King's personal valet and could not object to his master's fumblings.

"Your Grace?" Taylor stood beside the bed.

Behind him, Darnley could see Nelson, Symonds, Glen, MacCaig and the pageboy, also ready for bed. They sat in a circle sharing the last cup of wine, hiding their obvious disappointment at having to stay with their master whilst the rest of the servants indulged in revelry at Holyrood.

"My lord?" Taylor repeated.

Darnley kept staring at the doorway. "Why is the door unhung?" he demanded.

"Your Grace, you may remember, it was taken off to cover your bath and keep the water warm?"

"Make sure the house is secure," Darnley insisted, remembering the dark looks from several of the lords. "Who has remained?"

Taylor smiled ever ready to brush away his master's fears.

"Your Grace is most safe here. As the Queen left, Bethon, her chamberlain, locked the doors behind her. Bonkle the cook and the other servants have now left. Your Grace, it is Carnival Sunday. There are a few grooms and members of your retinue in the cottages and outhouses outside."

Darnley nodded and smiled secretively at Taylor. "And no one knows?" he said. "No one," Taylor whispered.

Darnley, satisfied, waited whilst Taylor went belowstairs to ensure that all was well. The rest of the servitors came to the bedside. Darnley pointed to the prayerbook in Nelson's hand.

"Thomas, you have a fine voice. Perhaps a psalm?"

"Your Grace, will you accompany me on the lute?"

The King shook his head. "I do not feel in the mood, man!" He pulled himself farther up on the bed. "Let others dance and feast," he declared self-righteously. He plucked the book from Nelson's hand and, opening it, chose the Eighth and Tenth Psalms. With Nelson leading, they began to chant.

Lead me, O Lord, in thy goodness, because of mine enemies.
Make thy way straight before my face.
Destroy thou them, oh God;
Let them fall by their own counsels.

Taylor returned and, when the psalm was over, Darnley clasped his hands. "A good-night drink," he commanded.

Nelson hurried to fill the goblets of wine, cleaning up the room now that the noblemen had left. Darnley sipped from the cup, reminding his henchmen that tomorrow they would leave early. After that most of the candles were doused. Taylor slipped between the silken sheets beside his master. The henchmen, their clothes neatly piled, made themselves comfortable on the straw-filled palliasses in the gallery.

For a while Darnley lay staring at the moonlight streaking through the casement window. Somewhere in the cemetery beyond, an owl that nested in the ruins of St. Mary's hunted amongst the gravestones under a clear, freezing sky. Darnley strained his ears. Now and again he caught the faint sounds of merriment or even the occasional reveller returning to his house on the edge of the city. Darnley thought of Mary and smiled. Tomorrow all would be different. He would come into his own. Now he would sleep for a while. His eyes grew heavy and, licking his finger, he snuffed out the beeswax candles on the table next to his bed.

At Holyrood Palace the wedding banquet drew to an end, only to be followed by a splendid series of masques, featuring regiments of centaurs, Moors, Moriscos, highlanders and demons. These either assaulted or defended a fortress specially constructed for that purpose. Outside, fireballs pierced the dark sky, whilst in the galleries the royal musicians played a series of lilting tunes as courtiers, splendid in their raiment, gathered round the Queen, the guest of honour between Christiana Hogg and Bastian Pages. The shouts, music and laughter filled the entire palace. As the groom and his bride retired to a specially decorated chamber, the Queen abruptly left the festivities to be closeted for an hour with the Earl of Bothwell and Captain John Stewart of Traquair, yet few thought their business could be serious. In the city itself some of the common people stared up at the palace, listening enviously to the faint sounds of celebration, or watched the lights burning in the windows. Generally Edinburgh was quiet: as midnight approached, revellers left the taverns and inns to quickly make their way home lest they be apprehended by the watch who faithfully patrolled the city.

In the fields, to the east of Kirk o'Field, a group of horsemen trooped quietly through the country lanes led by Andrew Ker of Fawdonside. A rebel, a man detestable to the Queen and a lifelong opponent of the Earl of Bothwell, Ker was a born killer. Had he not been present at the murder of Rizzio almost a year earlier? Had he not pressed his pistol against the very belly of the pregnant Queen? If he were spotted so close to Edinburgh at this moment, his presence would raise a few eyebrows. For such heinous treason, Ker had been declared an outlaw and put to the horn, but now he had slipped back, taking up a position in a wooded copse only a mile from Kirk o'Field.

James Stuart, Earl of Moray, was also thinking about Edinburgh as he prepared to take the ferry across the Forth to his estates in Fife. Moray was a worried man. He had seen Mary's accord with Darnley and wondered how events would proceed. How could Walsingham be so sure that matters could be turned on their heads? Moray had had carried out Walsingham's instructions, but he still wondered at their simplicity. A barrel of gun-powder had been prepared and carefully hidden away at Kirk o'Field, but what next? Moray shook his head. If matters did not change and Darnley was restored to royal favour, what could the future hold for Moray? The illegitimate son of a King who had already plotted unsuccessfully against his Queen? Moray's first failure had been treated with clemency, but what would happen if he tried, only to fail again? Moray drew his cloak about him and stared out across the icy, dark waters. He quietly vowed that if the next few days failed to yield a harvest, he would either stay at home or cross the border and place his sword at the disposal of the English Queen.

In London, Secretary Walsingham was in his privy chamber, a woollen blanket round his shoulders. He sat before the fire carefully sipping a cup of warm posset and watched the sand trickle through an hourglass placed on the table before him. Outside all was quiet, though now and again Walsingham heard the crunch of boots on gravel, a sign that his own private guards were doing their turn of duty, protecting their master against attack from any foreign agent. Walsingham watched the sand slip away. He heard the bells of a church chime midnight and turned the glass over. All the time, as the grains slid to the bottom, Walsingham thought of what could be happening in Edinburgh. Mary would be at her junketing: Darnley, sulking, brooding, would be plotting at Kirk o'Field. Walsingham felt a flicker of nervousness. He had moved all the pieces carefully along the board. If everything went according to plan, Elizabeth of England would be safe and Mary of Scotland neatly trapped like a coney in the hay. Walsingham closed his eyes and prayed that God would bless his cause and bring his subtle schemes and plots to full fruition. He opened his eyes; the last of the sand had sifted away. Walsingham's upper lip curled in a smile. He carefully doused the fire, blew out the candles and retired to bed. He was a happy man. In Scotland his Raven Master had spread his dark, death-bearing wings. The dice was thrown, the deed was done.

Segalla spent Sunday, 9th February, rather restlessly, alarmed at the Raven Master's impudent message. He was glad he had not gone to Holyrood to attend the festivities. Instead, he had supped alone in the tavern's taproom: Janette and Vartlett disappeared, apparently out on some mysterious errand. Segalla returned to his own chamber. He celebrated a short Mass and recited his office. In the light of the flickering candle, he carefully read the words of a psalm, followed by the Benedictus of Zacharias. After that, he went out into the gallery to ask a servitor whether his "good wife" and servant had returned. The man grinned sheepishly and shook his head. Embarrassed, Segalla returned to his room, quietly cursing. Soon he drifted into an uneasy sleep.

The sound of the explosion, like that of twenty or thirty cannon firing in unison, sent him staggering from his bed. He knew enough about firearms to recognise the sound of gunpowder, and as he hastily dressed he wondered whether some hostile force was attacking the city or laying siege to Holyrood. In the galleries outside, and downstairs in the courtyard, he heard servants and other guests running about and shouting. He grabbed his cloak and flung open the door to his room. Janette, heavy-eyed with sleep, dressed in a furred pelisse, her face white and startled, came hurrying up.

"What is it?"

Segalla glimpsed the small love bite on her neck and wondered what his "wife" had been doing. Vartlett, in a similar state of undress, joined them: a look at his tousled hair and sleepy eyes were sufficient answer for Segalla.

"Both of you lovebirds!" he snapped. "Get dressed!"

He paused to listen above the hustle and bustle of the tavern.

"What is it?" Janette repeated.

"At first I thought it was cannon fire, but there's nothing else; it must have been an explosion. Now dress and join me. I'll find out where it is."

Segalla raced down the stairs. In the taproom he paused to breathe more deeply and calm his thudding heart. The sense of dread that had haunted him ever since his arrival in Edinburgh now took a more substantial form. He seized the arm of a servant hurrying in from the courtyard.

"What's the matter, man?"

"May the guid Lord save us!" The fellow replied. "It's the ain King's lodgings at Kirk o'Field."

Segalla went out, shouting for his horse. He laid hold of a half-awake ostler. "My horse!" he bellowed.

The man stared blearily at him.

"Any bloody horse!" Segalla roared, slipping a coin into the man's hand.

The fellow sloped off. Segalla followed him into the stable. A shaggy-haired garron was brought out and harness tossed over it. Segalla fairly threw himself into the saddle and galloped through the tavern gates, sending people flying for cover. Outside, the alleyways were dark, the cobbles underfoot slippery with ice and a thin carpet of snow. The cold wind tore at his hair and face and tingled the sweat on his unprotected neck. One hand holding the reins, Segalla pulled his cloak closer, cursing his own recklessness yet shouting at people who were coming out of their houses to stand aside. He reached the Netherbow Gate and galloped through, along the country tracks that bore right to Kirk o'Field. Now and again, Segalla passed others running in the same direction. He turned a corner and, in the moonlight, glimpsed the outline of the old town wall and the ruins of St. Mary's church. People were running about, the pitch torches they carried faint pricks of light in the gloom.

Segalla also could see a large cloud of white dust. In the moonlight it looked like snow or smoke—but then Segalla pulled up.

"It is dust!" he said. "In God's name, what's happened?"

The white cloud lifted and spread. A man caught Segalla's horse by the bridle.

"It's the King's lodgings!" he cried. "Nothing more than dung or dross: not a stone left upon a stone!"

Segalla nodded, dismounted, hobbled his horse and walked towards the cloud of dust. Somebody was moving along the old town wall, fixing torches in its cracks and crevices: from where the lodgings had once stood there were cries and shouts. Segalla walked through a small postern gate that led from Thieves Row directly into the Old Provost's House. He stood within the entrance, mouth gaping, almost impervious to the dust that stung his eyes and the back of his throat. He thought the fellow who had stopped his horse had been exaggerating, but, indeed, the man had not told the whole truth. The King's lodgings were no more: nothing was left but a pile of rubble covered in the white dust of the plaster that had hung there for centuries. Segalla looked around even as he caught the acrid tang of gunpowder; the house had been blown from its very foundations. In the light of the torches, he could see how the masonry, including square, thick slabs of foundation stones, had been flung about like seeds of grain.

"Will you stand there and gape all day?" a voice shouted. "For the love of sweet Jesus!" We need help; the King himself could be buried here!"

Segalla coughed, cleared his throat and, pulling up his cloak, wrapped it firmly round his mouth and nose: he gingerly climbed over the pile of rubble. The man who had shouted was now waiting in the corner of the Old Provost's House where the gallery had stood.

"There's people here." He waved his torch at Segalla. "Come on, man!"

Slipping and slithering, Segalla huried across the rubble and helped the town bailiff pull aside a heavy beam. Beneath, in a hole, Darnley's servants Nelson and Symonds, their hair and faces covered in dust, stared beseechingly up at him. The town bailiff, Segalla helping, pulled each of them out. Nelson and Symonds immediately wandered off as if dream-walking. The bailiff grabbed Segalla's arm and pointed to a hand jutting out under a huge boulder.

"They were lucky!" he rasped. "The other poor bastards must be dead!"

Segalla nodded but hurried after Nelson and Symonds. Both men, arms crossed, crouched against the town wall. Symonds was whimpering to himself; Nelson just stared at the rubble, lips moving soundlessly. Both men were dressed only in thin linen shirts and breeches. Covered in dust, they looked like ghosts, except for their eyes round with fright and the trickles of blood from scratches on their hands, knees and feet. Nelson's lower lip was cut: he had a bruise under his right eye and small gashes on his forehead and cheeks.

Segalla seized him by the arms.

"Nelson, what happened?"

"I don't know," Nelson whispered. "I was asleep in my bed. There was a crash as if the heavens themselves were falling in." He glanced at Segalla. "I thought it was a nightmare. Then I woke up; the house was falling about me. Symonds was screaming." He stared down at his companion. "Then it was dark and the dust was threatening to cut our breath off." He looked back across the rubble. "My master," he moaned. "The King!"

If Segalla had not stopped him, Nelson would have run back across the rubble. "I must go," Nelson pleaded. "His Grace the King . . ."

"Oh, Lord, I am cold." Symonds now began to shake, as much from fear and shock as from the freezing night air.

"Come on!" Segalla ordered. "Both of you. Others will soon be here. The King will be safe."

Segalla dragged Symonds to his feet and pushed both men through the postern gate and out into Thieves Row. By now the track was full of hurrying people; cloaks were put around Nelson and Symonds, a wineskin produced, kindling collected and a fire lit. Others joined the searchers amongst the rubble of Kirk o'Field. Segalla returned with them and watched as the corpses of Glen, MacCaig and Taylor's young page were dragged from the ruins. Their battered bodies looked dreadful in the torchlight: heads, arms and legs crushed, staring eyes and blood-caked mouths. They were hastily wrapped in winding sheets and taken on makeshift stretchers to an adjoining building. The search continued, and more people arrived to look for the King's corpse. Vartlett came, explaining that he had told Janette to stay within doors.

The manservant surveyed the damage and whistled under his breath.

"Monsieur Segalla," he said quickly, speaking in French. "This was no accident."

"You have knowledge of explosives?" Segalla asked.

"A little. I served as a sapper with the Duke of Lorraine's forces against the Empire. To destroy a building like this—" Vartlett pointed to the quadrangle, now lit by torchlight. "See over there, those huge bricks. They are from the very foundations. A great barrel of gunpowder must have been used."

"A mine?" Segalla asked, pulling Vartlett into the shadows of the old town wall.

"Not necessarily," Vartlett said above the shouts and sounds of stone and rubble being shifted away. "A great deal of gunpowder in an enclosed space can also wreak terrible damage. And who has access to such supplies?"

"The Earl of Moray?"

Vartlett made a rude sound with his lips. "What about my lord of Bothwell?"

Segalla felt a shiver up his spine. So far they had been intent on finding the King, but like everyone else, he would start to wonder, and the gossip would begin.

"I will speak bluntly, Monsieur," Vartlett whispered. "Her Majesty has access to supplies of gunpowder. Bothwell is a trained soldier; the city is full of his henchmen, and the Queen did leave the King at Kirk o'Field for the revels at Holyrood."

Segalla looked up at the sky. "The Queen," he said, "would never stoop to such a murder."

"Perhaps she did not," Vartlett said. "Whatever, Master, the King is now gone."

"But is he dead?" Segalla asked and pointed to the people clambering about in the rubble. "So far there's not a trace of him. They have searched the place where his bed lay: they have discovered its remains but no sign of Darnley or his body squire Taylor."

Further conversation was impossible as Bothwell and the captain of the Queen's guard arrived, protected against the cold by their cowled cloaks. They were accompanied by a group of halberdiers from the castle and other able-bodied retainers. Bothwell immediately ordered the ruins to be cleared, telling the bailiffs to disperse the crowds. He pointed at Nelson, who was standing on the wall urging people to dig for the King.

"Come down, man," Bothwell ordered tartly. "If the King is not there"—he glanced at Segalla, who still stood in the shadows of the wall—"then God knows where he is!"

After a great deal of confusion, the crowd of helpers began to disperse. The soldiers, under Traquair and the careful direction of Nelson, began to dig where the top storey of the Old Provost's House had been. Vartlett slipped away into the darkness as Bothwell, his face hidden in his cowl, walked over to Segalla.

"Does the Queen know?" Segalla asked.

"No," Bothwell said. "So far, all I have said is there's been an accident. Perhaps a bolt of lightning." He glowered as Segalla laughed drily. "You find me amusing, Monsieur?"

"No, my lord, I do not, but such stories will not help the Queen." Segalla gestured with his hand. "Only a bairn or a fool would refuse to accept that Kirk o'Field was deliberately blown up. With what intent, and by whom, only God knows!"

"Master!" Vartlett, his face white, chest heaving, came running through the small postern gate. Lips moving, he pointed across Thieves Row at the large orchard and fields beyond. "Master." Vartlett leaned against the wall to steady himself. "I went for a walk, away from the crowds and dust."

He whispered hoarsely. "Darnley and his body squire. They are in the orchard." He shook his head wordlessly. "It's as if they are asleep."

Bothwell seized a torch from a niche in the wall; then he and Segalla followed Vartlett across the cobbled track. They entered the orchard and crossed the grass, lightly covered by a dusting of snow. They stumbled and slipped as they made their way through the trees to a small clearing, about thirty or forty paces from where they had entered. Segalla stared speechlessly down at the eerie scene. Darnley, in a furred pelisse, was lying on his back; his nightshirt pulled above his groin showed him naked beneath. A few yards away, lying on his face, hands under his chin, his nightshirt pulled above his waist, lay Taylor. Between them was a furred cloak, a chair, a pair of slippers, a dagger and, in the poor light, what looked like a heap of cordage.

"May the Lord have mercy!" Segalla whispered.

He knelt beside the King, pulling down the nightshirt to make his body respectable. Vartlett did the same for Taylor's corpse. Segalla just stared: at first sight Vartlett's description was correct: the King lay there, white-faced, eyes closed, mouth slightly open as if he were asleep.

"It's as if," Vartlett whispered, "someone lifted them from their beds and brought them here. There's no mark or sign upon the corpses."

Segalla grabbed the torch the manservant was carrying and, holding it as close as possible, carefully scrutinised the King's face, neck and torso.

"Not a mark. No bruise or contusion." He stared up at Bothwell, who just gazed strangely back.

"They could have been carried here," the earl declared. "By the force of the explosion."

"Nonsense!" Segalla whispered. "There are no burn, scorch or powder marks on his body."

He moved over to Taylor; he was the same as the King:

face a waxy white, lips half open, eyes closed. His body bore no mark. Segalla felt his corpse, then that of the King.

"What hour is it?" he asked.

Vartlett shrugged, his face grey in the torchlight.

"Between four and five in the morning."

"The bodies are cold." Segalla declared. "No warmth." He got to his feet. "They must have been dead for hours. But why here, eh? If the explosion was to kill the King, and it surely was, why not leave the corpses in the building? Why bring them out here?"

Vartlett pointed to the chair, furred pelisse, slippers, dagger and pile of cordage.

"They fled," he said. "They must have done, using the chair and rope they lowered themselves from the window. They then fled into the darkness, only to be met by their killers and, somehow, throttled or choked to death."

Segalla looked at Bothwell. "My lord. This is a bloody night's work. Those who cannot account for their movements will be held responsible."

Bothwell just stared back and, hitching his cloak around him, turned on his heel and strode off into the darkness.

Chapter 6

Segalla tried to ignore the gaze from the dead men's half-open eyes. The corpses looked ghastly against the frost-covered grass, and the flickering torches gave them a false impression of life. He turned away and carefully examined the dagger, slippers and furred robe all neatly placed at the side of the corpses. The pile of cordage received only a cursory glance as Segalla searched for any indications as to why these two men had been silently slain and laid out in this sombre orchard.

Bothwell returned with a company of soldiers carrying makeshift stretchers. Silencing their exclamations of horror at the two corpses, the earl ordered the bodies to be taken to the upper chamber of the New Provost's House, next to where the King had lodged. The soldiers obeyed, two of them providing tattered, stained cloaks to cover the corpses, which were then carried off.

"Should we also return, Monsieur?" Vartlett asked.

Segalla watched the black-garbed procession disappear amongst the trees: he heard the fresh cries of horror as the crowds round the ruined building learnt about the discovery of the corpses.

"Tell me, Vartlett," Segalla said. "You saw the chamber where Darnley was lodged. If you woke in the middle of the night because you believed assailants surrounded such a building, their hearts set on your destruction, what would you do? Remember," he added, "you have the keys to the chamber; the other set are held only by the Queen, who has left for

Holyrood. You must also remember"—Segalla held up his hand—"that you have four able-bodied retainers in your chamber and a few others in the different outhouses round the quadrangle." Segalla pointed to the doorway through which the procession had now disappeared, carrying the corpses as well as the chair, cordage and clothing of the dead King.

"Taylor had a dagger, and undoubtedly there were other weapons in the house." Segalla walked over to his manservant. "So, what would you do, Vartlett?"

Vartlett rubbed his lips. "If I went downstairs," he said, "and opened the doors, I might run into my enemies waiting for me. Moreover, the noise of their approach would have awakened the whole house, yet Nelson and the others slept throughout."

Segalla nodded.

"So." Vartlett scratched his head. "We know Darnley did not leave by that route. Hence the chair and heap of cordage. He must have let himself out by a window, lowering the chair and tying the loose end of the rope to some hook or point in the room. That," Vartlett concluded, "is how Darnley and Taylor escaped." He paused and gestured round the small grove of trees. "Darnley must have become suspicious: once he and Taylor escaped out of the window overlooking Thieves Row, they fled into the night, but the assassins chased and caught them."

"And what then?"

The manservant made a face. "Well, they would fight, struggle, put up some resistance." Even in the gloom Segalla could see the recognition dawning on Vartlett's face. "But there are no signs of struggle or violence here. No marks on the corpses!"

"Exactly!" Segalla said. "And if they were fleeing, why take the chair and rope? They would leave them, surely?"

Vartlett, dumbfounded, shook his head.

"Darnley might have escaped through that window overlooking Thieves Row, though we can't tell," Segalla added drily, "because it's now blown up. However, if they did, he and Taylor would have had to step over Glen, MacCaig, Nelson and Symonds. Surely they would have roused them, alerted them to the danger? But this didn't happen."

Vartlett chewed the corner of his lip, then laughed abruptly. "Perhaps they left by the other window, the one overlooking the garden, which stretches to the ruins of Blackfriars monastery."

"In which case," Segalla said, "my questions still stand. Why did they bring the chair and rope with them and why didn't they rouse Nelson and the rest?"

Vartlett spread his hands. "Monsieur, I do not know the answer."

"Neither do I," Segalla said, staring up through the gaunt branches at the dark sky now smeared by the first light of day. He suddenly felt tired and rubbed his eyes.

"Believe me, Vartlett," he said. "Darnley's murder was planned, devised and carried out by a most subtle mind." Segalla started as a bird, its black wings spread, sped across the orchard. "In London," he said, "Walsingham will be laughing his head off, preparing prizes and rewards for his Raven Master, whilst we must write to Archbishop Beaton and report we have failed."

"Monsieur, we did not fail." Vartlett took a step closer.

Segalla smelt the stale wine on his breath.

"Darnley may be dead, but the Queen and her son are safe," Vartlett said. "We delivered Beaton's letter and repeated his warnings. This plot, these deaths were planned for weeks. There is nothing we could have done." Vartlett tightened the sword belt round his waist. "The Scottish court," he rasped, "has the stench of death around it. The roots of this night's work stretch back years. Mary should never have left

France. She should never have married Darnley. She should never have brought him back into her grace and pardon."

Segalla stared at Vartlett's dirt-smeared, unshaven face.

"Do I look as unpresentable as you?"

Vartlett grinned and turned away: as he did so, Segalla caught the faint fragrance of Janette Lindsay.

"Are you lovers?" he asked abruptly.

Vartlett began to laugh quietly. "Monsieur, we are more than that. Didn't Archbishop Beaton tell you? In the eyes of the world, Janette Lindsay and you are man and wife. But in God's eyes, I am her husband." He grinned at the surprised look on Segalla's face. "Oh yes, we have been for at least twelve months. We were married on St. Blaise's day in a small chapel at Fontrevault."

"And you did not object?" Segalla asked. "To this present deception?"

Vartlett's hand fell to the pommel of his dagger. "Segalla, you are a mysterious man. Archbishop Beaton openly wonders where you came from. Nevertheless, you seem an honourable one, a priest, a Jesuit. I do not think you would abuse my wife." He tapped the hilt of his dagger. "Now and again," he whispered, "I kill not because my masters order me to kill but for Janette." His dark eyes held Segalla's. "I would slay any man who hurt her!" Vartlett stared again about the bleak orchard. "What are we doing here? Darnley is dead. Walsingham is gleeful and the Raven Master controls the game."

"We will wait," Segalla said. "As I have done before. They have brought us to the dance floor, Vartlett. They have whistled up their own tune, but our steps are still ours."

"So, where do we go now, back to the tavern?"

"No. I will take one more look at Darnley's corpse before the surgeons begin their bloody work." He pulled on his cloak and walked back to the orchard gate, but then he paused and gripped Vartlett's wrist. "You have done this before, haven't you?"

The manservant looked askance.

"Tasks, errands." Segalla explained. "For our good Archbishop."

Vartlett smiled and shrugged. "Of course, in France, the Low Countries and, on one occasion, beyond the Rhine."

"Rest assured," Segalla declared, "Janette is safe with me, whatever happens in the next few days. I only wonder . . ."

"Monsieur?"

"Why, this time, did Beaton send me with you?"

Vartlett glanced away. "You are French," he mumbled. "A Catholic priest. The Queen might confide in someone like you." He looked up under his brows at Segalla. "Why do you ask?"

Segalla shrugged and walked on.

They reached Thieves Row, where the crowd was beginning to disperse. From their scowls and dark mutterings, Segalla realised the gossips were busy at work: the words "regicide," "murder," "secret assassin" were bandied about loosely. Segalla ignored them as he hurried into the New Provost's House.

At the top of the stairs, to the left, was a whitewashed chamber stripped of any furniture except for two long trestle tables, on which lay the corpses of Darnley and Taylor. Already the curiosity-seekers were thronging into the room, eager to see the mighty fallen. Bothwell, who had been busy elsewhere in the house, came up the stairs and took Segalla aside.

"Truly a bloody night's work, Monsieur," he whispered. "I have studied the King's corpse."

Segalla glimpsed the genuine surprise in Bothwell's eyes.

"His flesh is as soft and unbroken as a newborn babe's," the earl said. "And the same is true of Taylor's."

Segalla pointed to the curiosity-seekers. "My lord, the

Queen would not like that. And I must, on behalf of my masters in Paris, view the King's body again."

Bothwell agreed: a few minutes later the chamber was clear and two of Bothwell's heavily armed mosstroopers were placed on guard just within the doorway, their hard-bitten, unshaven faces showing no surprise or dismay at having to guard a murdered King's corpse. Once Bothwell had closed the door behind the crowd, Segalla lifted the dirty cloak and studied the body.

"Do ye ken what I say?" Bothwell's voice was slurred, and Segalla tried not to flinch at the earl's breath, full of the sour smell of wine.

"A mystery indeed."

He examined each corpse carefully: white and waxen, they showed no bruises on the face, torso, legs or throat. He sniffed at the mouth of each dead man but caught nothing except the rich tang of wine. He then examined the fingernails but could see no abrasions or cuts, not even the minutest sign of any struggle, whilst the soles of the bare feet were coated only with a slight dusting of dirt and grass. Segalla finished his inspection and re-covered the corpses.

"You'd think they were asleep!" Bothwell said almost to himself.

Segalla grasped him by the arm. "My lord, you are a professional soldier. Have you ever seen the like before?"

Bothwell shrugged, though he refused to meet Segalla's eye, as if he resented the candles and torches that bathed the chamber in light. "It could be done."

"What do you mean, it could be done?"

"If they were smothered or choked with a piece of silk or had a napkin soaked in water pushed down their throats."

"But they'd struggle?" Segalla asked.

"Not if they were held down. But, Monsieur, what shall we tell the Queen?" Bothwell now stared directly at Segalla, who caught the panic in the nobleman's eyes.

"Tell her honestly. Her husband is dead, foully murdered by person or persons unknown whilst this dwelling at Kirk o'Field was violently rent by gunpowder."

Segalla paused as he led Bothwell farther down the chamber, out of earshot of the two mosstroopers. He recalled the warning he had received from the Raven Master but decided to keep quiet. He had no proof, no evidence, yet he sensed Bothwell's unease and wondered what this border lord had to hide.

"The Queen," Segalla whispered, "must ask herself a number of questions. Firstly, was the explosion intended for her as well as her late husband? Secondly, how was her husband so skillfully murdered, some forty paces away from a house which was then blown up? Thirdly, who had the power to obtain so much gunpowder? Store it quietly away, then have access to Kirk o'Field to organise its firing? Fourthly, who will profit from all of this?" He saw Bothwell flinch. "Finally, tell Her Majesty to act prudently. She knows where I am. My advice and my sword will be at her disposal."

Segalla left the chamber and went downstairs. Vartlett was waiting for him in Thieves Row; two shapes in black cowls stood near him. As he drew nearer, Segalla realised they were women, rather old and dressed in tattered cloaks, though their faces were alive with excitement.

"You have new admirers, Vartlett?" Segalla asked.

The manservant grinned and shrugged. "Monsieur Segalla, may I introduce Mistress Barbara Mertyon and Mistress May Stirling. They live in Blackfriars Wynd, a street which leads down to the western approach of Kirk o'Field."

"The road back into Edinburgh?" Segalla queried.

"Aye," Vartlett replied. "But listen, they have a story and a half to tell."

One of the old ladies did not even wait to be asked but, clutching Segalla's arm, began to chatter away so quickly in her clipped, singsong accent that Segalla had to smile and shake his head.

"Vartlett, I don't understand."

Vartlett pushed a coin into each of the women's hands, thanked them gracefully and, grasping his master by the arm, led him farther away from Kirk o'Field: behind him the women showered down upon him a thousand thanks for his generosity.

"Keep walking, Monsieur," Vartlett whispered. "For these ladies have told a story. Shortly before the explosion they looked through their windows, which overlook the street leading down to Kirk o'Field. They saw a group of masked men approach. After the explosion, the same men were seen running away. Barbara Mertyon ran down into the street after one of them and took hold of his cloak; it was of pure silk."

"And?" Segalla asked.

"They heard Bothwell's name mentioned."

Segalla stopped and whistled softly under his breath. "But it was pitch dark. How could they possibly see at the dead of night?"

Vartlett just shrugged and kept silent until they had passed through the Netherbow Gate.

"There's something else," he added. "One of the ladies claims that a certain William Blackadder, a sea captain and a friend of Bothwell, was taken up by the watch as they hurried to Kirk o'Field. He was lodged in the Tolbooth for a while."

Segalla tried to suppress his chill of apprehension: if Bothwell was implicated, then what about the Queen?

They arrived back at the Crucible to find Janette waiting for them. Segalla ordered the surly taverner to bring them fresh wine and something to eat, then glanced round the musty taproom: even though it was just after dawn, the place was open. Certain citizens, disturbed from their sleep by the recent explosion, now sat in corners whispering amongst themselves. Janette followed Segalla's gaze.

"It's all over the city," she said. "I hired a link boy to walk me down to the Tolbooth and back. The explosion at Kirk o'Field and the King being found strangled is on everyone's lips!"

"Strangled?" Segalla asked. "Who told you that?"

"Two of Truth's worst enemies: Rumour and Gossip."

"And what else did these two wretches say?"

Janette paused whilst a sleepy-eyed scullion brought them a platter of bread and cheese with small cups of watered wine.

"Isn't there anything hot?" Vartlett grumbled.

The boy mumbled something in reply. Segalla caught his drift: the fires had yet to be kindled. Moreover, what did they expect when good Christian folk were sent scuffling from their beds by mysterious explosions and bloody-handed murder?

Janette watched the boy's retreating back. "You see what I mean, husband?"

"I am not your husband." Segalla smiled. "Vartlett has told me the truth."

She simply shook her head and laughed. "It wasn't just a game, Monsieur. If I had told you, perhaps you might not have acted the part." She looked archly at Vartlett. "Oh well, I suppose you had to know eventually."

"I asked you about Rumour and Gossip?"

Janette bit into a manchet loaf. "Oh, they are fanning the news across the city: how Kirk o'Field has been blown sky high. How the King and his servant have been strangled in a garden."

She offered the platter of bread to Segalla and he took a piece.

"And is this the truth?" Janette asked.

Segalla described the destruction of the Old Provost's House, how Nelson and Symonds had been dragged from the ruins and how Darnley and Taylor had been found dead in a nearby orchard.

"But were they strangled?" she asked.

"Not a mark upon them," Segalla said. "Lying as if they were asleep. Their nightshirts on them, nearby a fur robe, a chair, a pair of slippers, a dagger and a pile of cordage."

Janette's mouth opened and shut in surprise. "Then how?"

"I don't know. But now is not the time nor the place to discuss it. What else do Rumour and Gossip say?"

"Well, the tongues are clacking: they talk of a group of men marching through the city led by Bothwell, who caused the explosion. A barrel of gunpowder has been found: rumours are rife about Darnley pleading for his life."

Segalla sipped from his wine cup. "About what hour is it now?"

"About seven," Vartlett volunteered. "Seven o'clock in the morning."

"And, Janette, when did you hear these rumours?"

She grimaced. "Like you, I was woken by the explosion. I stayed here for two or three hours. As soon as the sky began to lighten, I decided to walk around and see what was happening. It must have been about five when I left the tavern." She shrugged. "I had been back here at least an hour before you arrived."

Segalla cursed under his breath.

"What is it?" Vartlett asked.

"Well, the explosion occurred about two o'clock. The King's body was found about three hours later, at five. Mistress Lindsay began to hear rumours about what had happened almost at the same time we were viewing Darnley's corpse. Now, rumour and gossip may spread quickly—" He lowered his voice. "But we arrived back here to discover Janette knows as much as we do."

Segalla used his fingers to emphasize his points.

"Firstly, there's been an explosion at Kirk o'Field. Secondly, Darnley and a servant were not killed in that explosion but found dead in a nearby orchard. Thirdly, within a very short space of time, Bothwell is already cast as the villain of the piece, slipping out under cover of darkness to carry out this dreadful act." He rubbed his eyes wearily. "Fourthly, and more importantly, these rumours show the murder was well planned. The result of subtle ploys and devious plans."

"For God's sake!" Vartlett demanded. "Speak plainly!"

"It's obvious," Janette said. "Whilst Kirk o'Field was being blown up and Darnley murdered, the gossips were already spreading the rumour in the city. The crime is done, but within hours the blame is immediately laid at Bothwell's door."

"And that means," Segalla added smoothly, "a well-organised coven of conspirators: some at the explosion, perhaps others taking care of Darnley whilst the rest fan the flames of gossip in the city. By noon every ale-swiller in Edinburgh will be priding himself on knowing how the explosion was caused and a feckless Darnley killed. Yet, that will only be the beginning."

"The beginning of what?" Vartlett asked.

"When he was alive, Darnley was universally despised. I would wager good silver that by the end of the week Darnley will be portrayed as some tragic hero, the innocent lamb led to the slaughter, whilst others, innocent or not, will be depicted as his red-handed murderers."

"But could they work so quickly?" Vartlett asked.

Segalla stared round the taproom. Now and again he caught the glance of a beggar man or some shabby tinker and realised their raised voices and frequent lapses into French must be attracting attention.

"Not here."

They retired to Segalla's chamber. Vartlett and Janette sat on the bed. Segalla pulled up the table. He laid out parchment, ink horn and other writing implements.

"Very well," he said, sitting on a stool. "Let us begin." Janette watched Segalla write carefully across the stretched piece of vellum.

"Why?" she asked abruptly.

Segalla looked up. "Why what, Janette?"

"Why are you bothered?" she asked. "You brought Archbishop Beaton's letters. You delivered his warning. You counselled the Queen. Are you so frightened of failure, Monsieur Segalla?"

Segalla gave a lopsided smile. "Firstly, because the game is not over. Secondly—" He paused and stared across at the daylight now seeping through the window shutters. "Secondly, a long time ago"—his voice dropped to a whisper—"longer than you think, I betrayed a trust."

His face became fierce. Janette noticed how the skin tightened: his mouth grew thin-lipped as if the very memory opened a scar deep in his soul.

"I'll never find peace," he said, "unless I keep faith in what I have been given." He sighed. "Finally, there is Mary: Mary the Queen, Mary the woman. Oh, I know, I delivered Beaton's instructions." He smiled self-consciously. "But she touched me."

Janette leaned forward, her eyes full of amusement.

"So, you are smitten, Monsieur Segalla, you, a Jesuit priest?" She wagged a finger in mock disapproval.

"All a priest does, Janette, is give up his right to know and marry a woman, but never his attraction for them. Now." He picked up the quill. "How long was Darnley at Kirk o'Field?"

"A full week," Vartlett said. He looked curiously at Segalla; he was also surprised that this dispassionate man could now care so much either for the truth or for a queen he had just met.

"So." Segalla rested one arm on the table, pen poised. "We know there are traitors about Mary, not just the Raven Master but the Great Lords, like her half brother, the Earl of

Moray. They were given a full week to store gunpowder in the cellars."

"But could they?" Janette queried. "If the house, as you say, was lifted from its very foundations?"

She paused as Segalla looked at her quizzically.

"Well," she continued, "that would mean a great deal of gunpowder. Someone can't just walk into a royal palace and store such deadly merchandise where he wishes. If the house was lifted from its foundations, the powder must have been stowed in the cellar. However, we know from the servants' chatter that the cellars were used as a kitchen."

"Moreover," Vartlett added, "Mary may be surrounded by traitors, but there are others who wish her well. The captain of her own guard, Stewart of Traquair, seems a capable officer. Surely searches would have been carried out?"

Segalla listened to them, steepling his fingers together. "If I follow what you say, the powder must have been placed in Kirk o'Field only a few hours before the explosion."

Both nodded.

Segalla picked up his pen and scratched his brow. "Let us leave that for a while," he said. "Let's concentrate on Darnley's death."

He took his pen and drew a rough plan of Kirk o'Field house which he then held up. "Look. Here is Thieves Row; the Old Provost's House, the New Provost's House, the orchard, the quadrangle and the Flodden Wall. Master Vartlett, if you were an assassin, which direction would you take into Darnley's lodgings?"

"If I came through the quadrangle," Vartlett said, "I might awaken the other servants, whereas the other side is bounded by the old town wall as well as the brick face of the two houses. The only sensible direction, therefore, is to come from Netherbow Gate."

"Yes, I accept that." Segalla turned the paper round.

"When the murderers came they would seek entrance by the quietest route."

"But to do that," Janette said, "from whatever direction they came, they would still need keys to get into the house?"

"There is another way," Segalla mused. "What would happen If there were some passageway, probably through the cellars, from the New Provost's House into the Old?"

"You mean interlinking cellars?" Vartlett asked.

"Perhaps. That's one way to bring the gunpowder in. It could have been stored there and then moved by the murderers only hours before the explosion occurred." He smiled. "But that poses further problems: unless this passageway was very secretive, someone would have noticed, and even if they got into the cellar, they would still need keys to penetrate farther into the house."

"That's the nub," Vartlett said. "What did happen in the upper chamber of Darnley's room at Kirk o'Field? He wasn't killed there, that stands to reason; the assassins couldn't have entered without disturbing the rest of his retinue."

"So, how did Darnley get out?" Janette asked.

"There are two windows," Segalla explained, going back to his drawing. "One which overlooks the ruins to Blackfriars and the one over Thieves Row, directly opposite the gate into the small orchard where Darnley's corpse was found. I suspect he used the latter." Segalla sighed in exasperation. "But why didn't his departure arouse the rest?"

All three sat in silence for a while. Segalla stared down at the parchment; he seized another and began to draw, in minute detail, a plan of Kirk o'Field and the orchard beyond. His companions sat admiring his skill: Segalla then opened his writing case and slowly began to use watercolours to fill in his pen-and-ink sketch.

"A skilled artist," Janette murmured.

Segalla rubbed his eyes and put the pen down.

"In this great mystery," he said, "it's the only thing I can do; there seems no solution."

Chapter 7

Segalla finished his drawing. Janette exclaimed in pleasure at the picture, which caught the scene of destruction at the Kirk o'Field and the half-naked corpses of Darnley and his servant. She leaned so close that Segalla could smell the rosewater she used to wash her hands.

"You have a gift, Monsieur."

Segalla smiled over his shoulder at her. He took another piece of parchment and began to copy the scene again.

"What will you do with those?" Vartlett asked, suddenly jealous of his wife's open admiration of the Jesuit.

"I'll keep one; the other I'll send to Beaton in Paris."

Janette took the first copy to the window and, in the growing light, carefully studied it.

"You have even remembered the chair and the rope," she exclaimed, then shook her head. "I can't understand it. Why should Darnley and his servant flee, in their night robes, out into a freezing February night? And yet, at the same time, bother to take such impedimenta as a chair and cordage?"

"They used it to escape," Vartlett said. "When the Queen escaped from Holyrood, after the murder of Rizzio, she used the same method, a lowered chair and some rope. Remember, Darnley was weak after his long illness."

Listening to them, a vague idea occurred to Segalla. He laid his pen down on the table.

"We must accept," he began slowly, "and all the evidence points to this, that Darnley and his servant left Kirk o'Field of their own volition."

"Why should they leave in their night robes?" Vartlett asked.

Segalla chewed his lip. "But we don't know that they did," he said quickly. "What if Darnley and his squire secretly left their chamber, dressed, then went somewhere else? Yes, yes!" He rose excitedly to his feet. "Perhaps they met their assassins, who, God knows how, smothered or subtly choked them. Their bodies were then stripped, redressed in their night-clothes, taken out to the orchard and left there, the chair and rope put beside them to make it look as if they had died fleeing from the Old Provost's House."

"So, why the explosion?" Vartlett asked.

Segalla smiled. "A number of paths now open before us. Did Darnley blow the house up himself? Later he was killed and his corpse left in the orchard?"

Vartlett shook his head. "I doubt it: don't forget, Monsieur, as soon as the explosion occurred people ran to Kirk o'Field."

Segalla lifted his hand. "I concede that, but Darnley could have fled to Kirk o'Field and met his murderers. They kill him and Taylor, dispose of the corpses, then blow the Old Provost's House sky high?" Segalla clapped his hands with excitement. "That's it, to hide the fact that Darnley escaped!"

"But what about all these stories concerning Lord Bothwell?"

Segalla shrugged. "Perhaps it was Bothwell who killed him?" He paused. "Or someone else?" He paced excitedly up and down the room. "It's possible! Remember, when we visited the King's chamber, Darnley talked of his great horses being ready to travel to Seton?"

"But that was with the Queen," Janette said.

Segalla shook his head and stared at his drawing. "That's it," he said. "Darnley knew it was Carnival Sunday, that his wife was to attend the wedding of Bastian Pages. It was a holiday: all the servants would either be at Holyrood for the rich pickings or in the taverns in the city. Darnley deliberately chose such a night to flee."

Janette put the drawing back on the table. She glanced quizzically at Vartlett. "Monsieur Segalla, I think you have it." She drummed her fingers prettily against her lower lip. "When we went to Kirk o'Field, something was missing. Darnley was very conscious of his status. The wearer of the Crown Matrimonial, he wanted the Crown Absolute. A vain, empty-headed young man, Darnley liked the trappings of power, yet at Kirk o'Field his retinue was very simple. Oh, he had protection: Nelson, Symonds and the rest. But where were his musicians and the rest of his household?" She sighed. "But all this still leaves one major problem. With whom was Darnley conspiring to flee?"

Segalla shook his head and went back to his drawing. He and his companions had reached a consensus that Darnley's departure from Kirk o'Field was part of his secret plot to escape the Queen. But whom had Darnley met? How had they killed him? And why blow up the Old Provost's House?

The morning wore on. Vartlett went down to the kitchens and brought back a jug of wine, some kidney stew and small loaves of coarse rye bread. They were halfway through the meal, still discussing possibilities, when they heard the sound of mailed feet on the stairs and a pounding on the door. Vartlett drew his sword and Segalla grasped his dagger as the door was flung open and Stewart of Traquair strode in. Behind him, Segalla glimpsed the boiled leather jackets of his retinue of archers.

"You come unannounced!" Vartlett shouted.

Traquair dismissed him with a glance of contempt; his hard, unshaven face and red-rimmed eyes showed he had had little sleep the night before. He bowed to Segalla, then to Janette.

"Monsieur, I apologise for my graceless entrance, but these are pressing matters. Her Majesty the Queen demands your presence immediately at Holyrood." Traquair forced a smile, as Segalla's hands still rested on the hilt of his dagger. "You are safe," Traquair said. "The Queen wishes to take secret council with you. Madame." He bowed again in Janette's direction. "I must ask you to remain behind."

Segalla picked up his cloak and nodded at Janette. "Take care of my drawings." He smiled.

"And do not go out into the city," Traquair warned. "The King's death at Kirk o'Field is now known to all and the crowd's mood is both fickle and ugly." Again the false smile. "We Scots, at the best of times, do not like strangers!" He spun on his heel.

Segalla hastily took his sword belt and followed him down the stairs and out into the yard.

Traquair was in no mood to brook any opposition. Customers and scullions fled before this grim soldier dressed in half armour, his helmet held in the crook of his arm, his other hand not far from the great two-handed sword that swung from a ring on his belt. The rest of the retinue were equally well armed, and royal archers, wearing Mary's personal livery, had the horses ready in the stableyard. Segalla's mount was brought out and quickly saddled and, with Traquair leading, they entered Edinburgh and made their way up the High Street towards Holyrood Palace. The mounted archers formed a protective shield around Segalla, and he soon learnt why. Despite the freezing cold, the streets were thronged as much for gossip as for commerce, and Segalla glimpsed the dark looks the Queen's livery attracted. Now and again there was the odd catcall; a piece of rock, followed by fistfuls of dung, narrowly missed Traquair's head. The captain of the guard turned, as did the outriders, swiftly notching arrow to bow, and the troublemakers slunk away. They entered the great marketplace before the Tolbooth. The butchers' stalls were covered with slabs of meat, chicken giblets, pickled sides of pork and heaps of minced beef, their rottenness carefully disguised under a thick coating of salt and herbs.

Trade was brisk, but behind all this, people chattered and gossipped, stories were exchanged; Segalla had seen the same happen in Paris whenever some great crisis of state occurred, and he recalled his conversation with Vartlett and Janette. This gossip, these black looks were being carefully encouraged by secret agents, their malicious chatter speeding through the runnels and alleyways, whipping up resentment. But who was behind it all? Moray was miles away in the Fife, whilst the Earl of Morton was in self-imposed banishment in St. Andrews.

Segalla shook his head to clear it and stared around. Traquair was finding it impossible to cross the square because of the punishments and executions being carried out. Two river pirates were in the process of being hanged: hoisted up the ladder, their half-naked bodies were cast into the air to dance and jerk, whilst, below them, the crowds stood and watched, enjoying the sight of the pirates' faces turning black, their necks twisting, tongues protruding through clenched teeth. On a nearby platform, minor punishments were also being inflicted. A blasphemer was having his ears nailed to the stocks: a blowsy whore, having been caught for the third time, had her nose slit.

Meanwhile, a madcap entertained the crowd, offering to drink a gallon of ale in a minute, then vomit it just as quickly. Segalla had to steady himself in the saddle: the stench, the crowd, the brutal swiftness of the executions reminded him of scenes from Dante's *Inferno*. At last the punishments were ended.

"So are punished all who offend against the Queen's peace!" The bailiff roared from the steps of the Tolbooth.

"Aye!" Someone shouted. "But what happens if Her Grace falls from grace?"

"Puir Darnley!" a woman yelled. "Killed in his ain beid!"

The grumble of the crowd turned into a shout, and the throng turned as if to confront Traquair. The captain of the guard rapped out an order; swords were drawn and the mob parted like swirling water, fleeing from the upraised blades and sharpened hooves of the horses. Once they were across the square and cantering along the High Street, Segalla drew alongside Traquair.

"Sir, was this the best way to come?" he asked.

"Sir," the soldier replied, "we are the Queen's men and this is her city."

"You know what is happening?" Segalla insisted, fighting hard to control his horse.

Traquair noticed this and slowed down. He sheathed his sword and wiped the sweat from his face with the back of his gauntlet. "Aye. This is no spontaneous outburst of feeling, Frenchman. The Queen's enemies have been busy in the city."

"And how is Her Majesty?"

"She is withdrawn, white as silk." Traquair glanced sideways at Segalla. "She reminds me of the stories about her father. After Solway Moss he became like a child, swooning in fear and turning his face to the wall."

"Will the Queen recover?"

Traquair hawked and spat. "God knows, Frenchman. Darnley's death has shocked us."

"When did the Queen leave for Holyrood?" Segalla asked.

"About an hour before midnight, laughing and singing." Traquair allowed himself a half smile. "A grand sight, Frenchman. You should have been there. Torches and candlelight, dancing in the halls. Well, well. I doubt if the Queen will ever dance again."

"Sir John." Segalla leaned closer. "You are a man loyal to the Queen, as I am. You are also a soldier. What do you think happened at Kirk o'Field?"

Traquair made a face. "As you say, Monsieur, I am a soldier. I carry out orders. It is not my duty to speculate on the doings of the great ones, but I tell you this, I personally searched the Old Provost's House from cellar to garret. There was no gunpowder there yesterday."

"And who had keys to the chambers?"

Traquair shrugged. "The King had a set and so did Bethon, the Queen's chamberlain. But you have heard the rumours?"

"I have heard many," Segalla answered drily.

"Aye, and so have I. They are now talking of duplicate keys being fashioned."

"But you don't believe that?"

"No!" Traquair snapped. "I do not."

"And you have seen the King's corpse?"

"Aye, he was a bonny lad in life; even in death he still looks bonny."

"So, how did he die?"

Traquair shook his head. "If he was strangled, there would be marks and bruises on his neck." Now he seemed to lose some of his calmness. "I have seen similar corpses. Though I have not told the Queen. Two years ago, one of my soldiers smothered his wife, held a bolster over her face. If you want the truth, Frenchman, that is what I think happened to Henry Darnley, our King Consort of Scotland."

"But how?" Segalla asked.

"God knows!"

"And nothing untoward happened last night?"

Traquair urged his horse a little faster, and Segalla did likewise.

"Sir, I asked you a question."

"I am a soldier," Traquair said. "Such questions should be asked of Her Majesty."

"Did Lord Bothwell leave Holyrood yesterday evening?"

"Not to my knowledge, but there again, sir, such questions should be directed towards him."

They cantered silently up the High Street and turned into the gates of Holyrood Palace. Grooms came to take their horses, and Segalla marvelled at the change in the atmosphere. Where days before all had been jolly, somberness reigned. They went up the staircases and along the galleries to the Queen's private quarters. The servants were already hanging black tapestries against the walls, whilst broadcloth and purple buckram covered the furniture and chairs as a sign of mourning.

Traquair brought them into a small antechamber, where the funeral cloths had also been hung. The windows were shuttered, and in the flickering light of the torches the room looked like a mausoleum. Two men sat on a bench against the far wall, heads together. They looked up as Segalla entered.

"Monsieur Segalla." Paris got to his feet and, with Nelson trailing behind, hurried over to shake the Frenchman's hand.

"Thank God, sir, you've come. The Queen needs good counsel."

Both men looked badly frightened. Nelson still bore the marks and bruises from the night before: he kept nursing his right arm and walked with a slight limp, though he put a brave face on it.

"The Queen is within," he said. "She and Lord Bothwell are closeted together."

"Monsieur Segalla." Traquair peered from the doorway leading to the Queen's chamber. "Her Majesty will see you now."

Traquair ushered Segalla into the chamber, closing the door behind him. Segalla's attention was immediately caught by the Queen, who sat in a tall chair at the head of a long, oval table. She was dressed like a nun in black crepe and satin, her face hidden by a lace veil. Segalla caught the tension in the air, like some invisible smoke, and saw it reflected in the faces of the men sitting round the table: the Earls of Argyll, Huntly, Cassalis and other lords of the court.

"Monsieur." The Queen's voice was firm. "It is good of you to come at such short notice."

"Madame, I am your loyal servant."

Segalla sank to one knee even as the Queen clapped her hands and ordered Bothwell to clear the room. Segalla remained kneeling as the lords filed out.

"Nicholas!"

He was touched by the Queen's use of his Christian name.

"Please rise; sit here to my left."

Segalla got to his feet. The room was now empty. Only Bothwell, also dressed in black, lounged next to the Queen, his weatherbeaten face now grown paler. As Segalla took his seat, Mary lifted her veil, and he tried to hide his shock. She was no longer the pretty French princess or elegant lady of the court; Mary's face looked as if it had been carved out of the whitest porcelain and would shatter at a touch. Her lips were thin and bloodless, her skin stretched tight across her high cheekbones, though it was her dark-ringed eyes which frightened Segalla. They had the gaze of a woman under some heavy opiate.

"Ma—Madame," Segalla stammered, preparing his words carefully. "Madame, my deepest condolences."

"Her Majesty is in shock." Bothwell leaned across the table. "She cannot accept that her husband is dead."

Mary's gaze still held Segalla's. "You brought me a warning, Monsieur, and I did not heed it," she said softly. "I thought I was safe. I never thought . . ."

Segalla felt like kneeling before her. "Your Majesty," he said. "I failed you."

Mary just shook her head and allowed a ghost of a smile. "Monsieur, if the angel Gabriel had come down from heaven, what could he have done to prevent this tragedy?"

Segalla glanced across the table. He was tempted to discuss the presence of an English secret agent amongst her court, but he was too suspicious of Bothwell. Was he the Queen's man?

119

Or was he Walsingham's? Did he have his own secret dreams and ambitions? Despite the tragedy, the border lord lounged in his chair next to the Queen with a proprietary air. Bothwell seemed to read his thoughts.

"Frenchman." He rapped his thick fingers on the table. "No man or woman is above suspicion; this is a dastardly crime."

"They intended to murder me," the Queen broke in abruptly. "Yes, they intended to kill me as well as my husband. Seize my baby son and rule the kingdom in his name."

Segalla caught the wild glance in the Queen's eyes and decided, for the moment, not to contradict her.

"They plotted this." She stared down the room as if talking to herself. "Nobody, not even Beaton, could have stopped them."

"Your Majesty," Segalla said. "Who are they?"

Mary laughed abruptly. "The Great Lords of the Congregation. Moray and Morton's pack of traitors!" She spat the words out.

"Your Majesty must heed your words." Segalla said bluntly. "You must remember that Moray, Morton and Maitland of Lethington were well away from Kirk o'Field when your husband died. I beg you, Your Majesty, not to make allegations you cannot prove."

Mary put her face in her hands and began to sob quietly. Then she let her hands fall away. "I do not understand: before God, I'd leave this kingdom in my kirtle and go elsewhere."

"Monsieur Segalla." Bothwell said. "Her Majesty has asked you here to seek your advice. All Europe will be waiting for her response!"

"Then let Europe wait!" Segalla snapped. "Your Majesty, you must set up a Commission of Enquiry."

Mary dabbed at the tears on her cheek with the cuff of her dress. "I have done that," she said. "Tomorrow the Earl of Argyll opens a Commission at the Tolbooth. Proclamations will be issued, offering a pardon to any who will confess as well as a reward of two thousand pounds for the apprehension of my husband's murderers." She looked sharply at Segalla. "You can speak bluntly in front of my lord Bothwell." She smiled faintly. "He has my best interests at heart."

Segalla went cold. He glanced across at the table at Bothwell, then back at the Queen. Bothwell might be a powerful laird, but Segalla was not sure of his innocence in these matters. The Queen, however, had that lost, troubled look on her face. Segalla realised her mind was drifting: sometimes she would focus her energies on the problem at hand, and other times she seemed lost in a dream. Segalla recalled the fate of Mary's father and knew it would be this which decided her fate. If she confronted her problems she might win. If she retreated, if she trusted her fortunes to the likes of Bothwell, all would be lost.

"Your Majesty." Segalla stirred in his seat, deciding that honesty was the best path forward. "Your Majesty," he repeated. "I do not believe the assassins intended to kill you. They deliberately chose the evening of Carnival Sunday, knowing you would be absent at Holyrood Palace at the wedding celebrations of one of your ladies."

"What do you mean?" Bothwell cried.

"Your Majesty, my lord, I will be blunt. The gunpowder could not have been moved to Kirk o'Field until you left for Holyrood. In effect, how it was moved and fired is immaterial." He held up a hand to still Bothwell's questions, pleased that he now had the Queen's attention. "Your Majesty, the real mystery is why your husband's corpse was found, without a mark on it and dressed in his bed robes, lying in an orchard forty yards away from the Old Provost's House and surrounded by such items as rope, a chair and a dagger. The explosion at Kirk o'Field is only a minor mystery. It is your husband's death which poses all the riddles. Your Majesty, I believe," he added quickly, "that your husband plotted to flee

Kirk o'Field. He secretly left the Old Provost's House and went to meet his murderers, thinking they would assist him in his flight. Instead, they took him to another place. They smothered him and laid him out in the orchard with the chair and rope to make it look as if he had been caught fleeing from the explosion at Kirk o'Field. That explosion was to cover all signs of your husband's flight."

"Spoken like a Frenchman," Bothwell gibed.

Segalla glared at him. "My lord, what I am is neither here nor there. I am Her Majesty's loyal servant and the faithful envoy of her Ambassador in Paris."

"Who would encourage Darnley to flee?" Bothwell retorted.

"My lord, I don't know."

And Segalla quickly went through the conclusions he had reached: how Darnley's flight from Kirk o'Field, without wakening the other servants, could only be explained if the King had left of his own accord. The Queen listened attentively throughout.

"You speak the truth," she declared. "My lord Bothwell, you know he speaks the truth." She smiled tearfully at Segalla. "I admire your logic, sir: you have reached a conclusion with very little evidence. Some of that evidence we have."

Segalla's heart leapt. "Your Majesty, what evidence?"

Mary rubbed the corners of her mouth with her long fingers and then played with her mermaid ring.

"Small matters," she said. "First—" She paused and stared round the table. "What was it I was going to say?" She looked up at Segalla. "Surely I should be with my husband's corpse?"

Bothwell leaned across the table and squeezed her arm gently. "Your Majesty," he said, "such matters are in hand. It is important that we hear what you have to say."

"Firstly—" Mary smiled at Segalla, who hid his concern at how quickly Bothwell seemed to have gained an ascendancy over the Queen. "Firstly," she repeated, "we know our late husband had a ship stocked and well provisioned waiting in the Clyde. We do not know whether he was going to use it and, if he had, where he would have fled to. Still a staunch Catholic, Darnley once mentioned seeking the protection of Philip of Spain's forces in Flanders." She stared down at her ring. "Whether that was mere posturing or not, we do not know." She paused, rocking herself gently in the chair.

"What else, Your Majesty?"

"Secondly, we have received intelligence that last night, Carnival Sunday, Darnley's father, the Earl of Lennox, journeyed south but turned back after an attempt was made on his life."

Segalla stared open-mouthed as he reflected on the significance of this. "Your Majesty," he said. "You are sure?"

"We received the intelligence early this morning," Bothwell put in. "Well, Frenchman, you with your nimble wits?"

"The assassination attempt could be seen from a number of viewpoints. Did the assassins intend to wipe out Darnley and his father on the same evening? With all due respect, Your Majesty, they would have cleared the table of two trouble-makers in one fell swoop."

The Queen shook her head to acknowledge that Segalla meant no insult. "And what else, Monsieur?"

"Darnley and his father may have been in the same conspiracy. Did Lennox intend to meet his son in some place and raise rebellion, perhaps even seize the infant James?" He paused. "How was the Earl of Lennox attacked?"

"A gun was fired," Bothwell said.

"Then it could be pretence," Segalla said. "A ploy to make it look as if someone in Scotland wanted to remove Darnley and his father for their own mysterious purposes."

"Whom do you mean?" Bothwell asked.

"My lord, go into the city." Segalla said. "Wander the streets and alleyways, stand before the Tolbooth and listen to what people say. Your Majesty, I will be blunt to the point of rudeness: they point the finger at my lord Bothwell. I have no doubt that, in a few day's time, they will be pointing the finger at you."

Bothwell sprang to his feet, enraged. "You should be careful about what you say, Frenchman."

"My lord, you miss my point. It does not really matter what I think but what the world says."

"Sit down." The Queen drew herself up, but she allowed the veil to fall back over her face. "Jamie." She turned to Bothwell. "Sit down. Monsieur Segalla only repeats what we have heard already."

Bothwell took his seat, still glaring at Segalla.

"My lord of Bothwell," the Queen whispered. "Tell Monsieur Segalla what you know about Ker of Fawdonside."

Bothwell snorted. "A year ago," he began, "here in Holyrood the Queen's secretary, David Rizzio, was brutally stabbed to death." He waved his hand airily. "I know, I know the late King had a hand in that bloody business. But one of the knaves, a hellhound, a border lord named Andrew Ker of Fawdonside, was recently seen in the vicinity of the city. We marvelled at this impudence. The news was brought by a servitor, John Shaw, who claimed that Ker had even been seen in taverns in the city boasting that there would soon be a change in court."

"But would Ker dare do that?" Segalla asked. "Return from exile and travel to a royal burgh under sentence of death?"

"We wondered at that," Mary said. "I sent for my register of Privy Seals. Amongst its documents I found a pardon issued to Andrew Ker of Fawdonside. To put it bluntly, Monsieur, I did not issue such a letter of pardon. The only person who could have done was my late husband."

"Her Majesty was alarmed," Bothwell continued. "So I and some of my retinue left Holyrood and went to see if Kirk o'Field was safe. We reached Netherbow Gate: we saw all was well, so we returned."

"And what happened to Ker of Fawdonside?"

"We don't know," Bothwell said. "He disappeared. What we now think is Darnley issued that pardon to Ker in order to obtain his assistance."

Segalla gazed at the black-creped cross hanging against the wall of the Council chamber. Was this the truth? he wondered. Or was Bothwell, even the Queen, hiding something? Was this a story to explain the Earl of Bothwell's movements around the city the night Darnley was killed?

"So, my lord, you think that Ker came to assist Darnley in his flight?"

"More than that!" Bothwell snapped. "Perhaps Darnley reached him. Ker was a bloody killer. How do we know that he did not kill Darnley and his servant Taylor, lay their bodies in the orchard, fire the explosion and then flee?"

"Because," Segalla replied, ticking the points off on his fingers, "why should Darnley and Taylor flee in their night robes without disturbing the other servants? Secondly, how would Ker get into Kirk o'Field unopposed? Thirdly"— Segalla smiled bleakly at the Queen—"and this is the great puzzle, Your Majesty. I can understand, if not accept, some great lord's hatred of your late husband, God rest him. But, why kill Lord Darnley and then blow up Kirk o'Field and so risk possible capture or detection?" He tapped his hand against the table. "This last point lies at the nub of the mystery. Someone like Ker might kill a vulnerable man and his servant, though how he could do it without leaving mark or injury would puzzle me. However, to blow up a royal palace and escape unscathed?" Segalla raised his hands.

"I am pleased," Bothwell gibed, "that you seem as baffled as we are, Frenchman."

"And you, my lord?" Segalla retorted. "I ask you this, as

one man to another, are you pleased my lord Dárnley is dead?" Segalla glimpsed a fleeting look of triumph in Bothwell's eyes.

"Frenchman, there's no mystery. I confess, yes, before Her Majesty the Queen, there is not a lord in Scotland who will weep over Darnley's corpse."

Chapter 8

"M onsieur?"

Segalla whirled as he left the council chamber.

"Monsieur Segalla, please."

The Jesuit peered through the gloom.

"Why, Master Nelson, what is the matter?"

Segalla took a step closer, trying to control his unease after his recent meeting.

"How goes it?" Nelson asked curiously.

Segalla slapped his leather gloves against the palm of his hand. "Not very well. In fact, Master Nelson, I would appreciate a word with you." He glimpsed the anxiety in the man-servant's tired eyes. "No, no, nothing serious." Segalla smiled. "And what do you want from me?"

"A word, sir. Perhaps even protection."

"How can I give you protection?"

Nelson touched him gently on the elbow as a sign that they should walk on, raising a finger to his lips. Segalla shrugged, intrigued by this little man's apparent concern. They went back down to the stableyards. Nelson collected their horses, and they rode back into the city.

"Well." Segalla nodded back towards the palace and gestured at the wooden houses on either side. "No court spies here, Master Nelson. So, why should you need my protection?"

Nelson pulled his sorry-looking mount closer to Segalla's. "You are French," he began. "The accredited envoy of

Archbishop Beaton. Symonds, Standon, Hudson and the rest, we are all retainers of Darnley, an English lord, who has now been murdered. Who will bother about us, Monsieur?"

"Has the Queen offered you protection?" Segalla asked.

"I was interrogated this morning before the Council," Nelson replied in a shaky voice. "I told them exactly what I told you." His glance fell away. "Though there are other things, which I can only say, er, when my position is more assured."

"What things?"

Nelson reined in and pointed to the Blue Mantle tavern, a spacious hostelry on the corner of the paved High Street, now thronged with merchants and tradesmen as they gathered to break their fast, taking a short respite from the day's labors. Segalla shrugged again and agreed. They dismounted, stabled their horses and took a table and two stools in the far corner of the parlour at the back of the tavern. Segalla ordered wine, bread, cheese and dried pork, though the latter proved to be so heavily salted they left it alone. Segalla noticed the bruises and cuts on Nelson's face and that the manservant's nails and fingers were still chapped and scarred.

"You are frightened, Master Nelson?"

"Of course I am. The Queen's Lords asked me what happened and I told them. Now I am bound to appear before Lord Argyll tomorrow at the Tolbooth. Monsieur Segalla, what can I say? I fell asleep. The King, my master, was in his bed with Taylor. I was awakened by the explosion." He put his cup down and spread his hands in a gesture of helplessness. "I know what I'll be asked," he wailed. " 'Who had keys to Kirk o'Field?' 'Why, my lord,' I'll answer, 'the Queen's people had.' " Nelson looked piteously at Segalla. "My lord of Bothwell will not be pleased with such a reply."

"The Queen will protect you," Segalla insisted.

"Her Majesty has offered me, Symonds and the rest, a place in her own household." Nelson shook his head. "I doubt if we will take it. Why should Englishmen stay at a foreign court where our master has been slain?"

"Who else is there?" Segalla asked.

"Well, there's myself, Symonds and the King's musicians, led by Hudson. They are still in Glasgow, as are the Standon brothers."

"What were they doing there?" Segalla asked, intrigued. "Surely they should have been with their master?"

Nelson refused to meet Segalla's gaze.

"So, what will you do?" Segalla asked.

"We will all go south."

"Wouldn't Darnley's father, the Earl of Lennox, protect you?"

Nelson made a rude noise. "Like father, like son, Monsieur. Ah no! Now, Darnley's mother, the Lady Lennox, she's in London. We might go there. The Lady Lennox is a woman of integrity. She will protect us."

"Then, why are you so frightened?" Segalla asked bluntly.

"Because," Nelson said, "I know the questions. If my master, the King, was murdered in his own chamber, then why weren't we murdered with him? If he tried to escape, then why didn't he rouse us?"

"Your master was trying to escape, wasn't he?" Segalla asked quietly.

"Oh yes," Nelson answered slowly. He caught Segalla's arm. "Sir, we are poor men; will you provide us with silver, some money to journey south to the border? Perhaps a letter of protection, at least until we reach Berwick?"

Segalla smiled and patted his hand. "Just tell me what you know."

Nelson drank his wine greedily. "The King came to Kirk o'Field," he began in a rush, then paused as a scullion came to refill their cups. "He was afeared of his life and plotted to flee. He wanted to be near the baby James and intended to seize him as well." Nelson stared into his wine. "Nothing was ever said to us, but we knew Darnley was in communication with his father and Ker of Fawdonside. He ordered Glen and Mac-Caig to have his horses ready for this morning. That's all we knew."

"What do you think happened?"

"Last night," Nelson continued, "the King talked to us for a while and we shared wine. We were all exhausted and soon fell asleep: Glen, MacCaig the page boy, Symonds and myself. The house was locked. Other than the Queen, only Darnley had keys." Nelson blew air through his lips. "We all fell into a deep slumber, but I don't think my master or Taylor did. They must have risen immediately, dressed and left Kirk o'-Field to meet those who were to spirit them away. Instead they ran into their murderers, who killed them, laid the charges in the house and blew the building from its foundations." Nelson's hands shook as he put the cup back on the table. "Now you can see why I am frightened, sir. If the assassins didn't care last night, why should they care now?"

"Do you have any proof?"

Nelson smiled thinly. "Always proof," he muttered. "You know, sir, before I entered Lord Darnley's service I was with the Lord Chamberlain's men, a troupe of actors. The words 'Always Proof' figured in many of the plays we acted in the villages and towns round London. I never thought my life would depend on them. Yes, I have some proof, and I also have gossip. But"—he tapped his wallet—"now I need money."

Segalla handed over some coins.

"Darnley's planned escape was no great secret," Nelson continued. "Oh, we knew every lord in Scotland wanted Darnley dead. You have heard the story? How, on our way to Kirk o'Field, when the Queen took Darnley there in a litter, a large raven shadowed our passage?"

"A warning?"

"More like a prophecy. Last Friday, the Earl of Moray's men advised Darnley that his life was not safe."

"What?" Segalla sat forward. "Darnley was warned he was in danger?"

Nelson looked at him strangely. "Oh yes, sir. Didn't Her Majesty tell you? A violent confrontation took place between Darnley and the Earl of Moray's men; their hands were going to their daggers until the Queen appealed for peace."

Segalla sat back against the wall and stared at the rush-strewn floor of the small, crowded parlour. He heard the phrases "Kirk o' Field" and "bloody murder" and realised that what he and Nelson were discussing was on the lips of every man in the city. Segalla's unease deepened. Nelson was correct. If the King Consort could be slain in such a barbaric fashion, under the very nose of his Queen, what protection could be afforded to English menials? Or even envoys from Paris? Particularly himself, a Jesuit in a city renowned for its commitment to the Reformed Faith?

"Monsieur?"

Segalla hid his smile at Nelson's odd lapse into French. "We all have to tread warily, Master Nelson," he said. "If you must leave Scotland quickly, then so do I." He recalled Mary's dark-rimmed eyes in her beautiful white face. "Who do you think killed your master?" he asked.

"Oh, the Great Lords," Nelson answered quickly. He snorted with laughter. "In most murders the question is asked, 'Who did it?' When it comes to my lord Darnley, it would be easier to ask, 'Who didn't want him dead?' "

"But how was it done?" Segalla asked. "The timing, the speed, the efficiency of it all. Anything could have gone wrong. Grooms and others were about Kirk o' Field. They could have been disturbed by the sound of men laying the gunpowder. They could have seen Darnley escape. And why didn't he fight back? Did he go like a lamb to the slaughter?

And if his corpse, together with Taylor's, not to mention a chair and a pile of rope, was taken out to an orchard, why wasn't this seen? The murderers ran a great risk and yet were successful." He looked sharply at Nelson. "But you and Symonds were saved?"

"Aye, because we were sleeping in the gallery. Both Symonds and I thought about that: the gallery must have fallen last. If not, we could have been buried with the rest." Nelson leaned closer. "But there's other gossip," he whispered. "Have you noticed, Monsieur, how no one wished to stay at Kirk o'Field? They all, including the servants you mentioned, followed Her Majesty to Holyrood for the festivities. There are some"—he paused—"men like Sandy Durham, who made no bones about their fear of staying there."

Segalla recalled the young man he'd met the previous Saturday.

"He was the dead King's porter?"

"Aye."

Segalla sipped at his wine. What could he do? Nelson was correct. Everyone wanted Darnley dead; Mary seemed to have known he would be killed. But how would this save the Queen's reputation? Segalla understood the drift of what was happening. How would it look in the courts of Europe? Mary, dancing and revelling at Holyrood, whilst her husband was viciously slain.

"You talked of proof," Segalla said. Nelson drained his cup. "And, sir, you must give it in return for protection." He gripped Nelson's wrist, surprised at the the young man's strength as he flexed his arm in fear.

"Then come back with me," Nelson said. "I have a draft of a letter in my chamber. I had it in my wallet when Kirk o'Field was blown up. It proves Darnley was writing to his father and hoped to join him soon."

They gathered their cloaks and retrieved their horses from the stables. Segalla let Nelson ride ahead but paused when he saw a group standing on the Tolbooth steps. He told Nelson to wait and rode closer. Over the heads of the crowd, Segalla read the placard pinned to the Tolbooth doors.

OUR KING HAS BEEN FOULLY MURDERED, the red daubs said. AND THE WRITER OF THIS PLACARD WILL, IN GOD'S OWN TIME, NAME HIS FOUL AND BLOODY-HANDED MURDERERS.

Segalla found it difficult to follow the loud murmuring of the people around him, and he dared not reveal his accent by asking questions. Nevertheless, he heard the name Bothwell and, from the mouth of one well-dressed woman, the phrase "Aye, and Bothwell's ain paramour." They are working hard, Segalla thought. Whoever planned Darnley's murder are spreading their poison quickly through the city. He pulled his horse's head round and followed Nelson down an alleyway to a mean, narrow tavern with an ale bush pushed under its battered eaves.

"It's the best we could do," Nelson apologised.

They hobbled their horses and paid a ragged ostler to guard them. Nelson led Segalla into the tavern. On the rickety stairs a rat, bold as brass, was chewing a scrap of food and lazily moved away at their approach. As they climbed, Segalla noticed that the windows were covered with scraps of parchment; the dirt and grease lay inches thick on ledges, shelves and the rickety balustrade. At the top Nelson stopped before a garret door and knocked gently on it.

"Symonds!" he called. "Open up. It's me, Thomas; we have a visitor."

No answer. Nelson tried the battered metal latch but the door held firm.

"Symonds!" Nelson raised his voice. He smiled apologetically over his shoulder at Segalla. "He's probably asleep. He was hurt and shocked." Again he knocked.

"Perhaps he's left," Segalla said.

"What's the matter?" A blowsy harridan came up behind them. Her black hair hung loose and greasy; her face was broad and sweaty and a large purple scar stretched above her mouth where her nose had been.

"Yuir bloody Sassenach!" she snarled, hands on her hips. "Ye dinna ken the affray ye're causing."

Segalla dug into his purse and drew out a coin. The woman's mood changed instantly. A smile, even a curtsey.

"Is my friend in?" Nelson asked.

"He has na left," the woman replied, her eyes never leaving the coin.

"But he won't answer."

"Gie out of my way!"

She pushed by them, stood before the door, lifted her foot and kicked the door just beneath the latch. It shook on its leather hinges but refused to move. The woman held out her hand for the coin. Segalla handed it over. Again her boot hit the door with a crash, sending it flying open. Segalla and Nelson followed her into the room. The landlady took one look at Symonds sprawled on the bed and turned away, gagging, at the jagged gash that ran from ear to ear and the blood soaking his jerkin and the filthy sheets. She cursed and fled the room. Nelson slumped to the floor, quietly moaning, his arms across his chest. Segalla stood over the bed and fought down his rising gorge. The smell in the room was terrible. Segalla's stomach lurched as he saw a rat jump from beneath a grimy bolster and disappear behind the bed. He touched Symonds's cold cheek, then looked at the open casement window.

"Why should someone murder poor Symonds?" Nelson breathed.

Segalla tore his glance away from the blood-soaked cadaver on the bed and pointed to the far corner where Nelson's and Symonds's possessions were strewn about. "They were looking for something."

Nelson lumbered to his feet and searched amongst the bits of clothing. He picked up a battered belt with its leather wallet.

"Empty," he moaned. "They have taken the few coins we had as well as the copy of the letter I was carrying."

Segalla closed his eyes, picked up a threadbare blanket from the floor and slung it over Symond's corpse. He walked to the window and stared into the filthy alleyway below. The tavern walls were uneven, with cracks and gaps that would make it easy for anyone to climb into or out of the garret. He stared at the door and noticed that the bolts on the inside had been broken by the force of their entry.

"Who knew you were here?"

Disconsolate, Nelson sat on the floor, shaking his head. "I don't know," he wailed. "We collected what meagre possessions we had and came here this morning. At Kirk o'Field one of Bothwell's men, I forget who, told me to present myself at Holyrood." He nodded towards the bed. "Symonds was still weak and nervous. I told him to be careful. He bolted the door behind him."

"Was the window open?"

Nelson walked across and pushed the casement closed.

"It's got no lock or catch," he said despairingly. He clasped his arms about his chest and came back to stand before Segalla. "Monsieur, I am leaving here. I have had my fill of Scotland and its bloody practices."

Segalla seized him by the shoulders. "Nelson, look at me!"

The manservant looked fearfully up.

"Whoever killed Darnley followed you and Symonds here. They climbed the wall, forced the window and cut his throat. They ransacked your belongings for anything you may have taken from Kirk o'Field." Segalla let his hands drop. "They may have come to kill you because you saw something untoward. Some thread which will lead us back to Darnley's murderers. What was it, Thomas?"

Nelson turned and walked to the bed. He stared down at the coarse blanket covering his dead companion. "I don't know. As the Lord is my witness, I really don't know." He glanced over his shoulder. "But I am not staying here, Monsieur."

"You can come with us," Segalla said. He picked up his cloak.

"And what about Symonds?"

"You have read the Gospels: leave the dead to bury their dead."

Segalla, however, felt uncomfortable. As a priest, he should bless the corpse or whisper the words of absolution in the dead man's ear. He also had a duty under Canon Law to ensure that the body was given a fair burial. He fished in his purse and took out a coin, quietly thanking God that Beaton had furnished him with the necessary monies for this journey.

"Here, take this to the landlady downstairs. She will be curious about what has happened. Tell her to see that Symonds's corpse is taken away, dressed and given proper burial. Go on, now!"

Once Nelson was out of the room, Segalla knelt beside the small cot and pulled back the rough blanket. The dead man's eyes gazed sightlessly up at him; the face was slack-jawed, with that awful wound in his throat. Segalla stared at the window, then back at the corpse. He could imagine the scene: Symonds would have been fast asleep after the shock of the previous night: the soft-footed assassin would have opened the window and slipped through, padding gently across the floor, the knife descending on Symonds's throat before he could even stir. Segalla opened his eyes. He made the sign of the cross and, overcoming his distaste, leaned down and recited the phrases of absolution, willing the dead man's soul, in the name of Christ, to go out and meet his maker. Segalla sketched a hasty benediction, grabbed his cloak and went downstairs. The old harridan who owned the inn had quickly agreed to Nelson's request.

"I shall check," Segalla said, his face inches from hers. "One of my lord Bothwell's men will come here to ensure that the corpse is given a decent Christian burial. You have the coin?"

The woman nodded.

"Then make sure you do what we've asked." He paused. "You heard no clamour? No affray which would explain that man's murder?"

The harridan looked greedily at the coin in her grimy paw. She pointed at Nelson. "I heard the Englishman leave. I was on the stairs and heard him and his companion talking." She wiped her mouth on the cuff of her dirty dress. "As the Laird be my witness," she brayed, "I dinna hear a thing until you returned."

Segalla thanked her. He and Nelson mounted their horses and rode back through the crowded streets into the Crucible tavern. Segalla immediately called the landlord to arrange lodgings for Nelson.

"You can stay here, Thomas," he said kindly. "But then what?"

Nelson shrugged. "I'll obtain licence from the Queen, and, believe me, I'll leave Edinburgh as fast as I can."

Segalla nodded and went up to his own chamber. The room had been swept and cleaned. Some winter roses, small and white, had been placed in a small jar on the table next to his bed. Segalla smiled as he recognised Janette's touch, then wondered where his "dear wife" and manservant were. He felt tired, so he lay down on the bed and stared up at the multicoloured tester.

I should say Mass, he thought, but decided against it. The rules of the order were quite explicit. If in danger, or in a place or circumstances where the celebration of Mass might be too hazardous, a priest could dispense himself from discharging his daily office. Segalla mouthed a prayer and let his mind drift. Images emerged: the heap of rubble at Kirk o'-Field: Darnley's body lying in that freezing orchard: Bothwell, nervous and agitated: the Queen in a state of shock.

Nelson eager to be away; Symonds, his throat gashed. Segalla placed his hands behind his head. He was sure of one thing. Darnley had escaped from Kirk o'Field. He had been offered protection and assistance, then cleverly trapped by his murderers, who had proceeded to blow up the Old Provost's House.

But who?

Everyone wanted Darnley dead. However, thinking of the deed and wishing it done were worlds apart from carrying the foul act through. Was it Bothwell? Had he really gone out to ensure that all was well at Kirk o'Field? Or did he and his henchmen meet Darnley and Taylor and quietly smother them in the open countryside or in some other place? And if it was Bothwell, had the Queen held up her hands and looked through her fingers at the deed? Or was it Ker of Fawdonside? Or the Earl of Moray? But had he not been absent in Fife? Whilst the other great lords had made sure they were nowhere in the vicinity. Segalla chewed his lips. Beaton had warned him about Walsingham's spy, the Raven Master. Was he the actual killer? The man, whoever he was, had acted with brutal efficiency. But how could an English spy lay his hands so easily on so much gunpowder and transport it with such impunity into the royal lodgings? Was the Raven Master a spy? Or a Scottish lord in Walsingham's pay? Beaton had said someone close, such as Bothwell. Did he have his own secret plans? Segalla recalled the message the Raven Master had left for him and admired the man's cool effrontery. He heard a tap on the door and his hand slid under the bolster, where he had placed his dagger.

"Come in! Come in!" he shouted.

A thin, white-faced slattern entered. She paused nervously in the doorway, her face hidden by greasy locks of hair. Segalla swung his legs off the bed.

"What is it, girl? Don't be afraid."

She walked across the room. "A man left this for you."

"What man?"

"Downstairs."

She handed him a sealed package. He turned it over; written in blue-green ink in a bold hand was his name. Segalla froze. The letters "S.J.," signifying "of the Society of Jesus," were scrawled beside his name. Segalla hid his alarm and smiled at the girl.

"Did you receive it?"

"Aye, sir. I was cleaning the table. The man comes in, dressed in a cloak he was."

"How did he speak?"

"Softly in the Scottish tongue. The landlord told me to bring it up."

Segalla thanked her. "Do you know what the writing says?"

She made to retreat. "Ach no. I canna read but he said your name." She closed the door quickly behind her.

Segalla stared down at the packet. Who knew his identity? Only the Queen? He undid it swiftly. Inside were two glossy black feathers. The message on the parchment was simple. Pray for Symonds, pray for yourself and pray for the Queen. It was stylishly signed, The Raven Master.

Segalla found it hard to control his anger. He took one further look at the parchment and walked to the corner of the room, where a small capped brazier glowed weakly. He lifted the lid and thrust the message inside. Hastily he filled a goblet of wine and sipped it greedily, ignoring its bitter, stale taste. For a while he just stood, rolling the cup in his hands, trying to master his panic. The Raven Master knew not only his identity but his every movement. He was certainly responsible for Symonds's murder and now was quietly taunting Segalla. The Raven Master's cool boldness was no mere bragging, but served to demonstrate how cleverly he controlled the game.

Segalla sat back on the bed. "Her Majesty knows," he said

to himself, "that I am a Jesuit. But does anyone else?" Walsingham might know: his agents at the French court would scrutinise everyone and might have seen through the disguise. Segalla went cold. Two others knew his identity: Janette Lindsay and Thomas Vartlett.

"Impossible!" He spoke to the bare wall, then reflected. "Nothing's impossible," he conceded. He bolted the chamber door and lay back on the bed. Why had Lindsay and Vartlett been sent? To assist him? To provide him with a disguise? True, the Queen was readier to speak to him than to any of them, but did Beaton really trust them? Was that why Beaton had warned him not to trust anyone? Was it possible that Lindsay and Vartlett were in Walsingham's pay? They knew his true identity. They kept to themselves; God knew where they went. They had been with him at Kirk o'Field on his first day in Edinburgh, deep in conversation with servants like Paris and Sandy Durham. And on the night of the explosion? Segalla turned on the bed restlessly.

"Is it possible?" he said. "Did Janette and Vartlett play a role in the King's death?"

He got off the bed and took out his ink horn, quill and parchment, followed by his Book of Hours. He opened this at the back and, using the cipher Beaton had taught him, began to draft a letter to the Archbishop in Paris describing the explosion at Kirk o'Field and Darnley's mysterious death. He kept the letter stark and blunt, detailing exactly what he had seen, the Queen's reactions and what dangers now beset her. Once he had finished he wrote it again, seeking to make his sentences more incisive. He then took a copy of the drawing he had made, put that in the letter, rolled it up and sealed it.

He was just finishing when he heard Vartlett's and Janette's voices in the gallery outside, followed by a rap on his door. Schooling his features, he opened it. Janette pushed past him into the room, drawing back the cowl of her cloak, her face cheerful. Vartlett, too, looked invigorated, stamping his hands together and blowing on his fingers. Janette flounced down on the bed.

"Husband, why lock the door against us?"

Segalla shrugged and smiled. "We live in stirring times."

"And how is Her Majesty?"

Segalla described his visit to Holyrood and his meeting with the Queen and Bothwell. He deliberately painted a picture of the Queen as stronger and more determined than she really was. Janette studied him curiously.

"What's wrong?" she asked. "Don't lie to me, priest!" she whispered. "Your smile is false: it never reaches your eyes. You've brought the shutters down on your soul. Why?"

"Is it Symonds's death?" Vartlett asked. "We found Nelson below in the taproom feeding his face, happy as a pig in muck. He believes you will protect him."

"Yes, yes, Symonds's death," Segalla answered, more flatly than he intended. "Nelson now fears for his own life, as I do mine. The Raven Master"—he held Janette's gaze—"knows who I am. On two occasions he has threatened me."

"Then we should leave," she retorted. "We have delivered the Archbishop's letters to the Queen. We have carried out our task."

Segalla turned and walked to the window so that they could not see his face. "Before I left Paris," he said slowly, "Beaton gave us another task."

"To clip the Raven Master's wings," Vartlett said.

Segalla turned. "Oh no, Master Vartlett, we are going to do more than that. As God is my witness, I intend to kill him!"

"Kill?" Janette rose to her feet. "Monsieur, are you mad?" All the laughter had died out of her eyes. She stood lacing her fingers together. "We are envoys, not assassins!"

"We came to bring you news," Vartlett interjected, standing between them. "The King's body is about to be embalmed. And . . ."

"And what?"

"They have found the barrel which held the gunpowder near Kirk o'Field."

Chapter 9

The scene at Kirk o'Field looked even more desolate in the light of day. The dust had settled, revealing a spectacle of devastation. Crowds from the city flocked out to ogle the spot where their King had died; soldiers in royal livery were cordoning the place off, whilst retainers from the Queen's household, led by Archibald Bethon, her chamberlain, sifted amongst the rubble.

"From the very foundations," Janette breathed as she stood next to Segalla. "How could it have been done?"

Segalla glanced sideways at her. He had hardly spoken to her or Vartlett since they had left the tavern. He was still pricked by suspicion about his two companions. "Wait here!" he ordered.

Janette caught his arm. "Nicholas." Her face was anxious. "What is the matter?" She waved a hand at the ruins. "This is not our doing."

Segalla pulled his arm free and picked his way gingerly across the rubble. One of the royal archers went to stop him, but Archibald Bethon, his robes covered in dust, shouted to let Segalla through. The chamberlain was crouched, digging amongst a pile of loose plaster, oblivious to the dirt staining his robes. His long, mournful face looked even more sombre than usual.

"Monsieur Segalla, not a stone left upon a stone." The chamberlain narrowed his eyes. "You were at Holyrood this morning?"

Segalla nodded and crouched beside him.

"The Queen values your counsel," Bethon said. "She wishes to see you again, soon." The chamberlain tossed away a piece of plaster. "So, your arrival has saved me a journey to the city." He stared about him. "I have wasted enough time here."

"What are you looking for?" Segalla asked.

"Oh, anything valuable." Bethon led him to where a large hole had been excavated. "According to what I remember," the chamberlain explained, "the Queen's room was under her husband's, so Darnley's possessions should be in this area."

"But have you found anything?"

Bethon gazed at the crowds thronging behind the line of archers. "People come to plunder," he remarked. "That's why I am here. Oh, we've come upon the odd trinket and bauble, but everything's been smashed. However, what I find mysterious is that I've discovered the remains of the Queen's writing desk but no trace of any parchments, ink horn, or quills she left here." He got to his feet, flicked the dust from his hose and glanced up at the overcast sky. "If it snows," he said, "the task of clearing will be made impossible."

"Do you think the house was plundered," Segalla asked, "before the explosion occurred?"

Bethon scratched his unkempt reddish beard. "In a word, Monsieur, yes, I do. But how could it be? I held the Queen's keys; the King held his own."

"Perhaps Darnley himself took the missing items?"

"You mean as he fled from the house?"

"Perhaps he didn't flee," Segalla said, 'but left of his own accord."

"So, why should he take the Queen's writing implements, pens and seals? There's a casket," Bethon continued. "A silver casket. The Queen had it on her desk, yet there's no trace of it."

Segalla left him to his search and walked back to his two companions.

"What's the matter?" Vartlett asked.

"The mystery deepens," Segalla said. "According to Bethon, the Queen's chamber, and possibly Darnley's, were plundered before the house was blown up. But"—he smiled wryly—"according to Bethon that's impossible, unless the King did it himself." He shook the dust from his cloak. "Now, where's that barrel of gunpowder?"

Vartlett made enquiries of one of the archers, and they walked through the gardens of Kirk o'Field into the small quadrangle. In the centre was a well with an ornate cover, and beside it a large iron-bound cask.

"According to the archer," Vartlett explained, crouching beside the barrel, "they found this near the entrance which led from the quadrangle to the Old Provost's House."

Segalla looked into the barrel. He ran his fingers round the inside, then sniffed at the fine coating of greyish dust. It smelt of sulphur. He wiped his hands on his jerkin. "It's gunpowder," he said. "But if it was used to blow the house up, where did it come from?"

He was about to walk across the quadrangle when Janette blocked his way, Vartlett beside her. Janette's her eyes were calculating. "Come, come, husband," she whispered. "Neither you nor I believe this farrago of nonsense."

"What do you mean?" Segalla asked.

Janette pointed to the barrel. "That was meant to be found. I know it and you know it. The assassins never plundered the Queen's chambers, whilst Darnley, though feckless, was not stupid. He would hardly run out into the night dressed in his bed robes, carrying a chair, if he knew his enemies were outside." She stepped closer. "He left of his own accord, did he not? Husband, why do you distrust us so much?"

"I am not your husband," Segalla snapped. "And I don't

distrust you. But, Mistress Lindsay, since we arrived in Edinburgh, you and Vartlett have gone your way and I have gone mine. You are a mysterious pair. Why did Beaton send you with me?"

Segalla took a step forward, but neither Vartlett nor Janette gave way.

"Tell us the truth, husband," Janette mocked.

"I'll tell you my truths," Segalla replied, "when, Madame, you decide to tell me yours!"

Janette looked at Vartlett, who nodded almost imperceptibly.

"We think," Janette began, "that Darnley intended to flee Kirk o'Field. He had his own madcap schemes, to seize the baby Prince and either flee abroad, or raise rebellion with his father. The Archbishop told us this before we left Paris." She caught the look of annoyance on Segalla's face. "No, don't be angry with our master. You were ordered to advise the Queen. We had our own separate instructions. If Darnley escaped, and I repeat, only if, we were to act as though sympathetic to his cause, furnish him with help and advice until"—Janette paused as if choosing her words carefully—"until the danger he posed could be contained. Now Darnley is dead, no longer any danger to the Queen. Our task is finished. If you wish us to stay with you, we will. But if not, then, Monsieur Segalla, it's heigh-ho out of Scotland!"

Segalla gazed at her steadily. "Yes, I believe Darnley escaped Kirk o'Field: those who pretended to assist him, killed him, possibly re-dressed his body in those nightclothes and left the corpse in the orchard. After that, those same people blew up Kirk o'Field. The barrel over there was left deliberately; whether it was used or not is neither here nor there. The stage is now set; the next few days will tell us how the play will go."

"What if Darnley himself had gunpowder secreted away in one of these outhouses; he laid the charge himself and blew the house up?" Janette said, "After all, this would keep people guessing whilst he made his escape; then he was killed by his so-called allies?"

Segalla tried to hide his surprise.

"Husband dearest," Janette said, "you are not the only one who thinks. What would happen," she continued, "if there were further variations on the theme? Darnley blew up Kirk o'Field to hide his departure, even as a ploy so that he can later proclaim that he escaped mortal danger by the skin of his teeth. The possibilities are endless."

Segalla was about to reply when he heard his name called; Bethon the chamberlain, shaking dust from his robe, walked into the quadrangle.

"Monsieur Segalla, do you wish to accompany me? The Queen's apothecary is now attendant on the King's corpse. Perhaps it's best if you are present: there may be questions to be asked."

"May we come?" Janette asked.

Segalla glanced at her and shook his head. He touched his fingers gently to her lips and winked at Vartlett. "I did you a great injustice," he said quickly in French. "Your thinking is clearer than mine. I have a letter for the Archbishop in Paris. Perhaps it's best if you both take it?" He smiled at them, then hurried after Bethon.

Segalla let the chamberlain go ahead up the stairs, claiming he had to use the privy closet. Once Bethon was out of sight, Segalla sat on a bench and stared down at his hands.

"You are making a mistake, Nicholas," he said to himself. "And you should know better than that."

He closed his eyes, leaned back and reflected on what Janette had said. Was he wasting his time? There were so many possibilities: Janette had shown him how events could be interpreted any way people wanted, and that that was the dreadful beauty of Darnley's murder. However it was twisted, in the end the Queen would take some, if not all, of the blame. If Darnley had been fleeing, what had he been so frightened of? If he had been forced to flee, why hadn't his wife protected him better? And Janette's and Vartlett's theories? Segalla opened his eyes. There was something dreadfully wrong, but he could not put his finger on it.

"Monsieur Segalla, are you coming up?"

He climbed the staircase. Bethon stood at the top, leaning against the wall, watched by the two grinning archers who stood on guard outside the chamber.

"I wish I hadn't come," Bethon whispered. "The surgeons are embalming the King's corpse." And, pressing his hand to his mouth, the chamberlain hurried back down the stairs.

Segalla nodded at the guards and opened the door: he immediately understood what had made Bethon so nauseated. The Queen's apothecary and master surgeon, Master Pitcairn, stood by the trestle table on which Darnley's corpse lay. He had sliced the body from chest to crotch: the entrails were piled in bowls and the air was thick with the cloying smell of corruption, mingled with the herbs and spices Pitcairn was preparing. Assistants in dirty leather aprons were busily washing the entrails in buckets of water, pickling them before they were doused in herbs and placed in caskets. Segalla's jaw tightened and he tried not to breathe in. He glimpsed Sandy Durham, the King's porter, standing by the window, his back to the proceedings.

The King's master surgeon looked up: a small man with a neatly cut moustache and pointed beard. He immediately broke off what he was doing and stared at Segalla.

"Should you be here, sir? For God's sake, this corpse is like any other. It is not some mummery at a village fair!"

Sandy Durham, his face completely white spun round and came past the table. He walked a little unsteadily: Segalla did not know whether it was due to nervousness or whether the man had been drinking heavily. He was about to order Segalla from the room when suddenly he recognised him and smiled.

"Master Pitcairn, this is Monsieur Segalla, the Queen's special envoy from France."

The master surgeon smiled in apology and went back to his task as Durham gently ushered Segalla out of the room.

"A bloody business, Master Durham."

"Aye, and it's my task to guard the corpse. The Queen intends to bury it in the Chapel Royal at Holyrood." In embarrassment the porter looked away. "It's not the easiest of tasks," he said in a low voice. "I stand looking out of the window, pinching my nostrils, praying to God the barber surgeons will soon be finished."

Segalla grasped Durham by the elbow, pushing him along the gallery to a window seat that overlooked the ruins of the Old Provost's House.

"I have questions for you, Master Durham."

The porter gazed brazenly back. "Everyone has questions, Monsieur Segalla."

"Why weren't you with Darnley when he died? After all, you were his porter."

"Why, sir, do you wish me dead?"

"No, but I would like to know why you were so desirous of leaving Kirk o'Field."

Durham grew even paler, his eyes darting from left to right as though someone might lurk behind the wainscoting. He leaned forward. "What are you implying, sir?"

"Gossip, Master Durham. The gossips say that you were desirous of leaving Kirk o'Field on Sunday."

Durham looked down, studying the cheap ring on one of his fingers. "You have no authority to ask me such questions."

"No, but the Queen's Justices do. As do her torturers."

"I have friends," Durham mumbled without looking up. "Powerful friends."

"You mean those who planned the explosion at Kirk o'-Field?" Segalla gibed.

149

"No, Frenchman, patrons at court."

"You still haven't answered my questions. The King's death is treason." Segalla gestured back towards the chamber. "The King's bowels are being removed, but he is long dead. What must it feel like, Master Durham, to be hanged, cut down when you are half dead and have your entrails plucked out and burnt before your eyes?"

Durham leaned back in the window seat, crossing his arms to control the trembling of his body. His eyes filled with a mixture of panic and hate. "Stay out of this!" he hissed. "Frenchman, you do not know what you are meddling in. Leave me alone." He made to rise.

Segalla swiftly drew his dagger and blocked his way. "Why were you so desirous to be away from Kirk o'Field?"

"I was ill."

Durham seemed to sag.

"You are a liar. Tell me the truth."

Durham gazed through the window at the ruins. "You visited the house, Monsieur. You felt the tension. Any man who had a brain knew Death and Murder lurked in the shadows. I left Kirk o'Field because of that as well as to attend the revelry at Holyrood."

"Did your master, the lord Darnley, intend to flee?"

Durham sniggered. "My master," he answered slowly, "blabbered like a bairn: his noddle was full of madcap schemes and subtle stratagems. Yes, he may have intended to."

"Did he talk to you about this?"

"He did not."

"Did you have a key to the King's chamber?"

"I did not, only to the cellar. Where Bonkle the cook worked."

"And the night of the explosion?"

"Bonkle doused the fire, cleaned out the ovens, set out

plates of cold meat and wine should the King be hungry and, like the rest of us, left to drink his wits away."

"And you locked the cellar door?"

"Of course! Just before the Queen left for Holyrood."

"And you had the only key?"

Durham snorted with laughter. "In God's name, Monsieur, how can I know that?"

"You didn't lend this key to anyone else? Or arrange for the cellar door to be left open?"

"Why should I do that?"

"Because," Segalla answered tartly, "I know a little about gunpowder. Oh, I have seen the barrel left outside, but that's only to whet our curiosity. However, what I do know—" Segalla pointed out of the window. "To destroy a house such as that with stone foundations, supported by vaulted arches: to lift it entirely off the ground, to do that, sir, the gunpowder must have been put in the cellar." He smiled thinly. "And how could they do that if you locked the door?"

Sandy Durham sprang to his feet and pushed his face into Segalla's. "I don't know, Frenchman. But now I tell you this: there are those who both know and resent your meddling."

And before Segalla could stop him, Durham strode down the gallery and back into the chamber, slamming the door behind him. Segalla sat on the window seat and stared out over the ruins of Kirk o'Field. He must have waited for at least half an hour before the chamber door opened. He heard Pitcairn the surgeon talking to the archers on guard outside and stepped out of the window embrasure.

"Master Pitcairn, of your courtesy, a word, please?"

The little doctor smiled, shrugged and walked slowly down the gallery towards Segalla. Now free of his broad leather apron, he wore a puffed-out, quilted jacket over a high-necked linen shirt, knee breeches of the same dark red velvet, elegant hose and high-heeled shoes with gold rose buttons.

He carried a silver-topped walking cane, and his fingers were covered in little rings, carved with the signs of the zodiac. From one lace cuff draped a silken handkerchief; in his other hand the doctor held a silver pomander studded with gems from which, now and again, he would sniff languidly. He held out one limp hand for Segalla to shake.

Segalla grasped the man's hand and noted the shrewd expression in his eyes. "I have some questions," he said.

The doctor laughed and held the pomander up to his nose. "Questions, questions, haven't we all, sir? But I am hungry. I tell you, sir." He leaned on his walking stick. "There's nothing like peeling a corpse and bottling the innards to give a man an appetite."

Segalla gestured towards the stairs. "Then, sir, be my guest."

Pitcairn collected his cloak and high-bonneted hat and, swinging his cane, led Segalla out of Kirk o'Field and back in the direction of Netherbow Gate.

"At times," he remarked as they walked, "we Scots can be terrible cooks. I have studied in France, at the Sorbonne." He kissed his fingers. "Once you have dined in the Paris eating-houses you are spoilt for life. But, come, I'll show you a small oasis in this desert of poor food."

"You are Scottish-born?" Segalla asked.

"Oh yes, and proud of it. The second son of an impoverished laird. I fled as quickly as I could. First Paris, and then I studied under Vesalius when he was professor of anatomy at the University of Padua. Have you ever read his book *The Fabric of the Human Body?*"

Segalla hid his smile and shook his head.

"Superb," the little doctor continued. "A brilliant mind. Do you know"—his voice fell to a hoarse whisper as if he were telling Segalla some great secret—"he proved Galen was wrong." Pitcairn sighed. "But what does it matter here, eh? The Queen wished me to be in Scotland, so here I am."

"And will you stay here?" Segalla asked.

The doctor stopped and leaned on his cane, his head to one side. "Monsieur Segalla, I am no fool. I look at a man's face, his eyes, his hair, his nails. I am trained to detect the evil humours, the rise of black bile or the onset of yellow phlegm." He walked on, swinging his cane. "And so it is with the body politic. The common people of Scotland are God's own, but its nobility is rotten. It's a foolish man who puts his hand into a stinking corpse, and no man stays in a room infected by the plague. I spend my time, Monsieur Segalla, cleaning wounds and balancing the humours. I do not like killing, and in Scotland the killing will soon begin."

"You will desert Her Majesty?" Segalla asked bluntly.

Pitcairn paused to pluck a pair of elegant gloves from his belt and put them on. "Did I say that, Monsieur? But the Queen is finished. I have given her my advice." He nodded back at Kirk o'Field. "After this business how can she prosper? She is ill, Monsieur Segalla. She has a proud, courageous spirit, but her body betrays her."

"What is her illness?"

The doctor tapped the side of his head. "In here, Monsieur; think of it." Pitcairn stopped; they were nearly at Netherbow Gate. The doctor sat on a wall. "What I say here is for your ears only, Monsieur Segalla. Once Durham told me who you were"—he smiled apologetically—"if you had not invited me to supper, I would have extended the invitation myself. The Queen is a beautiful woman," he continued as Segalla sat next to him. "Her father, James V, died within a week of her birth in a state of mania, terrified by visions, brought on by a deep melancholia. Some kind of insane frenzy which exhausts both the body and the mind." Pitcairn's voice fell to a whisper. "The Queen's father, if the truth be known, suffered from the petit mal, the falling sickness. Mary is no different. On her return to Scotland, the hardships she has had to face brought these attacks about. Six years ago she fell from a horse after a sudden seizure. Other attacks followed, and, after the murder of Rizzio, she being pregnant, her labour was prolonged and excessively severe. Four months ago, at Jedburgh, the Queen suffered her most serious fit. She became as dead: her members cold, eyes closed, mouth fast, feet and arms stiff. Only myself and the other doctors, as well as the Queen's unbounding courage, brought her back to consciousness. Now, after such seizures, the Queen is weak, at least in body. I can prescribe philtres and potions, but my lord Bothwell, who has a reputation for dabbling in necromancy and the black arts, also gives her potions."

Segalla stood up, stunned. "Monsieur Pitcairn, you must be mistaken."

"Monsieur Segalla, I am not. The Queen is exhausted. In the wrong hands, under a more baleful influence"—Pitcairn also rose to his feet, steadying himself on his cane—"God knows what might happen." He grasped Segalla by the wrist. "Her Majesty must be removed. She must flee back to France, take her infant son with her, allow her body and mind to recover. Her kinsmen there, the Guises, will give her sanctuary, and then, at a more suitable time, she can return to Scotland." Pitcairn smiled and shivered. "But come, it is cold and that promised meal awaits us."

Chapter 10

I n a small eating-house just within the city gates, Pitcairn hired a special table partitioned off from the rest of the room. For a while Segalla sat and watched with amusement as the little physician, who had so recently been cleaning a cadaver, ate with gusto: minced mackerel, goose slices in sauce and loin of pork with horseradish sauce. Every so often he would take sips from a deep cup of claret. Segalla still felt a little queasy and confined himself to small bread rolls and a Paris pie.

At last Pitcairn dabbed his mouth and toasted Segalla with his cup. "Well, Monsieur, I cannot read minds, but I suspect it is the dead that concern you rather than the living."

Segalla nodded. "We will talk in French," he replied. "Softly." He looked about. "Even in this private place, the walls may have ears."

Pitcairn agreed.

"How did Darnley die?"

The physician sipped the wine, then smacked his lips. "He was a tall man, of good constitution, though syphilis had made itself felt."

"Any poison?" Segalla asked.

"None that I could detect. Most of the principal ones, arsenic, belladonna, henbane or foxglove, stain the stomach and cause a most pungent smell. All I can say, Monsieur, is that our King drank deeply the night before he died."

"And no scorch marks on the body?"

"None whatsoever!" Pitcairn laughed. "I, too, have heard

the ridiculous stories. How the King's body had been blown up in the air only to fall into the orchard along with a dagger, slippers, a chair and a net." He saw the startled look on Segalla's face. "Surely you don't believe that the king's body was blown into the air?"

Segalla shook his head. "No, I was puzzled by your reference to a net. I saw a heap of cordage." Segalla paused as he remembered he had only glimpsed it in the dim light of dawn.

"Well, I have seen it," the doctor said. "In a heap, it looks like a pile of cordage, but it was a large net, the type used in warehouses to lower goods into the hold of a ship. Darnley must have used it when he escaped from Kirk o'Field."

Segalla rubbed his fingers along the tabletop. He thanked God that somewhere in the tavern, two wandering musicians had struck up with tambour and flute, drowning their conversation.

"If Darnley was not blown up, stabbed or throttled, how did he die?"

"I suspect his breath was stopped."

"Suffocated?"

"Possibly."

"But wouldn't he struggle?"

The physician spread his hands. "I, too, have thought about that, Monsieur. What happened if they used drugs or Darnley was held down?"

Segalla recalled Nelson's words about Darnley's sharing cups of wine before they all retired. "Could Darnley and his party have been drugged?"

"Possibly, Monsieur, a heavy sleeping potion. The assassins crept into the room, killed Darnley and his squire and transported the bodies out of the window." The physician shrugged. "It could happen. There are housebreakers and riflers in Edinburgh who could walk through a man's house, even his bedchamber, steal and slip away." He studied Segalla's troubled face. "But you don't believe that, do you?"

"No, I don't." Segalla put down his wine cup and leaned across the table. "Who could drug Darnley?" He shook his head. "And they'd need keys to get in. I believe Darnley and Taylor left that house of their own accord and went out to meet their murderers."

Pitcairn played with the crumbs on the table. "So, if I follow your logic, Monsieur, Darnley rises, dresses and, accompanied by Taylor, slips from Kirk o'Field. He goes somewhere else, where they are seized by their murderers, who suffocate them. They then strip the bodies, dress them in their nightgowns and take them out to that orchard with a chair and netting to look as if they had died fleeing from the assassins?"

Segalla grinned. "You can read minds, Master Physician."

"And would Darnley have taken his possessions?"

"Possibly, a sword and dagger."

Pitcairn leaned back against the wooden partition. "Darnley was a prince," he said. "According to you, Monsieur, he is fleeing for his life in the dead of night. For what purpose, God knows. I agree, he would dress, take sword and dagger. But let us go back to that chamber. If you were fleeing, Monsieur Segalla, would you bother to take your night robe with you?"

Segalla sat back, surprised. "I—I hadn't thought of that," he stammered. "Darnley would not have taken it with him. The assassins would scarcely go back to Kirk o'Field just for that, nor would they use anyone else's."

"Whatever happened," Pitcairn continued, "I do not think Darnley was fleeing. Not only because of what I've told you, but I've washed Darnley's legs and feet: there was no mark or dirt on them. No sign of being dressed, being stripped and then re-gowned. In fact the opposite. His night robe was of wool; pieces of that wool still clung to the hairs of his leg. No, no, Monsieur, it is my view that Darnley was smothered in his bed, then taken out of Kirk o'Field, which was later blown up."

"But two others survived. Nelson and Symonds."

Pitcairn pulled a face. "Then we must reconsider what I said earlier. Were Darnley and his party given a heavy opiate, drugged wine or . . ."

"Or what?"

"There is another possibility: did Darnley and Taylor drug the wine of their servants before slipping quietly from the room? Did they meet the murderers elsewhere in Kirk o'Field? Both men were still in their night robes. The assassins then killed them and moved their bodies to the orchard."

Pitcairn tapped the table and grinned at Segalla. "Just like a game of chess, is it not?" His face became grave. "We do not know, Monsieur, whether Darnley deliberately met his murderers in Kirk o'Field or, hearing some sounds, roused his manservant and went down, either into the *salle* or the Queen's chamber, which lay beneath his." Pitcairn lifted his eyes. "But if that is so," he whispered, "who had the keys to Kirk o'Field? And the answer is the Queen. Did she go back there? In her youth, Her Majesty did have a passion for dressing in men's clothes for the purpose of masque or revelry. Or did she give the keys to someone else?"

"Could Her Majesty do that?" Segalla asked.

Pitcairn looked away, chewing the corner of his lip. "The Queen I serve—" He shook his head. "No, I do not think so. But, Monsieur Segalla, what happens if the Queen's mind, as I described earlier, became paralysed with fear?" He wagged a finger at Segalla. "Don't forget, Darnley's period of sickness and official withdrawal was coming to an end. On Monday, tenth February, he was to rejoin the court." Pitcairn gripped Segalla's hand. "Can you imagine it, Monsieur?" he said hoarsely. "The Queen at her revels knowing that, in a few hours, the polluted Darnley, the husband who betrayed her, who organised the murder of Rizzio, was once more to share her bed and life." Pitcairn shook his head. "Could you blame the Queen if her mind turned to murder?"

"But the deed was planned," Segalla said. "The gunpowder must have been prepared."

Pitcairn sipped his wine. "Aye, Monsieur, you can lay the gunpowder, but it takes only a passing thought to light the train."

✻ ❈ In Whitehall Palace in London, Elizabeth of England, with her red hair and green eyes, sat wrapped in a thick, sable-edged robe before a roaring fire in her private chamber. The windows were shuttered; the air was thick with the fragrant herbs which had been hidden amongst the logs and in the silver chafing dishes placed about the room to fend off the February chill.

Below, Elizabeth heard the wind rattling the wooden barriers in her father's old tilt yard and the creak and groan of his ancient palace, which, she said to herself with a quiet curse, had seen better days. She cradled the cup of posset in her hands.

"I should be at Richmond," she muttered, gently rubbing her right cheek, wishing the toothache would go away. "God save us from physicians!" Sooner or later, she would have to go to the barber surgeon and subject herself to his skillful ministrations. She grinned. The man was so nervous, she didn't know who was the more terrified: she at losing a tooth or he at having to draw it. She heard sounds in the gallery outside, followed by a knock on the door.

"Come in!" she snapped.

"Your Majesty, Sir Francis Walsingham waits below."

Elizabeth's eyes remained on the fire. "Tell him to wait," she replied. She glanced at the hour candle burning in the corner. "As I have had to wait. Tell my Black Tom." She stretched one hand out to the fire. "Subjects should not keep their princes waiting."

Elizabeth heard the door close behind her and smiled; her

159

narrow, oval face took on a girlish look like the one she had worn when her father used to summon her to this very chamber. Then she would hide, fearful of that great giant of a man with his legs like tree trunks, his narrow eyes and booming voice, which could reduce the most powerful nobleman to a quivering mass. Elizabeth gazed round the room. So many ghosts; Mary, her Spanish half sister, with her hard face, thin lips and suspicious mind. Young Edward with his gentle eyes and racking cough. Elizabeth gripped the cup. Now she held the orb and sceptre and wore the crown. Nine years a queen and already she had sipped from the chalice of bitterness. She touched the inflamed gum gingerly with her tongue and stared impassively at Holbein's painting of her father which hung above the fireplace. Her father had executed her mother, publicly calling her a whore and declaring her illegitimate, yet Elizabeth was still fascinated by him.

"No man like him," she murmured. "Except for Dudley, sweet Robin!"

Elizabeth heard footsteps in the gallery: Walsingham, "Black Tom," was waiting to tell her about a Queen who'd had the luxury of two husbands. Elizabeth opened the small pouch that hung from the arm of the chair. She took out the miniature of her cousin and read the gold letters round the frame.

"Marie, Reine d'Ecosse, France et Angleterre."

Seven years ago, Throckmorton, Elizabeth's Ambassador in Paris, had sent this miniature to her. Elizabeth felt a surge of anger. She stared down at the sweet, pale face that gazed back at her.

"How dare she?" Elizabeth had raged. "How dare she style herself Queen of England?"

Her two familiars, Walsingham and Cecil, had crept like Job's comforters about her. They wove their nightmare tapestry before her eyes; a Catholic Queen backed by French troops pouring across the Channel as her grandfather Henry

Tudor had some seventy-five years previously. In Scotland, the Great Lords, eager to avenge the defeats of Flodden and Solway Moss, would mass on the border, two swords to England's throat. But Francis had died and Mary had returned to Scotland. Elizabeth had secretly marvelled at her cousin's skill in managing her rebellious lords, sitting patiently whilst being lectured by fiery Knox on the new doctrines from Geneva. Mary had become an even greater danger until Darnley had checked her. Elizabeth's lips parted over her blackened teeth. She gazed up at the portrait.

"Trust a man," she said. "Trust a man to spoil everything."

She picked up the silver handbell from the table and rang it furiously. She did not stir as the door opened silently behind her.

"And how is my Black Tom?" she said without turning.

Walsingham coughed. "As ever, pleased to see Your Majesty. Eager to be of service."

"You are such a bloody liar!" Elizabeth retorted, grinning over her shoulder at him. "Don't play the courtier, Francis, it doesn't suit you." She waved him to a chair on the other side of the fireplace. "Come, sit down, my spinner of webs."

Walsingham eased himself into a chair, doffing his bonnet. He sat in a relaxed posture. Elizabeth always dispensed with the courtesies when they were alone. Walsingham gazed at the red hair peeping from underneath the silver jewelled comb on her head. He noticed the Queen's constant touching of her right cheek and how she almost hid herself in the folds of her great fur cloak.

"Your Majesty has the rheum?"

"Your Majesty, Tom," Elizabeth tartly replied, "is freezing from tip to toe." She glared round at the wooden wainscoting. "One of these days I will burn this place. Well," she said. "You have brought me into London."

Walsingham shook his head. "No, Madam, you chose to come to London. The Commons meet soon and, of course, the Earl of Leicester is due to return from the west country."

Elizabeth threw her head back and laughed. "What don't you know, eh?"

"Darnley is dead."

Elizabeth let the cup slip to the floor. "Dead!" she exclaimed. "The sickness or the plague?"

"Murdered, Your Majesty."

Walsingham picked up the goblet, wiped it with a napkin and filled it from the jug which stood warming on a stone in the inglenook. He passed it to the Queen.

"Drink," he urged. "It will ease the pain in your gums. I will have words with my lord of Leicester about a barber—"

"Shut up!" Elizabeth snapped. "Tell me what happened."

Walsingham briefly described the news he had received by fast courier from Edinburgh. Elizabeth forgot the pain in her gums and listened, round-eyed. When Walsingham had finished, she sat for a while.

"The Stuarts are cursed," she said. "Mary's father died mad. Her grandfather and great-grandfather were killed. Now she bears the curse. What will happen?"

"Civil war," Walsingham said. "Darnley's death will be laid at Mary's door. The lords will object, demand greater control. Scotland will be divided."

"She will get help from France?"

Walsingham shook his head. "The Catholic powers will be scandalised."

"Scandalised?"

"Aye, your Majesty, scandalised. Whilst your good kinsman Darnley died, Mary was revelling at a banquet."

"And who was responsible?" Elizabeth asked sharply, suddenly remembering her kindship with the dead lord.

Walsingham's gaze fell away.

"I asked a question, sirrah."

"The Great Lords were all party to his death. They may not have lit the fuse, but they looked through their fingers when it was done. The principal blame will be laid at Lord Bothwell's door."

"And do you have proof?"

"Soon, Your Majesty, we will have all the proof the world needs. Bothwell is a murderer and Queen Mary is his paramour."

Startled, Elizabeth let the fur robe slip. "To accuse a queen of adultery, Master Walsingham—" She tried to hide the quickening of her heartbeat and concealed her jewelled, clenched fingers beneath her robe. "To accuse a queen of adultery," she repeated, "is treason itself."

"There is proof, I believe."

"What kind of proof?"

"Letters between the Queen and Lord Bothwell."

Now Elizabeth glanced away, trying to control her chill of fear. In all her life she had feared two men: her father and Walsingham. She recalled her deep affection for sweet Robin and marvelled at the intricacies of Cecil, but Walsingham's mind! She had not wanted to send Darnley to Scotland, but he had insisted. She had been opposed to his marriage to Mary, but Walsingham had quietly favoured it. Now Darnley was dead. Mary would take the blame and Bothwell would become her paramour. Elizabeth recalled Amy Robsart and wondered for the hundredth time whether Amy had fallen or been pushed.

"And who killed my lord Darnley?" she asked abruptly. "And who lit the fuse?"

Walsingham gazed steadily back.

"You have an agent in Scotland," Elizabeth insisted. "The man you call the Raven Master."

"Your Majesty, who said it was a man?"

Elizabeth raised a clenched fist from beneath the robe. "Don't play games with me."

"Your Majesty." Walsingham paused and took a deep breath; he was about to enter the eye of the storm. "If the good of this realm and the happiness of your person is enhanced by the death of Darnley, and, believe me, Your Majesty, it surely is, then who cares if we extinguish the life of a hapless young man and bring the House of Stuart crumbling to ruins? Seven years ago," he continued coldly, "Mary of Scotland sat on the throne of France and threatened England: one dagger to its heart, another to its throat. Both daggers have now been knocked from her hand, and the danger has passed. The Raven Master, if he is a man, will continue to do his damage and work for your security. That is all I can say."

Elizabeth tapped her foot. She was already, in her mind, composing a letter to Mary Stuart, working out the subtle hints and silken threats. She glanced up at Walsingham and for a moment he could have sworn she winked.

"Black Tom. Black Tom," she murmured. "Go back to your spider's web. Keep me and Master Cecil appraised." Her face became grave. "It is time you sat higher at the Council table, Sir Francis. Such loyalty and dedication will not be forgotten."

Walsingham rose. Elizabeth proffered her hand for him to kiss, then squeezed his fingers.

"In the presence of your sovereign," she whispered hoarsely, "you kneel."

Walsingham's hooded eyes never changed in their expression, nor did a muscle flicker in his granite face. He sank to one knee and stared into the green eyes of his Queen.

"Tell your Raven Master," Elizabeth whispered, "that what is to be done is to be done, and it's best if it was done quickly." Elizabeth squeezed his fingers again. "But tell him, and take heed yourself, not a hair on the head of Mary Stuart is to be harmed. No man nor woman has the right to lift his or her hand against the Lord's anointed. You understand? It is the prerogative of monarchs to deal with other monarchs, not for their subjects. Sir Francis, I have your word? Not a hair on her head."

Walsingham nodded and Elizabeth let go of his hand.

"We are finished," the Queen said.

Her spy master walked towards the door.

"Walsingham!"

Sir Francis turned, his hand on the latch.

"Mary of Scotland has a string of black pearls. When the House of Stuart has fallen, those pearls must be given to me."

"I understand, Your Majesty."

"Oh and Walsingham."

"Yes, Your Majesty."

"Six years ago Amy Robsart died at Cumnor Place."

"Yes, Your Majesty, God rest her soul."

"Aye, Master Walsingham, God rest her soul. One of these fine days I must ask you, where were you on that bright autumn day?"

"As always, Your Majesty, at your beck and call."

Elizabeth heard the door close behind him. Elizabeth gazed up at the portrait of her father.

"Truly the psalmist is correct," she muttered. "Nothing is new under the sun and all men are liars."

Feeling uneasy after his conversation with Pitcairn, Segalla left the eating-house near the Netherbow Gate and made his way towards the Tolbooth.

A bell from a nearby church struck the hour and Segalla, his hand grasping his sword, pressed on and entered the great square. People were gathering round the steps of the Tolbooth, where archers from the royal household were forcing a passage, led by heralds shouting, "Make way! Make way for the Queen's Commissioner, the Earl of Argyll!"

Segalla stopped in a doorway and stared round. The marketplace was frenetic, but he sensed the danger and noticed how many of Bothwell's soldiers, well-armed mosstroopers wearing the livery of the Hepburns, mingled with the crowds. Segalla made his way across the square and, by a combination of bribery and showing the letters he carried, managed to squeeze past into dark, stale-smelling Tolbooth hall. One section of it had been cordoned off and, at the far end on a dais, the Earl of Argyll sat at a table covered in green baize, officials, clerks and scriveners on either side. People thronged in, pressing against the balustrades, shouting and swearing, waiting for the proceedings to begin. Water tipplers and pedlars selling food and drink shouted for business: at last the two heralds raised their trumpets and gave short, shrieking blasts. Segalla climbed onto a windowsill, peering over heads as the heralds came and stood before the Earl of Argyll.

"Hear ye! Hear ye!" one of them shouted. "All ye that have business before the Queen's Commissioner!"

The rest of his declaration, about an enquiry into the death of Lord Darnley and the rewards offered by Her Majesty for the apprehension of his murderers, was drowned in strident catcalls. Segalla's stomach lurched as he gazed at the crowd. The Queen's enemies had apparently organised a claque. Segalla heard shouts of "Bothwell!" and "Hang the murderer!" Only more trumpet blasts and a file of royal archers who came out of the door stilled the clamour.

Argyll rose to his feet and read from a proclamation empowering him to hear the matter, and the first witness was called. Thomas Nelson, an archer on either side, came through a side door and sat on a chair in front of the baize-topped table. Argyll leaned forward.

"Give your name!" he barked.

Nelson obeyed. In a halting voice he described his position in Darnley's household.

"Tell me what you know," Argyll commanded, "about the events of Monday last when your noble lord was slain."

Nelson cleared his throat and gave a cogent description of everything that had happened. As he reached the end, his voice faltered. "I knew nothing else except that I woke to find the house falling all about me."

"Who had the keys to the house?" one of the lawyers sitting next to Argyll asked in a loud voice.

Nelson lowered his head and mumbled something.

"Speak up!" Argyll shouted.

"Aye," a voice called from the hall. "Let us know the truth."

"The keys were held by Her Majesty's chamberlain."

Nelson gave the same answer he had to Segalla, and immediately confusion broke out. Shouts and cries, curses against Bothwell leading the Queen. Segalla looked over the crowd, which stretched from the Tolbooth out into the market square. The claque, and whoever was leading it, were proving very effective. A shout was taken up.

"The truth! The truth! The truth!"

This rose to a swelling chorus. Argyll and the herald tried to impose order, but it was useless. Eventually the Earl flung up his hands in despair and stalked out of the hall. The master herald cried that the proceedings were suspended, and Segalla, fearful that violence would break out, slipped from the windowsill and out of the Tolbooth.

The mob in the square were no more pleasant than the claque in the hall. A company of soldiers wearing the Bothwell arms were accosted by a group of apprentices, who did not desist from their jeers and catcalls until the soldiers drew their swords.

Segalla hastened through the side streets back to the Crucible. He wanted to hide in the silence of his own chamber and think, but Janette and Vartlett were waiting from him in the taproom.

"You have been to the Tolbooth?" Janette waited for Segalla to sit, then leaned across the table, her face concerned. "Husband dearest, you look as if you have seen a ghost."

Segalla gazed at her and Vartlett, admiring their cool impassivity.

"I have seen the death of the Queen's cause in Scotland," he said and briefly described the scene at the Tolbooth.

"There's worse to come," Vartlett whispered. He pushed his hand inside his leather jerkin, drew out some grubby pieces of parchment and handed them over.

Segalla studied them carefully. The first was an anonymous placard whose writer claimed the two thousand pounds' reward offered by the Queen for the apprehension of her husband's murderers.

I CLAIM THAT REWARD, the writer had scrawled. BECAUSE THE EARL OF BOTHWELL IS THE PRINCIPAL ADVISER OF THE MURDERER AND THE QUEEN ASSENTING, THERETO, AT THE PERSUASION OF THE SAME EARL OF BOTHWELL.

The placard went on to name other people: Balfour, who owned the house: Chalmers, whom Segalla knew to be one of the Queen's legal advisers, and Black John Spens.

"Who is this latter?"

"One of Bothwell's principal henchmen," Janette replied. She picked up the cup of wine the servitor had brought and thrust it into Segalla's free hand, caressing his fingers as she did so. The Jesuit blushed and glanced up, but Janette just grinned at him.

"Don't fret."

Segalla envied her calm demeanour; her face looked fresh, eyes bright, lips slightly painted with carmine.

"Do you care?" he asked.

Janette looked quickly at Vartlett.

"What happens if this is all true?" she said. "What happens if the battle is lost before it is even fought?"

"You mean Bothwell is the murderer and the Queen did assent to it?"

"Possibly," Janette said. "But tell me, how do they know so much? Oh, we can have an English agent, the Raven Master, pecking away at Her Majesty's reputation. So, what happens if, for all his cawing, the truth is as these placards say?"

Segalla shook his head and went back to the manuscripts: more proclamations written anonymously, boldly asserting that Bothwell was the murderer, that he had keys to Darnley's lodgings and that a smith, who had made these duplicates, was prepared to confess all. The final poster was libellous in the extreme, depicting Queen Mary as a mermaid, making fun of the dolphins in her coat of arms as well as implying she was a whore. The picture also depicted Bothwell as a hare, a reference to his coat of arms. The mermaid was crowned and langorously drawn. Segalla marvelled at the craft of the author: even the poorest beggar in Edinburgh, unable to read, would look at these drawings and know what they meant. A mermaid was a sailor's euphemism for a prostitute. The hare, noted for its cunning and skill, stood for Bothwell; and the way the drawings were placed, one above the other, clearly proclaimed Mary and Bothwell to be lovers bound by a murderous pact. Segalla threw the parchment back on the table.

"Whoever did that," he said, "is skilled, subtle and devious."

"They are all over Edinburgh," Vartlett announced. "As are pictures of Bothwell with the word 'assassin' scrawled underneath." He grasped Segalla by the hand. "Monsieur, what more can we do?"

Segalla remembered the letter he had written to Archbishop Beaton in Paris. For a moment he was on the verge of instructing Vartlett and Lindsay to pack and flee the city, but then he remembered Mary's dark-rimmed eyes and pallid face. He sipped from his wine goblet.

"Please God," he prayed. "The Queen is no murderer."

Chapter 11

"M onsieur Segalla?"

The Jesuit lifted his face from his hands as Nelson slid along the bench in front of him. The fellow was clearly terrified. Janette ordered him a goblet of wine, which Nelson gulped noisily, slamming it down on the table.

"That's it!" he exclaimed. He glared at Segalla. "You were there?"

The Jesuit nodded.

"Tomorrow morning," Nelson continued, "I intend to prostrate myself before the Queen and seek licence to leave Scotland."

"Where will you go?" Vartlett asked.

"To Berwick, then on to Lady Lennox's estates in England. I am going to hide there, bury myself for years. Lord Darnley is dead. The rest are killed or dispersed. Symonds is murdered." He looked down at his shaking hands. "Last night, outside in the alleyway, a knife was thrown at me."

Segalla grasped him by the shoulder. "Why?" he asked. "Why should the murderers of your master still pursue you? What did you see?"

Nelson put his face in his hands and began to sob quietly. "I don't know," he wailed. "Before God, Monsieur, I don't know!"

"Lord Bothwell is bringing more troops into Edinburgh," Janette abruptly declared.

"Is the situation so perilous?" Segalla asked.

"Well, a broadsheet published this morning claims that

Darnley's father has petitioned Mary to hold a court. He implicity accuses Bothwell of his son's murder."

"He did it," Vartlett said in a surly tone. "Bothwell gambled and he may yet win."

"What do you mean?"

"Darnley was not loved. No one liked him, so the mob outside have been well paid, but by whom God knows."

"Should we investigate that?" Segalla asked.

Vartlett laughed. "For God's sake, Master, you have seen similar placards posted in Paris. It would take months to hunt the printer down, only for another to spring up in his place."

"You were talking about Bothwell?" Segalla asked, trying not to look at Nelson, who now sat, half dazed, the tears still welling in his eyes.

Segalla winked at Vartlett, a sign that he should say nothing that might betray them.

"Bothwell may outface his accusers," Vartlett explained. "He might even style himself as the avenger of wrongs; Darnley had little support apart from his family."

"Or," Segalla put in, "Darnley may be portrayed as the martyred lamb. In which case, God help us all!" Segalla dug into his purse and passed a coin to Nelson. "Get yourself something to eat," he said. "Stay within the tavern. Pack your belongings. Tomorrow Vartlett will give you the wherewithal to reach the border."

Nelson fairly sprang to his feet. Segalla grasped his arm.

"If you remember anything new, Thomas, tell me!"

The servant shook his head and shuffled off.

Janette, playing with one of her earrings, watched him go.

"We should do likewise, Master. We are finished here. We should leave."

Segalla was forced to agree. "I have a letter," he said, "to the Archbishop in Paris, and one of my drawings of Kirk o'-Field. In two days' time, leave for France."

"And you?"

Segalla stared at a mongrel gnawing at a collection of bones. "I don't know," he said. "I have not decided." He shrugged. "Only one person has said anything untoward: Sandy Durham, the porter of Darnley's chamber. Vartlett, do you remember him?"

"Vaguely, yes."

"I want you to take him a message: say that I intend no harm. However, if he would speak to me and satisfy my curiosity, he will be the richest porter in Scotland." Segalla got to his feet. "And, once I have done that"—he exhaled heavily—"then perhaps we can leave this den of vipers and go back to our master."

Segalla returned to his chamber. He stayed there for the next two days, writing down everything he had learnt, poring over his plans of Kirk o'Field, trying to recall every conversation. Now and again, Vartlett and Janette would visit him, and the news they brought from the city grew worse. Scotland was slipping towards civil war. The placards on the streets grew in number as well in the intensity of their allegations. At night, sepulchral voices could be heard shouting from the crossroads in the city or from the tops of houses that Darnley had been viciously murdered and Bothwell was the killer.

Segalla worked on, trying to make sense of the jumble of facts, but each time he reached an impasse. Vartlett reported he'd delivered his message to Durham, but Segalla despaired at receiving any reply. Instead messages came from Holyrood: the Queen sought his counsel, but Segalla claimed he was unwell. He dared not go. How could he face the Queen? She would read the message in his eyes and, if she believed Segalla was lost to her cause, might shut him out forever.

Four days after Vartlett had delivered his message to Durham, Segalla received his reply late in the evening: the porter appeared, tapping on his door, his hostility at the previous meeting apparently forgotten.

"I thank you for coming." Segalla shook the man's hand and waved him to a chair, but Durham shook his head.

"If you wish to learn the truth, Monsieur, then you must come with me."

Segalla stepped back. "Where?"

"You must trust me."

"Whom will I meet?"

Durham's boyish face broke into a smile. "You really must trust me."

Segalla stared at the half-open door.

"And by yourself, Monsieur. Put on your boots and cloak. Leave your sword and dagger and come with me."

"I—I am an accredited envoy," Segalla stammered.

"Those you meet intend no harm," Durham said.

Segalla told Durham to wait for him in the taproom below. He locked everything away, put on his boots and cloak and went down. Vartlett and Janette were gone. Outside, the night was freezing cold. Segalla went towards the stables, but Durham plucked at his sleeve.

"You'll not need your horse," he said, smiling through the darkness.

They left the tavern yard, and the circle of men closed immediately around them. Segalla had no time to resist or shout out. His arms were seized and pinioned, a gag thrust into his mouth and coarse sacking pulled over his head. He heard voices, the clatter of hooves; then he was hoisted into a saddle, and he and his captors set off at a gallop. Segalla panicked as he lurched in the saddle, fearful of falling off though the riders on either side held him firmly. He realised they meant him no immediate harm; he struggled with the gag, trying to control his breathing whilst listening to the sounds about him. He heard the noises of the city, revelry from the taverns and the cries of beggars. Then it grew silent, and the smells of the city faded as they entered the countryside. Still they rode on: no sound, no talking, just the galloping of hooves along rutted tracks, the creak of harness and the occasional bone-chilling cry of a night bird. Segalla began to freeze. His mind grew numb as dreams and pictures from his long past began to surface—images and memories that he had firmly controlled. He tried to talk to himself but found that the gag choked him. He struggled to move his hands, but they were lashed firmly to the saddle horn. He felt he was floating in a nightmare, being taken through the air by dark-winged succubi; then he heard shouts. A gate swung open and, through the sacking, Segalla caught the flicker of torchlight. Rough hands pulled him from the saddle; the sacking was removed and his bonds cut. He began to cough and would have collapsed, but men dressed in half armour, with swords and daggers clattering against their sides, gripped him by the arms. Segalla glimpsed candlelit windows, turrets and gables and realised he had been taken to some manor house outside the city.

Inside the manor, the passageways smelt sweet and the walls were freshly painted. Segalla tried to turn his head, but the movement sent shivers of pain down his back: he kept his eyes fixed on the soldiers walking ahead of him. Polished oaken doors were flung open. They were crossing a tiled floor; the room was warm and smelt as fragrant as a summer's day. Sconces on the walls threw pools of light, illuminating the gold and silver thread of the gleaming tapestries hanging there. Segalla was placed gently in a high-backed chair, soft cushions under him, its arms and back carefully padded. He looked up. On the dais in front of him was a long table; the men sitting behind could see him clearly because of the flaring lights from the beeswax candles. Segalla blinked and rubbed his eyes.

"What—what is this?" he stammered.

"Welcome, Monsieur Segalla. We apologise for your rough passage. We do not wish to frighten you. However, you keep asking questions, so we will provide you with answers."

Segalla held up a hand. "I can't see you."

"Bring him closer!" a voice ordered.

Burly soldiers lifted him, still in the chair, closer to the dais. Other servants, wearing the livery of the Earl of Moray, the royal arms of Scotland with the black bar sinister drawn across them, shifted the candelabra on the table. A silver goblet brimming with wine was thrust into Segalla's hand.

"Drink," the voice ordered. "Don't worry, there is no potion."

Segalla obeyed: the rich Bordeaux cleansed his mouth and warmed his stomach. He relaxed and sat back, staring straight into the crafty face of the Queen's half brother.

"You know me, Monsieur Segalla?"

"Aye, my lord."

"And my companions? May I introduce James Douglas, Earl of Morton?"

Segalla stared at the white face with a red beard framed by its ornate ruff and black steeple hat. Douglas gazed at him unblinkingly.

"You have heard of my lord's reputation?" Moray murmured.

Segalla had, but he kept his mouth shut. Morton had spent his youth hiding from the Crown and had risen to power in the past ten years as a leading Reformer. A cold, cruel man, sly in peace, ferocious in war, or so Beaton had described him. Morton ruled his estates with an iron fist. Those who offended him were hurried to the gallows, often pricked by spears.

"I don't think the Frenchman's met me."

The man on the other side of Moray leaned forward into the pool of candlelight. He wore his dark mustache and beard in the French fashion, carefully cut and tended. The face under the skull-cap was that of an angel: lustrous dark eyes, finely etched eyebrows, sensuous lips and ivory face; his every movement was delicate. Segalla forced a smile and bowed.

"I know you by reputation, Sir William."

He stared at Sir William Maitland of Lethington, Secretary of State for Scotland: a man who hid behind the arras and worked in the shadows. A veritable shadow, but one who made his presence felt. He would prepare the pistol for another to fire. Sir William held Segalla's gaze and smiled most amicably.

"We do apologise for your rough treatment, but we understood from Master Durham that you are a seeker after the truth."

"I did not know Master Durham's friends sat so high on the Queen's Council," Segalla replied. "If I had, I would have spoken to him earlier." He stirred in his seat and glanced behind him. He glimpsed the line of soldiers dressed in chain mail. "Am I your prisoner?" he asked.

"No, Master Segalla, you are our guest." The Earl of Moray rapped the table. "You may, if you wish, leave immediately. No one will hinder your return, but if you go, the questions you keep asking will never be answered."

"So, I will be told the truth?"

"Oh yes, and we wish you to take this truth back to your friends in Paris."

"You have proof?" Segalla asked.

Moray rose to his feet. "Come with us."

All three noblemen left the dais and swept down the hall; Segalla and his military escort followed.

With Moray leading, they went along one of the galleries and stopped before an iron-studded door, a soldier on guard on either side. Moray snapped his fingers; the soldier opened the door and, taking a sconce from the wall, led the earl and the rest down dark, cold steps into the crypt below. A cavernous circular room, once probably used as a kitchen, it was lit by torches. These flared in their iron holders, bathing the man stretched out on the rack in a ghostly light: it gave his white flesh an extra sheen and emphasized the lines of blood that flowed from his manacled hands and feet. He was naked except for a loincloth; his face was a mass of bruises, his thick beard, moustache and hair matted with dirt and gore. The cavern was hot from the braziers that stood round the room, and near these, like demons from hell, a group of masked torturers heated up the pincers and burning irons.

"He lives still?" Moray asked.

One of the executioners, the top half of his face hidden by a red leather mask, grunted something.

"Good! Good!" Moray walked towards the racked man, signaling Segalla to follow. "It's a pity," Moray said. "But, its a fact of life, Master Segalla, that the soft thud of the torturer's mallet, hooks and pincers glowing red-hot, not to mention the skinning knife slipping in a gory hand, can search out the truth quicker than any questions."

The man on the rack turned, pushing his tongue through swollen lips. "Water!" he gasped. "For pity's sake, water!"

Segalla glanced away; he tried not to stare at the empty socket and the bloody rope mark round the man's forehead. The eye had been forced out.

"For pity's sake," he whispered. "Give him some water."

Moray snapped his fingers. One of the torturers hurried up with a bucket of water and roughly splashed it in the man's face.

"Let us," Lethington remarked, going round the other side of the rack, "introduce you to Patrick Wilson, one of my lord Bothwell's most trusted mosstroopers." Lethington smiled down at the tortured man. "Master Wilson has a story to tell, haven't you, Patrick, my boy?"

He seized the man's face and twisted it towards him. Morton, silent as the shadow of death, drew his dirk and neatly sliced the man on either side of his neck, razor cuts that sent the blood bubbling out.

Segalla watched aghast at the cold, implacable cruelty of these great nobles.

"Wilson is a murderer," Moray declared. "He and others from the retinue of Lord Bothwell were party to Lord Darnley's death. Of course, Master Wilson is accustomed to having his fingers dirtied in Bothwell's filthy affairs." He leaned down, his mouth inches from Wilson's face. "He's Bothwell's pimp: this woman, that tiring lady, anyone who catches Bothwell's fancy."

"Lord, mercy," the racked man whispered.

"Mercy?" Lethington tapped him on the cheek. "Tell your story, Patrick. Let us hear it for one last time."

Wilson grimaced in agony.

"For God's sake!" Segalla whispered. "Give him some comfort."

Moray snapped his fingers and the torturers loosened the rack, easing the strain on the prisoner's legs and arms.

"Tell your story, Patrick!"

"At ten o'clock," the prisoner began. "I and Willie Powrie had orders."

"When?" Lethington demanded.

"On Sunday, the night before Darnley was killed."

"Continue!"

"We received orders to collect gunpowder which my Lord of Bothwell had taken from Dunbar Castle. We were to carry it to Blackfriars Gate. The powder was packed in polks." Wilson stared at Segalla. "Small leather bags," he explained. "Placed inside a portmanteau. We took it there on a grey nag, making two journeys."

"From where?" Segalla asked.

"My lord of Bothwell's quarters."

"Just the two of you?" Segalla asked.

"No, French Paris and others of Bothwell's coven. I helped them carry the polks through the east garden of the Old Provost's site. We then went back to the horse, but he had bolted, so we stayed in the dark and waited. Then we entered the Provost's House. Ormiston, Bothwell's lieutenant, forced

178

Paris to unlock the doors. He had counterfeit keys. We took the gunpowder into the Queen's chamber."

"Then what happened?"

"Ormiston told me: 'You know what to do when all is quiet above? Fire the lint and come away.' After that the rest of the gang left. Paris locking the door."

"Was Bothwell there?"

"Aye, Master, he was. Paris had forgotten to wash his hands. He was covered in dirt and dust." Wilson stopped to lick his lips. "Water, please, for the love of God!"

A fresh bucket of water was brought, and this time Segalla grasped the ladle and scooped the water into the gasping man's mouth. Wilson coughed and spluttered. Morton, standing in the shadows, came forward and laid his knife at the man's throat.

"Tell the Frenchman," he said in a grating voice, "about the Queen."

"Her Majesty saw Paris and said 'Jesus, sir, how begrimed you are.' The company then left the house for Holyrood." Wilson stopped and licked his blood-encrusted lips. "After midnight my lord of Bothwell changed from his carnival clothes. He dressed in a black canvas doublet and a soldier's riding cloak. He met me and others in the palace grounds and led us up Canon Gate."

"What happened then?"

"We were challenged by the watch but Bothwell answered. We reached Kirk o'Field; Bothwell had keys to the Old Provost's House and let us in. Hay and two others of my lord Bothwell's coven had remained hidden there. They prepared the gunpowder, lit the fuse and we all hid in the garden."

"What happened to the King?" Segalla asked.

Wilson shook his head. "God knows. He must have heard the clamour and left the house, escaping out of one of the windows. My lord of Bothwell must have known of this:

there were others hiding in the orchard, but I saw nothing." Wilson's remaining eye rolled in panic. "I swear to God I saw nothing of that! The fuse was lit and the house went up with a great crack, stones and masonry lifted off the ground."

"But at the time?" Segalla asked quietly. "You believed the King was still in his lodgings?"

"Aye," Wilson whispered. "It was only the next day, after dawn, that we heard rumours of the King being found slain in a nearby orchard."

"And you swear this is the truth?" Lethington asked.

"As God is my witness. For pity's sake, sir."

"Pity?" Moray stepped between Segalla and the rack. Again he leaned over and pushed his face close to Wilson's. "Pity? What pity did you have on my lord Darnley? You are a traitor, sir. You will be hanged, drawn and quartered, the parts of your sorry corpse pickled in salt and brine, packed in a wicker basket and sent to be stuck on the gates of the city." Moray drew himself up. "Continue the racking!" he ordered the torturers hidden in the shadows. "See how tall you can make this little man and whether there are further truths to be told." Moray looked at his two colleagues, but Lethington and Morton were already moving towards the door. Moray followed, grasping Segalla's arm. "So, Monsieur, your questions are answered."

Segalla only shrugged, relieved to be out of the crypt. The Lords took him back to the council chamber. This time the servants had put the chairs in front of the table, set in a half-circle before Segalla's: a small table stood between them with a tray containing a silver jug and pewter goblets. They took their seats; Lethington, smiling as courteously as ever, served Segalla wine.

"You have your answers, Monsieur Segalla? Or should it be Father Segalla, member of the Jesuit order?"

"Whatever I am," Segalla retorted, "I am an accredited French envoy. You have no authority or jurisdiction over me. And believe me, sir, if you took me down to that rack and stretched me out until my arms and legs cracked, I'd confess to being Queen of the fairies or even Macbeth, fresh from hell. Any confession wrung by torture has no force in laws."

Lethington shook his head. "There are others who will confess the same."

"A thousand on a torture rack sing the same song," Segalla snapped.

"But we have other proof," Moray said. "Oh yes, Monsieur Segalla, we have written proof that Her Majesty and Lord Bothwell are lovers. Now, what say you to that?"

"I believe a cat could jump the moon if the proof were offered," Segalla replied, trying to hide his disquiet.

"We have letters," Moray said. "Love letters from the Queen to Bothwell. These betray her true feelings towards my lord Darnley."

"I don't believe you!"

Moray leaned down and drew from a leather bag a thin roll of parchment, which he tossed to Segalla.

"Read it, Monsieur. It's not the original but a fair copy."

Segalla undid the red cord: it was a letter, undated, and, studying it quickly, he recognised that it was a letter from the Queen to the Earl of Bothwell. It began abruptly without any salutation.

"Being gon from the place where I had left my harte, it may be easily judged what my countenance was . . ."

The letter continued in affectionate and amorous sentences, describing . Mary's journey to Glasgow to collect Darnley and bring him back to Edinburgh. Segalla glanced up. The three Lords gazed impassively back, and Segalla tried to control the panic seething in his stomach. At first he was tempted to dismiss the letter as a forgery, but the contents could be known only to Mary: Darnley pleading with her to lodge next to him: how he blamed his sickness on Mary's "being so strange unto him" and criticised Mary for her cruelty in not accepting his offers of repentance. The letter—Segalla quickly gauged it must be at least two thousand words long—went on to refer to other matters that could be known only to the Queen, including Darnley's plans to flee on an English ship.

"Monsieur Segalla, what do you think?"

The Jesuit glanced at Lethington's smiling face.

"See," the Secretary murmured. "What the Queen writes about my lord Darnley: how he believes Mary will never harm him though there are others who might. Do read on, Monsieur."

Segalla obeyed and the chill he felt deepened.

"God forgive me," the letter ran. "But God knit us for ever. For the most faithful couple . . . This is my faith, I will die in it."

One phrase caught his eye: "Alas I have never deceived anyone but I submit myself totally to your will. . . . What ever happens to me, I will obey you."

Segalla read it through, keeping his features impassive, and tossed it back at Moray. "Where is the original?"

The earl smiled. "Come, come, Master Segalla. Don't play the Jesuit with us. You know that letter was written by Mary."

"It does not prove she killed her husband."

"It proves she was a liar!" Morton snapped. "She blabbed to him that she would keep him safe, and, yet must admit, Frenchman, she never did that. Well, did she?"

Segalla could do nothing but quietly agree.

"It also proves," Lethington said silkily, "that Bothwell and the Queen are adulterous lovers: the letter was written when both were married. And haven't you heard the rumours? The Lady Bothwell is also sickening. Now, you have heard Master Wilson's confession. You have read our proof, but we have more."

"The rest of these casket letters"—Moray almost spat the

words out—"will prove that my sister is an adulteress, a liar and, if she did not murder her husband, was party to the decision and looked the other way." Moray leaned back in his chair and carefully rolled up the piece of manuscript. "Our picture's not yet complete," he said. "I give you that, but I tell you this, Frenchman. Bothwell blew up Kirk o'Field with the full consent of my half sister. Somehow or other Darnley escaped." Moray fingered his moustache and beard. "Perhaps Bothwell waited and Darnley escaped straight into the arms of another group of his henchmen."

"Yet Nelson and Symonds were pulled from the ruins," Segalla said. "They did not see or hear their master's hurried departure?"

"Have ye nae brain in yer head?" Morton brayed. "I wager, Master Segalla, that if the royal physician . . ." The heavy, secretive face relaxed, as if telling Segalla they knew all about his conversation with Master Pitcairn. "If the royal physician," Moray continued, "opened the corpses of the other puir victims he'd find they were sent into a drugged sleep. Nelson and Symonds were fortunate. Any effects of such a philtre would be put down as a consequence of the explosion and their narrow escape."

"And Master Durham's role in this?" Segalla asked.

"He knew of Paris's treachery. A porter sits and watches."

"What will happen to Wilson?"

"He will continue to give us names," Lethington snapped. "If he dies, he dies, and others will be invited into the dance."

Segalla gazed at these three powerful Lords. They were speaking the truth, he concluded, even if they were full of malice: they might have known about Bothwell's plot, but he must take the blame and the Queen with him.

"Why are you telling me this?" he asked.

"You ask questions, Frenchman. Now you have the answers," Moray said. "Go back and tell your master in Paris the truth about our Queen. Leave Scotland, Frenchman, and leave it soon. There's a storm coming, and no one knows who will be swept up by it." Moray spread his gloved hands and smiled. "You have heard our witness, you have seen the proof. Now you may go." The earl grinned. "More comfortably than you came."

He clicked his fingers. The soldiers behind Segalla moved forward and, without a second glance or another word, he was out of the hall and back in the courtyard.

Another fast ride, this time circled by mailed riders who hid his view. They thundered along the country lanes and clattered through a postern gate, reining in only when they reached the Crucible. Without a word they allowed him to dismount: their captain, his face concealed by his cowl, edged his horse forward.

"One more message, Frenchman."

Segalla looked up at the shadowy face.

"My lord of Moray is most insistent. You are to be out of Scotland soon." He turned his horse, and he and his party clattered off into the darkness.

Segalla found himself trembling. He had to restrain himself from running straight into the taproom; he walked in calmly. Janette and Vartlett were sitting in a corner playing cards with Nelson. They looked up expectantly, but Segalla kept up his pretence.

"Did you see Durham?" Vartlett asked.

Segalla hid his hands beneath his cloak and forced a smile. "Aye, I saw him."

"And?" Janette leaned forward, cupping her chin as she smiled up at Segalla.

"Tomorrow I see the Queen," Segalla said. "Then we pack our bags. Master Nelson, I would advise you to leave. Within the week, I hope to be back on board ship and away from this murderous place."

Segalla went up to his own chamber. He trusted no one,

not his companions and certainly not the Lords whom he had just met. The only person left was the Queen. Segalla smiled into the darkness; he was a Jesuit, a priest, and that might be the key to all this mystery.

Chapter 12

The following day Segalla rode through the early-morning mist to Holyrood Palace and demanded access to the Queen. Traquair immediately recognised him, and Segalla had to wait for only a few moments in an antechamber before being shown into the Queen's private room. Here, too, the walls had been covered in black crepe, and in the light of the candles and dancing torches, it looked like some burial vault, dark and sombre. The Queen was seated in a high-backed, quilted chair before the fireplace, dressed in black silk: the great puffed sleeves of her dress were covered with embroidered bands of gold and silver cord. On her head she wore a coif of black jet, with a lace veil concealing the upper part of her face.

"Monsieur, it is so kind of you to come. I have sent for you on a number of occasions."

Segalla caught the brittleness in her voice. He approached the chair, went down on one knee and kissed the Queen's icy hand. Looking up at the Queen, he was shocked at her expression of utter despair.

"Madame, I could not come." Segalla had to steel himself for what he had planned.

Mary waved him into a chair opposite. "Sit down! Sit down! More questions, eh, priest, before you take ship to France?"

Segalla looked at her quickly. The Queen just shook her head.

"No, I have no spies," she muttered. *"Mais tout est perdu,* all is lost. But there again, maybe it was lost before it even began."

"No questions, Madame," Segalla declared. "But you are right. I am a priest. I have come to celebrate Mass."

Mary lifted her veil slowly. "Why, Monsieur Segalla, I thank you." She indicated a small table behind him. "That can serve as your altar."

Segalla excused himself and opened the panniers of his saddlebag. He unrolled a small linen cloth across the table, set on it a small wooden crucifix, took out the pyx and smiled over his shoulder at the Queen, who was watching him intently.

"Your Majesty, I need some wine and a goblet."

The Queen pointed to a tray. Segalla filled a gem-encrusted goblet with wine and took it back to the altar. He placed one of his precious unleavened wafers on the table, then drew out the piece of consecrated silk that served as his stole. He sat down opposite the Queen.

"I know what you are going to ask, Monsieur." Mary smiled tearfully at him. "You live in the city: you have heard what my enemies are proclaiming. I have seen the placards." Her voice quivered. "The bare-breasted mermaid. I know all about the voices at midnight." She breathed heavily. Segalla sensed her quiet rage, as if the Queen would like to stretch out and crush her enemies.

"What was I going to ask, Madame?"

"You wished to hear my confession."

And before Segalla could reply or stop her, the Queen slipped elegantly to her knees before him, joining her hands in prayer. She intoned the ritual. "Bless me, Father, for I have sinned. It is two months since I was last shriven and these are my sins." The Queen fought hard to control her voice. "I confess my mistakes. I was born at a time when I should not have been. I dressed for summer when I was born into the coldest winter. I have loved and wanted to be loved but found nothing but hate. I was a Queen on two occasions, and each time the crown has been swept from my head. I have looked into the heart of human darkness and I now know what it is to hate. No." Mary held a hand up before Segalla could interrupt. "I have loved two men. One was a mere boy and died before manhood. The other I thought a man but he was really a sickly wolf with a ravenous hunger." She paused.

"And murder?" Segalla forced himself to ask.

"Yes," the Queen whispered, nodding. "I confess to murder, many, many times! In my mind, I have murdered Moray, Morton, Lethington and all the Great Lords!"

"And your husband, Darnley?"

"Yes, he, too, has been there. Many a time I have murdered him: with a stiletto, axe and rope."

"But the business at Kirk o'Field?" Segalla asked gently.

Mary's fingers flew to her face and she laughed. "All my murders, Father, are ones of thought, not deed. In truth, I have lifted my hand against no man. But, yes, I did hate Darnley." She breathed in again, her body slightly swaying, her eyes fixed on a point beyond Segalla as if she had forgotten him and were talking to some unseen spirit. "I hated Darnley." So I set myself a penance; I forgave him. I thought, in my stupidity, I could learn to love him again and forget the past. I could be wife and Queen in my own house and realm. When I moved into Kirk o'Field that was my intent."

"And the lord Bothwell?" Segalla asked.

The Queen gazed directly at him. "A lusty laird, high-spirited, devoted to my service. A man of many faults, but treachery, treason and murder do not sit in his soul."

She must have caught the look of surprise on Segalla's face.

"Whatever you hear, Father, whatever you are shown, it's a lie." She fumbled with the pouch beneath her cloak and drew out the most beautiful pearl rosary Segalla had ever seen. The Queen held this up by the crucifix. "I swear," she intoned. "I swear by the cross, by the Mass I shall hear, by the sacrament I shall take, by my life and by my eternal soul, neither I nor the lord Bothwell had anything to do with my husband's death."

Segalla leaned forward in the chair and gripped the Queen's cold hand. He squeezed her fingers softly as if he could rub his own warmth into them: he was pleased to see the old Mary return, the gentle mockery in her eyes, a co-quettish cast to her face.

"Why, Father, you are hearing my confession." Her eyes studied Segalla carefully. "What have you seen, Father? What have those devils from hell and, I say to you, they are devils from hell, told you?"

Segalla knew that Mary was being honest: the whole force of her personality and soul lay behind what she said. So he confessed everything: his discussions with Master Pitcairn and his suspicions about Vartlett and Janette; his own thoughts and reflections; and, finally, his late-night visit to the Earl of Moray and the rest. Mary rose from her knees, pulled a chair closer to Segalla and sat. At last he came to the subject of the letter, and Mary put her face in her hands. When Segalla fin-ished, she just sat rocking herself gently, not a murmur or a cry escaping her. Then she looked up, and Segalla flinched at the fury in her face.

"They have trapped me!" She said. "Oh, they've trapped me, boxed me in cleverly with my own words." She exhaled noisily. "Was the letter signed?"

Segalla shook his head.

"Did you see the original?"

"Do they have an original?" he asked.

"Oh yes." Mary laughed and rubbed her hands along the folds of her dress. "Oh, my clever bastard of a brother has the original. A draft of a letter I wrote to Archbishop Beaton in Paris. What they have done, Monsieur, is to take that letter and weave it ever so cleverly into a love letter I wrote to Darnley."

"But how could they do that?"

189

Mary stared into the fire.

"I have traitors in my own household; even the Lord Bothwell I do not trust fully. But, to answer you, priest, I had, in my chamber at Kirk o'Field, a casket of such documents; drafts of letters, memoranda, et cetera. I thought they had been destroyed in the explosion. As you know, I sent my chamberlain down: he could find no trace, so I thought they were gone, utterly destroyed." She shrugged. "Now I know the truth. When they broke in to murder my husband, they also stole into my own chamber and seized those documents."

"But, Madame, how did he die?"

Mary closed her eyes and her jaw tightened. "I don't know," she said hoarsely. "God be my witness, neither I nor Bothwell know. We left Kirk o'Field for the revels at Holyrood. Traquair informed us about Ker of Fawdonside being in the vicinity, so Bothwell and some of his henchmen went to see whether Kirk o'Fields was quiet, then they returned."

The Queen waved her hands in exasperation. "I thought my lord of Bothwell went to bed with his wife: his henchmen were too drunk to light a candle, let alone a fuse. So, say your Mass, priest. But, after the consecration, pause awhile."

Segalla, mystified and shocked by what the Queen had told him, rose and went to the table. He took his small missal out of the pannier, made the sign of the cross and intoned the opening verse of the psalm: "I will go unto the altar of God and to God give joy for my youth." The Mass swept on: Segalla, leaning over the bread and wine, whispered the words of transubstantiation and elevated host and chalice. The Queen, who had been kneeling at a prie-dieu behind him, rose in a rustle of silk and approached the altar. She placed both hands over the host and chalice and drew herself up, her face stern, full of majesty.

"I swear," she whispered, "over this most holy sacrament, that I was not party, nor did plot, nor seek to bring about, in any way, the death of my husband. I also swear, to the best of my knowledge, the Earl of Bothwell is guiltless in this affair. I also swear"—Mary's hands fell away—"that I tried to love my husband: I confess to a dreadful mistake in leaving him at Kirk o'Field: it is one I shall regret to the end of my life."

She went back to her place. Segalla continued with the Mass. He gave the Queen absolution, followed by the sacrament. After he had finished and packed his things away, the Queen brought him a goblet of sweetened wine and a plate of sugared almonds. She smiled easily down at him.

"You are a strange man, Segalla. Let us talk about you for a while. I am sure a man like you once served my mother. But is it possible, Monsieur, for a man never to die?"

Segalla kept his face impassive. "There are worse fates than death, Madame."

The Queen blinked and looked away. "Too true. Too true. "Father, do you think some people are cursed? I am a Stuart born and bred. My father died stricken; my grandfather was killed at Flodden; his father was murdered and his father before that. Do you think our blood is cursed? Do we bring destruction upon ourselves and all we touch?"

Segalla relaxed, relieved that the Queen had ceased her questioning him.

"Not cursed, Madame," he replied. "But, as you say, people are born at the wrong time in the wrong place and, like strange elements, mix and mingle with those they should not. Your half brother the Earl of Moray wants to be King. Elizabeth of England sees you as a danger. The French view you as a pawn to use in their dreams of a grand alliance." He sighed. "But what will you do, Madame?"

The Queen shook her head. "I don't know. Oh, I recognise my half brother and the rest of the Lords of the Congregation in all of this. I hear their mockery: soon sword and dagger will be pulled, and the rest is God's will."

"And the lord Bothwell?"

"He gives me comfort and counsel. If I abandon him I have no one and become the pawn of my half brother's coven. If I support Bothwell, then it will be war." Mary looked wistfully at Segalla. "Is it wrong to wish for death, Monsieur? Sometimes I feel I would like to ride into the centre of my enemies, lay down my sword and scream, 'Do what you will!' "

Segalla studied her anxiously and remembered the words of Master Pitcairn. "Madame," he said suddenly. "Does my lord of Bothwell give you medicines, philtres or potions?"

Mary lifted her hands and rubbed her temples. "He gives me powders to make me sleep. I must have peace. I must have rest." Her hands fell away. "Monsieur Segalla, you do believe me?"

"Aye, Madame, I do."

Mary looked down at the ring on her finger. "The Great Lords brought about Darnley's death," she said. "But who was the traitor, Monsieur Segalla, and how did he kill my husband?"

"Madame, I have failed you in that as I failed in removing the danger from you."

Mary laughed girlishly: she reached out and gripped Segalla's hands. "You did not fail," she said. "You could not have stopped what had been planned, plotted and most deviously carried through." Her face grew hard. "But avenge me, Monsieur Segalla. I, a queen, have sworn great oaths on your behalf." She pressed Segalla's hand against her heart. "Now swear, on the heart of this Queen, that you will hunt down the assassin of my husband." Mary's eyes blazed, brilliant with anger. "Catch the viper! Crush its head!"

She let his hand fall away and, rising briskly, walked to the far corner of the room and returned carrying a silver-hilted sword in a velvet scabbard studded with gems. She towered above Segalla.

"This is my father's," she said. "He brought it back from Solway Moss. Now it is mine and I am Queen, dispenser of justice in these realms." She held the sword up as if it were a cross. "I, Mary, Queen of Scotland, England and France, Lord of the Isles, do swear out this commission that you, Nicholas Segalla, are my justiciar in this matter. You will seek out the murderer of my husband, Lord Henry Lennox Darnley, King Consort of Scotland, most foully and mysteriously murdered. You are to act on the full authority of the Crown, and when you bring this foul assassin to boot, you have my full authority to carry out lawful execution." Mary lowered the sword. "Do it, Monsieur," she urged. "For my sake as well as the sake of God's justice!"

She sat silently for a while, then came and knelt like a young girl before her father or a girl beside her swain.

"Nicholas," she said. "Look at me."

"Madame?"

"We shall not meet again, Nicholas. You know that as I do. What happened at Kirk o'Field is the beginning of my end. I will face it resolutely, knowing that, through you, God will see justice done." She rose to her feet. "Now you must go. I have a message from the Archbishop in Paris. He wrote to me, warning me once again of a great danger. Soon he will realise how prophetic he was: Darnley's death is already rumoured in London and Paris. However, he sent one message for you, a postscript: 'Tell Segalla.' Mary paused. "Yes, that's it. 'Tell Segalla only the Queen, Lindsay and Vartlett know that you are a priest, a member of the Jesuit order.' " She saw the puzzlement in Segalla's eyes. "That is all he wrote." She extended her hand. "Now go, Nicholas. Do not come back here. I can say no more, but there is a great deal you can do."

Segalla kissed her fingers. For a few seconds Mary stroked the top of his head, then he rose, collected his cloak and saddlebag and walked to the door.

"Nicholas."

Segalla turned. The Queen came towards him, her eyes tearful but her mouth smiling. "In another life, Nicholas, perhaps in another life, we will meet again. I will simply be Mary and you a beau called Nicholas." She kissed him gently on each cheek, and he caught the faint fragrance of her perfume. "Go," she whispered. "And never forget me!"

Nicholas left Holyrood as quickly as he could, finding it difficult to hold back the scalding tears that pricked his eyes. He recalled Beaton's words in Paris, describing Mary as a fawn surrounded by wolves.

"How right you are," Segalla said to himself. "And now the wolves are closing in."

He returned to the Crucible and went to his own chamber. Taking out pen and parchment, he once again listed his conclusions about Kirk o'Field. He tried to imagine the scene, summoning up all the different theories he had formulated, desperate to reach a conclusion. He ordered some food; rancid meat in a watery gravy and a jug of wine were brought up by a slattern.

When he grew tired of his task, he forced himself to reflect on his meeting with the Queen until he recalled Beaton's cryptic message.

"Tell Segalla," he murmured to himself, "that the only people who know he's a Jesuit are Vartlett and Lindsay." Again and again he repeated this to himself. Beaton was sending him a secret cipher, but what did it mean? Mary had told no one. Then he recalled Moray's gibe and went cold. So simple, so obvious, so totally malicious! He then took his theory and began to apply it to his days in Edinburgh. Everything fitted, but instead of excitement Segalla felt as if he were in a trance.

"It must be," he said aloud. "That is the only way out of the entanglement. But how can I prove it?"

He retired to bed. Having slept deeply without dreaming, he awoke refreshed the next morning, determined what to do. He washed, shaved, quickly said his morning office and went down to the taproom to break his fast. When Vartlett and Janette joined him, Segalla smiled at them.

"I apologise for my recent lack of manners." He filled their cups and shouting at the scullion to bring more bread and dried meat. "But this business has tired me. You are to leave Edinburgh immediately."

The pleasure in their faces was obvious. Vartlett gripped his hand; Janette leaned across the table and kissed him on the cheek, her warm mouth a sharp contrast to the cold lips of the Queen.

"Thank you," she said.

"And will you come with us?" Vartlett asked.

Segalla stared down at the table. "No." He glanced up and grinned. "I know how Darnley was killed," he announced, enjoying the consternation in their faces. "I know the truth behind the explosion at Kirk o'Field." He glanced round the taproom and lowered his voice. "More importantly, I know who the English agent, the Raven Master, is. I need to collect some more proof; then I'll proclaim the truth to the world."

"Shouldn't we wait?" Vartlett asked hurriedly, glancing at Janette.

"No, both of you must leave," Segalla insisted. "Go today, seek passage on a ship from Leith. Take my letter to Beaton with one of my drawings of the explosion at Kirk o'Field. Tell him when I have finished I'll return to France."

Janette leaned forward. "But why don't you come with us?"

"I have things to do."

"Will you stay here?" Vartlett asked.

"Oh no. I still look for further proof at Kirk o'Field. The cottages around the quadrangle are empty. I'll seek permission to take up residence there." He smiled lazily. "Don't worry about me. Your master will surely reward you for what you have done." He stilled any further protests with his hand.

"Go now!" he urged. "Pack and leave. Master Nelson was correct: Scotland is now no longer safe for foreigners."

Vartlett and Janette looked at each other, then quietly obeyed. They packed and brought their baggage down to the stableyard, where Segalla had negotiated with the landlord for horses and a sumpter pony to take them to Leith. They shook Segalla's hand: Janette kissed him again, pressing her lips firmly against his.

"The Raven Master," she whispered. "Who is he?"

Segalla shook his head. "In time, Janette, in time everything will be clear."

She pouted prettily at him as he assisted her into the saddle. He stood waving until they had left the tavern yard. He returned to his own chamber, lay down on his bed and, closing his eyes, imagined Darnley in his chamber only hours before the assassins struck. Segalla could re-create in his own mind all that had followed and was now certain that the conclusions he had drawn were the truth. He spent the next few days constantly going over what he had learnt and waiting for a reply to a letter he had despatched to Master Pitcairn. Eventually it came: Pitcairn was puzzled but supportive. He had taken Segalla's request to the Queen and she had graciously granted it: he was to have use of one of the cottages in the quadrangle near Kirk o'Field as long as he wished. The other matter, the physician had written, had been easier to resolve: Master Vartlett and Mistress Lindsay had not left Scotland by Leith.

Segalla waited a few more days, then moved his belongings out, setting up house in a rather squalid cottage that bordered the quadrangle near the remains of the Old Provost's House. The crowds no longer flocked out to gaze curiously at the devastation: the ruins and the buildings around them were lonely and desolate. Rumours had begun to circulate that Darnley's ghost now haunted the place and his cries, as the murderers cut off his breath, could still be heard at the dead of night. Segalla dismissed this as scurrilous gossip. Once night had fallen, he lit a pitch torch and carefully examined the ruins, and what he discovered there only confirmed his suspicions. During the day he took to going to the city and realised the Queen's cause was lost. Bothwell might pack the city with his troops, but the tongues still wagged and dark stories circulated: Bothwell was the Queen's lover; Bothwell now intended to marry the Queen: Bothwell had taken great oaths to kill the other Lords.

Segalla wondered whether to return to Holyrood but realised he could be of little help. The city mob was now firmly against Mary, and the great Lords of the Congregation, Moray, Morton and Lethington, began to emerge from their hiding places. The Queen left the city, moving herself to Seton and her baby, James, to Stirling, whilst Bothwell was made Commander-in-Chief of all her land forces and Governor of Edinburgh. Segalla knew what was coming, and Pitcairn kept him informed. The royal physician, curious at Segalla's haunting of Kirk o'Field, invited him out to supper and told him about the tittle-tattle of the court.

"The Queen is grievously stricken," Pitcairn whispered across the candlelit table. "She cannot abide the light of day and hides in a darkened chamber. Even the flames of the candle hurt her eyes. She was like that when Killigrew, the new English envoy, presented his credentials."

"And what will happen now?" Segalla asked.

"Darnley's father, the Earl of Lennox, is beginning to move. He has not only demanded the trial of his son's murderers but specifically named Bothwell." The little physician sipped from his wine and shrugged. "If a trial takes place elsewhere, Bothwell will be found guilty and go to the block. If it takes place in Edinburgh, Bothwell will overawe the court and Lennox will refuse to come, decrying the whole process as a sham."

"Why doesn't the Queen flee to France?"

Pitcairn laughed softly. "Flight would mean admission of

guilt. And the English agents in Paris have been busy, or so the gossips say.."

"So what will happen?"

"The Queen will fight. If she wins, there will be a massacre: Bothwell will not leave Morton and Moray with their heads."

"And if she loses?"

Pitcairn sighed. "She will flee into England."

"What!" Segalla exclaimed. "Go into the camp of her enemies?"

"That is only my guess," Pitcairn hurriedly added. "But I have listened to the Queen carefully. Monsieur, have you ever served as a soldier?"

Segalla nodded, unwilling to give this inquisitive physician any further information about himself.

"And so have I," Pitcairn chattered on. "I have served in sieges as a surgeon and I have encountered a strange phenomenon, a matter of the soul rather than physic. Sometimes a soldier can become so battle-weary he actually welcomes death: he sees it as an escape from the horrors about him." He smiled thinly at Segalla. "The Queen's mind is of a similar mould." He slurped from his goblet and picked at the ruins of the chicken on the platter before him. "Anyway, in a month I will be gone. Perhaps go abroad again. And you, Monsieur?"

"I'll stay a little while in Edinburgh," Segalla replied. "But I need your services, Monsieur. One further favour. Two sturdy men." He held a hand up. "No, no violence. I want them to guard my cottage in the grounds of Kirk o'Field whilst I am gone. They are to watch carefully and report to me what happens, particularly any stranger in the area."

Pitcairn agreed, and the next morning two sturdy journeymen who had fallen on hard times, or so they described themselves in their guttural accents, presented themselves at Segalla's cottage in Kirk o'Field. They looked to be honest, reliable men, with open, chapped faces, unkempt and dirty but eager to do a day's work in return for the precious coins Segalla paid them.

"All you have to do," he directed, "is watch the ruins. If anyone approaches, act as if you are workmen clearing the site. If anyone asks after me, show them where I live, but don't betray anything else. You can do that?"

Both men, delighted at such lavish reward for such light work, quickly agreed. Segalla waited. He went into the city and bought himself two horse pistols, which he primed and loaded. In his cottage he made sure the window, firmly shuttered, hung loose, and he made up his bed so that in the dark it would look as if he were sleeping there, whilst he made himself comfortable in a shadowy recess beside the hearth. And he waited. The first week of March came and went. Then, on the afternoon of the ninth, as he returned through the gathering darkness, his two appointed spies were waiting for him. Usually their report was the same: some curious townspeople had come out, but no one in particular. This time it was different.

"We were approached," one of them explained. "The fellow was hooded and cowled and kept his face turned away. Yet he paid us generously, claiming he was a friend of yours. He asked where you were staying and what you were doing. We gave the reply you told us to."

Segalla thanked them. He shook their hands and gave them each a coin. "Then your work is now finished," he said. "Tomorrow I will be gone. Whatever is left in that cottage you may have." He shook his head at the puzzlement in their faces. "Go now," he insisted. "I must prepare for my friend."

Segalla returned to the cottage. He lit and built up a fire: the flames danced, shedding light on the small cot carefully made up. Segalla ate the bread and dried meat he had bought, locked and barred the door, then sat staring through the darkness of the half-open window. Night fell. For a while he slept, disturbed now and again by the sound of some hunting night bird. He kept staring at the hour candle; the flame had passed the twelfth red circle when Segalla heard a sound and saw the dark form of the Raven Master slither quietly through the window into the room.

Chapter 13

Segalla picked up one of the heavy pistols, straining his eyes in the darkness. He glimpsed the flash of a dagger as the cowled figure thrust and thrust again at the blankets on the bed. Using his other hand, Segalla pulled back the hammer. The click sounded like a crack of thunder in the silent chamber.

"Bienvenue," Segalla whispered. "Welcome, O bird of the night!"

The figure whirled round.

"Stay where you are," Segalla ordered. "Let your dagger drop." He edged into the circle of light thrown by the fire. "I have two pistols primed and loaded, so do not do anything you might regret. I have longed for this meeting. Now, stretch your hands out before you."

The black-gloved hands came up. Segalla knew the intruder was looking for an opportunity, any slip on his part, but the Jesuit had prepared the room well.

"Sit down," Segalla commanded; he pointed to the hearth. "See, I have another chair waiting for you and a cup of wine. Come, Master Thomas Nelson. It is Master Nelson, is it not?"

The cowl came back and, in the dancing flames, Segalla studied the smiling features of Darnley's porter and groom: the ever subtle Thomas Nelson.

"I knew you would come," Segalla whispered. "Now, please, sit down."

Nelson's eyes never moved: his smile went no farther than his lips.

"You are cursing yourself," Segalla said. "I can read your thoughts, Thomas: I've been inside your soul for many a day. I know you almost as well as you know yourself. Now, sit down!"

Nelson obeyed. Segalla indicated the goblet of wine warming on the hearth.

"You see, I was waiting for you. I knew you would come. So, let us sit here in the dark. After all, Master Nelson, we are both creatures of the night."

"You are a priest." Nelson picked up the goblet.

"Drink it, don't throw it," Segalla urged. "Before God, Master Nelson, I do not wish to kill you, yet. True, I am a priest, a Jesuit, a French envoy, but I am more than that. I have met people like you, Master Nelson, all the dusty days of my life. Men who wield power from behind the scenes, who slink amongst the great ones of the land. Well, what shall we talk about?"

Nelson relaxed, slouching in his chair. Segalla watched his hands cross his stomach and knew he must have a knife concealed there; he had already glimpsed the hilt of the throwing dirk in the top of the man's high-heeled riding boot.

"Oh yes." Segalla rested the pistol on his knee. "The destruction of kings, the overthrowing of princes, treason, treachery and bloody-handed murder. The bringing to naught of the good and the exaltation of the evil."

"I carry out orders," Nelson replied softly.

"Oh yes, you carry out orders: instructions from Master Walsingham in London, no doubt?" Segalla kept the barrel of the long, heavy hunting pistol aimed directly at Nelson's stomach. "Let me tell a story," Segalla began. "About a beautiful princess, the present Queen Mary. A woman born, or so some say, to wear the crowns of France, England and Scotland. Now, thanks to you, she is not even mistress in her own home. Mary is innocent: to quote the great Aristotle, she pursued the good, wanting nothing more than the prosperity and peace of her own subjects and the enforcement of law and rule. She returned to Scotland, where she won over harsh, cruel men and was accepted by the people. She is what this great country has yearned for many a year. Never since the rule of her own father has Scotland desired or needed a ruler to bind its wounds."

"Mary was a threat to England," Nelson said.

"No, she wasn't. Oh, she was popular, even admired: Mary took the title Queen of England, but that was when she was a young girl, following the orders of her father-in-law, Henri II.

"Scotland is England's back door," Nelson said.

"And Mary would have kept it shut," Segalla declared. "She wanted peace. Born a Catholic, raised a Catholic, nevertheless Mary came back here, committed to toleration for all faiths. Segalla saw the smirk on Nelson's face. "But, of course," he continued, "the men of power south of the border have their own twisted perception of the world; not a Scottish lord, apart from Bothwell, is free of English bribes. Time and again, Mary had to send Walsingham's envoys packing south because of their interference in the affairs of her realm."

"Which is the way of the world," Nelson replied, sipping from his goblet, his eyes watching the barrel of the pistol.

"No, it is the way of your spider master, Walsingham. He could not leave well alone. The bribes failed, so he sat in the shadows and studied Mary's weaknesses. Our Queen—" The phrase slipped out before Segalla could stop himself. "Our Queen is a great romantic. A great lover, she has the weakness of all great lovers, a weakness neither you nor your master would understand: she must love and she must be loved."

Nelson leaned forward and put his cup down on the hearth.

"Don't move so quickly," Segalla warned.

Nelson smiled. "I am listening to your story, priest."

"Then listen well. Walsingham glimpsed Mary's weakness, so he sent north the handsome, long-legged Darnley." Segalla shrugged. "A whited sepulchre: all beauty without but dirt and dross within. Corrupt, evil, weak-willed." He smiled. "But Mary still loved him passionately. Darnley was the prince she had always wanted and he cruelly betrayed her. And Mary the great lover? She still stretched out those beautiful hands in peace." Segalla sipped from his own goblet. "But, of course, what Mary didn't know is that when Darnley came north, Walsingham had placed a canker in the rose, one of his most subtle and practised agents, the Raven Master; not just a professional actor but a born one, Thomas Nelson. I wonder what role you played in Darnley's festering mind? Did you slyly encourage his sense of grievance? Emphasize his greatness? Point out every imagined slur and insult? Where were you when Rizzio was murdered?"

Nelson gazed back.

"Your task was simple," Segalla continued. "Drive a wedge between Henry Darnley and Mary Stuart: bring about conflict, rub salt into any wounds." As Segalla set his goblet down, he saw the flicker in Nelson's eyes. "I have another pistol," he said. "In your eyes, Master Nelson, I may be a priest, but in my time I have been an accomplished soldier."

"Your time," Nelson said. "What is your time, Monsieur? Sir Francis Walsingham in London is wondering about that. But your story?"

"At first you thought you'd succeed," Segalla said. "Mary and Darnley became enemies, but then the Queen in her greatness of spirit took you all by surprise. She forgave Darnley. She wished to reach an accord, and the tragedy of Kirk o'Field began to emerge." Segalla paused. "The tragedy originated in the subtle mind of Walsingham. He must have received your reports and become alarmed. On the one hand,

Mary was doing everything within her power to reach an accord with her husband: on the other, Darnley still nourished hopes of quietly fleeing the realm. Stories abounded about ships waiting in the Clyde or preparations to go abroad. Walsingham perceived the danger. If the Queen could win Darnley over and the marriage became harmonious, Mary would be as dangerous as ever. If Darnley fled, however, then Mary could claim she had been deserted by her husband and possibly seek an annulment from Rome. Only then did Walsingham probably give you the order to carry out murder and put the blame on Mary's head." Segalla shifted in his seat.

"And you are going to put the whole blame on me?" Nelson said. "But how did I know the Queen would be leaving Kirk o'Field for the revels at Holyrood? How could I get gunpowder? How could I make my master flee in the middle of the night? And how could I kill both him and Taylor?"

"I'll come to that by and by."

"And the gunpowder?" Nelson said. "Was it heigh-ho down to Canon Gate to buy the largest barrel?"

Segalla smiled. "Oh come, come! Did I say you worked by yourself? You were Walsingham's link with Moray, Morton and the Lords of the Congregation. They did not know who you were, but they certainly did what you asked. The gunpowder was the easiest part of it. Where was it stored, eh?" Segalla looked round the cottage. "Here? One of the outhouses? I am sure my lords of Moray and Morton could purchase it and stow it away carefully, once they knew where Darnley was going to lodge." Segalla shifted himself away from the heat of the fire. "Let me begin with the Queen's journey to Kirk o'Field. We both know Moray chose Kirk o'Field for her, probably at your urging, a good choice, near enough to Edinburgh but not too close to the baby Prince at Holyrood. You convinced Darnley to agree. The Queen quickly agreed: she journeyed down here whilst my lord of Moray, having received secret instructions from you, could see the opportunities the Old Provost's House offered and had the gunpowder hidden away nearby. So, the scene is set for your play."

"How did I know Darnley would be by himself?" Nelson asked.

"Oh, that was simple enough. Sunday, ninth February, was Carnival Sunday. A time of great rejoicing before Lent begins, and all servants and retainers are given leave of absence. On that same evening, one of the Queen's favourite ladies-in-waiting was being married, and the Queen had promised to attend the revels." Segalla caught the smile on Nelson's face. "Then, of course, there was the urgency of the situation. On Monday, tenth February, Darnley's period of rest was over. He might rejoin the Queen or, more probably, seize the opportunity of fleeing. Which is why he had been secretly negotiating with the outlaw Ker of Fawdonside." Segalla moved the pistol on his lap. "So, Sunday ninth February was ideal. Kirk o'Field would be empty. The Queen would be elsewhere, and it was the night before Darnley fled. He was going to flee, wasn't he?"

Nelson spread his hands. "Even a child could see that." Then he shrugged. "Or perhaps they couldn't. Darnley's mind festered with schemes. He may have fled, I don't know. Or he may have joined Ker of Fawdonside and tried to abduct the Queen."

Segalla looked at him in surprise. Nelson smiled grimly.

"You hadn't thought of that, had you, clever priest? Darnley may have fled, but I think he brought Andrew Ker of Fawdonside here to kidnap the Queen and the baby Prince."

"And, of course, you couldn't allow that," Segalla replied quickly. "Such an act would proclaim to the world what a feckless, rotting idiot Darnley was. Not a man, woman or child in Scotland would have objected if the Queen, as she certainly would have done once she escaped, either had her marriage annulled or sent her treacherous husband to the block."

Nelson reached down and picked up his cup, cradling it within his hands. "It is refreshing," he whispered, leaning toward Segalla, "to realise you don't know every step of the dance, Monsieur Segalla."

"Oh, it was a dance all right," the Jesuit replied. "A dance macabre which began as soon as the Queen left Kirk o'Field late in the evening of Sunday, ninth February, and made her way to the revels at Holyrood. In the Old Provost's House all fell silent. Bonkle the cook and the other servitors were gone. Many of Darnley's household had been sent elsewhere in preparation for Darnley's madcap scheme. Nevertheless, he felt secure, locked in his privy chamber with Taylor, Symonds, Gunn and, of course, Master Nelson, whom he never suspected."

The fire suddenly crackled, and Nelson started. Segalla gripped the pistol, levelling the barrel.

"It's only the flames," he said. "It was as silent as this in the Old Provost's House, wasn't it, Master Nelson? The wine is proffered, Darnley and his servants take a cup, but they don't know you've drugged it. After midnight—" Segalla cocked his head. "It was after midnight, wasn't it? You and your helpmate Symonds roused yourselves. The doors are locked, everyone is gone. You take a bolster and place it over the faces of your drugged companions and death comes quickly and silently. It's so easy. The men are tired and drugged: their murder is as simple as extinguishing the flame of a candle."

"And Darnley?" Nelson asked.

Segalla could see that the man's face had paled. He shook his head. "I don't know. Did you kill him immediately? Or did you and Symonds question him? Did he cry out as he realised the treachery he faced? Only God knows, because I am sure you will never tell me. Did you question him about the Queen's relations with my lord Bothwell? Whatever, the night is passing, not much time can be wasted, and so the Raven Master and his helpmate place the bolster over Darnley's face, sending his soul unprepared to eternity." Segalla paused. "Did you have Darnley manacled or fastened so as to leave no mark? It wouldn't be difficult: he was still weak, whilst you and Symonds were robust and strong. Once he was dead, however, you moved quickly. You had to make it look as if Darnley was killed fleeing from Kirk o'Field. You placed his corpse in a chair. No, no." Segalla held his hand up. "First, you go through the chamber searching for important documents, letters, anything which can be used to further your master's plans. You then hurry downstairs, smashing open the Queen's chamber. You hurriedly search it, taking away a casket of letters and any other document which may catch your eye; then you return upstairs. The bodies of Darnley and Taylor lie unmarked on the bed. You want to sustain that mystery, so you place Darnley's corpse on a chair and put it in the net you have hidden away."

"A net?" Nelson exclaimed.

"Yes, a net: the same used at warehouses when goods are lifted by crane to and from a wharf or cart. Only this net carries a grisly burden, Darnley tied in a chair. You open the casement window and, with the help of Symonds, lower Darnley's corpse to the ground." Segalla eased the muscles in his hand. "I suspect Symonds went down the rope and released Darnley's body, and took it into the orchard. He then returned and used the netting to climb back up to the casement window. And then it was Taylor's turn. The chair and net are raised, the corpse placed in it and lowered. After this, both you and Symonds clamber down. The net, containing the chair and Taylor's corpse, is taken into the orchard and placed next to his master's." Segalla paused. "You took them from the chair in the net, carrying each corpse in a way that the nightgowns were rucked back. You then left the chair, robe, rope and a dagger to make it look as if Darnley had been fleeing."

Nelson moved in his chair, and Segalla caught his sneer.

"Are you angry?" he asked. "Did you think your subtle plan was proof against any solution?" Segalla shrugged. "Indeed it was: a great mystery was posed. How was Kirk o'Field blown up? How did the King escape? And, if he was caught by his murderers, why was there no mark of violence on his body or that of Taylor's?"

"It would have worked!" Nelson snapped.

"Oh yes. You turned the entire matter on its head. How could people break into Kirk o'Field? If they did, how could they rouse Darnley but not his companions? If Darnley went down the stairs he would have met his murderers. If he climbed from the window in his nightclothes and jumped, then this would have left some mark upon his corpse. If he used the netting and chair, why didn't he rouse his companion to follow suit? And when he did escape—remember he was supposed to be fleeing through the night from his assassins—why bother to take a chair and netting with him?" Segalla changed the pistol from one hand to the other, wiping his sweaty fingers on his cloak.

Nelson saw the movement and tensed in his chair.

"I was as lost as any," Segalla declared. "But then I thought, why not start at the beginning? What if Darnley was murdered inside the house? And when I realised the netting was used, the pieces of the puzzle began to fit into place." He smiled again at Nelson. "The netting could only be useful to someone already in Kirk o'Field, and it also explained why the chair was left there. Finally, I put this question: if the rest were killed, why not Thomas Nelson? Here we have an explosion which levels the house, yet you and Symonds crawl out with a few cuts and grazes. You are even able to climb onto the wall and shout for help. Master Nelson, you would have made a good Jesuit. You acted the part so cleverly. The day you appeared before the Royal Commission in the Tolbooth you were still acting the role of the wounded innocent, loudly declaring that only someone from the Queen's household could have had access to Kirk o'Field."

"Aren't you running ahead of yourself?" Nelson snarled. "What about the explosion itself?"

"Oh, that was the easy part. Once you had laid the corpses out in the orchard, you slipped back into Kirk o'Field. Not through the casement window, but through the cellar door leading to the kitchen, fortuitously left open for you by Sandy Durham. In one of the outhouses, Moray or someone of his ilk had hidden away gunpowder."

"So, Master Durham and the Earl of Moray knew my identity?"

"Don't be stupid!" Segalla said. "They would receive their instructions from you, quietly and anonymously. Segalla paused as he heard a sound outside, but it was only the whining of the wind. "You and Symonds acted quickly: the powder was laid around the foundations, the fuse trail laid, and Kirk o'Field went up in a thunderous roar."

"But if Darnley was dead?" Nelson taunted. "Why blow up the Old Provost's House?"

"At first," Segalla replied, "I thought it was to deepen the plot and thicken the mystery. I suppose it did. However, the real reason for the explosion, and such a devastating one, was to cover up the crime you had committed in the house: the death of the other grooms, the violation of the Queen's chamber and the theft of her letters. After the house exploded, and the dust began to settle, you and Symonds raced back. You strip off your clothes, cover yourselves in dust, give yourselves a few grazes and bruises and, heigh-ho, the scene is set. Out of the wreckage these two innocent, bewildered, helpless servants are dragged. You continue to act such a part as long as you can." Segalla paused and pointed at the Raven Master. "No one will suspect you. Nor can your accomplices the Great Lords be blamed: Moray is in Fife, Morton is in St. Andrews and Lethington at Edinburgh Castle. Nevertheless, they seize the opportunity you presented, and a whispering campaign begins in Edinburgh. Placards are posted depicting the Queen and Bothwell as adulterous lovers, intent on murder."

Segalla, without dropping his gaze, sipped from his goblet.

Nelson leaned back in the chair and slowly clapped his hands. "Clever, clever priest. Why spoil a good tapestry, eh?"

"What do you mean?" Segalla asked.

"You were puzzled?" Nelson gibed. "Why Kirk o'Field was blown up but Darnley was found dead in an orchard yards away?"

Segalla kept his face impassive. Nelson, so proud of his achievement even in the face of death, did not want his grand scheme to be misunderstood.

"If Darnley had been killed in the explosion," Nelson said in a self-satisfied voice, "some people might claim it was an accident, or that Darnley himself was preparing to kill his own wife but the attempt went wrong. Or even that someone else lit the fuse, mistakenly believing the Queen had returned." He rubbed the side of his leg. "Darnley was hated," he spat out. "So he had to die in a manner which boldly screamed 'Murder!' but was tragic enough to arouse men's sympathy for him and suspicion against his wife."

"Of course!" Segalla said. "The young Prince, frightened of assassins sent by his wife, fleeing half-naked through the night."

"Precisely. Yet killed in a way which would intensify suspicion, with no mark or bruise. How could that be done in a muddy orchard at the dead of night?" He smirked. "Oh, I saw you puzzle about that. How your mind must have teemed! The really great mysteries, priest, are those which have as many solutions as there are questions. The explosion had to be seen as the reason for Darnley's flight as well as

211

concealing our plunder of the Queen's chamber. There had to be no doubt that Darnley was murdered during his escape." Nelson's grin widened. "So many mysteries behind an explosion, which also served other purposes."

"Such as?"

"Frightening off the cowardly Ker. He fled like a bird through the night. It was I who spread the rumour about his approach to Edinburgh: Bothwell's charging about the streets of Edinburgh looking for Ker truly was an unexpected reward. But go on, clever priest, now finish your story."

From the look in Nelson's eyes, Segalla knew the assassin was biding his time, waiting for some mistake or weakness on his part. He tightened his grip on the pistol.

"Once Darnley was dead and Kirk o'Field destroyed," Segalla continued, "you had two pieces of unfinished business. First, you hand over the casket of letters you stole from the Queen's chamber: Moray and the others can use these to draw up forgeries in the Queen's name which will serve as proof that she and Bothwell were adulterous conspirators to murder."

"And the second?" Nelson asked quietly.

"Oh, Symonds: he was useful, but no spy master trusts anyone. So you killed him. He'd served his purpose. You opened the window before you left that tavern, then climbed up the wall, cut Symonds's throat and ransacked his paltry pile of belongings. That made it look as if Darnley's murderers were still hunting you and, of course, gave you the pretext to both mislead and stay close to me."

Nelson stared back.

"Poor little Thomas," Segalla continued. "The hapless innocent feeding me tidbits, ever ready to help, always near, always watching. At last you concluded that your great scheme was prospering, so you fled south to Marshal Drury, the Governor of Berwick, Walsingham's eavesdropper on the Scottish march."

Nelson moved in the chair, his eyes on the pistol.

"Walsingham said you were clever," the Raven Master replied. "If I had my way, I'd have killed you. But there again, I thought you could be used. If Beaton's own envoy, a secret Jesuit priest, began to believe Mary was guilty—"

"And when I didn't," Segalla interrupted, "but began to hint that I knew the identity of the Raven Master as well as his role in Darnley's murder, you had to come back to kill me."

Nelson's eyes swept up to meet his.

"There was no need to kill me," Segalla said. "Why should you when there were two spies in my own camp? Master Vartlett and Mistress Lindsay: they work for Walsingham as well, don't they?"

"What makes you think that?"

"Only they and Beaton knew I was a Jesuit, yet Moray and the rest recognised me as one. True, some spy in France could have sent such a message, even Walsingham himself, but others seemed to know my thoughts and actions with an uncanny speed. The Queen I trust. Who else was left?"

Nelson did not bother to answer.

"Mistress Lindsay," Segalla continued, "knew so much about Darnley's death. Oh, not from you: the Raven Master was known only to Walsingham and confined himself to secret messages. Lindsay must have been closeted with Mary. Perhaps she and Vartlett knew Beaton mistrusted them: perhaps that was why he sent them with me: if they were traitors they would show their hands. Mistress Lindsay and Vartlett are, I suspect, professional spies who work for the highest bidder, and this occasion was no different. They told everything to Moray and, as I have said, you and that murderous lord have a secret way of communicating."

"But they didn't know who I was."

"No, they didn't, but, alarmed by what I had told them, they changed their plans. They didn't sail to France, but hastened to tell Drury at Berwick. Of course, the ubiquitous Thomas Nelson, the consummate actor, would listen to what they said." Segalla stood, gripping the musket more firmly. "You realised your house of cards was tumbling down. So back you came to kill me. I thought you would; it was too important a task to entrust to others."

"And, instead, I am trapped." Nelson smirked. "You cannot kill me, not you, a priest."

Segalla backed away. "I have the Queen's authority," he said. "Sworn under a great oath to carry out judgement against those who foully murdered her husband, Henry Darnley, King Consort of Scotland."

"No one would believe you," Nelson rasped.

"Who cares?" Segalla answered. "You have sown your seeds of destruction: Bothwell will be blamed for Darnley's death. His innocent walk through Edinburgh to search out the whereabouts of Ker of Fawdonside will, in time, become Darnley's gruesome death march. His followers will be captured. They will be tortured, broken and made to confess to anything their captors want." Segalla tightened his grip round the pistol's handle. "You even had the impudence to bait me, leaving messages at the tavern to unnerve and dismay me. Pride goeth before a fall, Master Nelson. I was led like a bullock with a ring through my nose. Moray and the rest thought they could even use me: I am shown the confessions of a tortured man and some clever forgeries so I will go back to France to tell Beaton that the Queen was guilty, somehow or other, in the death of her husband. Vartlett and Lindsay would simply confirm what I said."

Nelson forced a smile. "Fortune's fickle wheel," he said. "Vartlett and Lindsay are mercenaries. They work for both sides, though more for Walsingham than your parsimonious Archbishop."

"They signed your death warrant," Segalla retorted. "Lindsay was too pert, too swift in her conclusions, feeding me the accepted story, never wavering in her insistence that Darnley had been killed by forces outside Kirk o'Field. Once I knew she was a traitor, I concluded everything she told me must be an arrant lie. I also realised that what you said neatly agreed with her. Your air of bemused innocence became suspect, as well as your undue haste to leave Edinburgh. A matter of logic, Master Nelson: no one broke into Kirk o'Field, so why should Darnley flee? The murderer was one of his own household and now stands before me, guilty as Judas."

In the flickering firelight Nelson's face paled again; his eyes lost some of their arrogant certainty.

"You—you cannot," he stammered. "You will not kill me."

"I will carry out judgement," Segalla said. "I swear this before God: all those who had a hand in the murder of Darnley and the vilification of the Queen will face a bloody judgement in this world as well as the next. Look into my face, Thomas Nelson, and remember what your master has told you."

Nelson watched him fixedly.

"I am Nicholas Segalla, priest of the Jesuit order. Yet you have heard the whispers of your master! Where I came from and who I am are a mystery. In my long life, I must face one truth and accept it fully: betrayal, not death, is the greatest pain."

"Who are you?" Nelson whispered.

"Ask your master in hell."

"And what about Vartlett and Lindsay?" the Englishman snarled. "Will they suffer judgement?"

Segalla smiled. "Walsingham in London will gnash his teeth and quiver in anger at how those two fools were trapped into taking a message which sent his beloved Raven Master to his death. They will, in God's good time, pay for their treachery. Now—" Segalla deliberately turned his back, using both hands to cock farther back the pistol's hammer. "I must go," he said.

He heard a sound behind him and turned even as Nelson drew the dirk from the top of his boot.

"You were given your chance," Segalla said.

Nelson's hand kept rising quickly to throw the dagger, even as Segalla pulled the trigger of the pistol. The cottage became engulfed in smoke and the crack of the pistol sounded like thunder. The ball took Nelson straight full in the heart; his hand holding the dagger dropped. As the smoke cleared, Nelson, blood bubbling from the corner of his mouth, staggered forward. He stared glassy-eyed at Segalla, then crumpled to a heap on the floor.

Segalla placed the pistol on the table.

"Judgement is passed," he whispered. "Those who live by the sword shall surely die by the sword. You murdered by gunpowder in the dead of night, so you die by gunpowder in the dead of night."

Segalla shivered. He picked up his cloak and wrapped it round him. He then took a burning brand from the fire and threw it on the straw strewn on the cottage floor. The flames greedily caught at the dry kindling. Segalla picked up his saddlebags and walked out into the night.

For a while Segalla stared across the ruins of Kirk o'Field. Even as the cottage behind him burst into flames, he stood, recalling Mary, vivacious and flirtatious, the first day she had received him. Segalla made the sign of the cross and, turning away, strode through the darkness to his waiting horse.

Conclusion

A nn Dukthas sat in the small, very comfortable pub, the Golden Lamb, in a side street off Westminster. Through the window she could glimpse the spires and ornamental turrets of Westminster Cathedral. Now and again she smoothed the manila envelope containing the manuscript the mysterious Segalla had given her two weeks before. She had received a telephone call from him the previous evening, short and cryptic, instructing her where to go.

"Be there," he said. "Please, at one o'clock. "Your flight tickets and other papers will be waiting for you at the Aer Lingus desk at Dublin airport."

He had hung up the telephone before Ann could ask even one of the many questions that had teemed in her mind since she had finished reading the manuscript. A large grandfather clock standing in the far corner of the lounge began to chime quietly. Ann looked towards the door but could see no one so returned to her own thoughts. Was the Segalla who had given her the manuscript the same man who had worked so assiduously on Mary Stuart's behalf in those bleak, far gone February days in Scotland? How could it be? Ann had done her own research in this, at both the public and the university libraries. She had read the different histories of magic. Again and again, she had come across the legend of a man who had never died and who was known in successive epochs.

"Impossible!" she muttered to herself.

"Nothing under the sun is impossible, Ann."

She looked up; Segalla was standing before her. He was

dressed elegantly in a black coat, a woollen scarf round his neck, on his head a dark trilby, which he swept off and held as he smiled down at her. He stretched out a hand and took hers: his grip was warm and firm.

"I am sorry," he said as he sat opposite her. "But the traffic is growing impossible." He loosened his coat buttons, took his scarf off and threw it over the small briefcase he carried. "Do you wish to eat?" he asked. "They provide a very good lunch."

"No thank you." Ann smiled, silently cursing her nervousness. "Perhaps a vodka and tonic?"

Segalla smiled and called the waiter over. "A vodka and tonic and"—he smiled—"yes, a glass of your best claret."

For a while Segalla sat, staring down at the package on the table in front of Ann. Once the drinks had been served, she picked the package up and handed it to him.

"You want this back?"

"No, no." Segalla's dark face broke into a smile. "It's yours to do as you think fit: print it, publish it, burn it or dismiss it as a piece of madness."

"Are you the same Segalla?" Ann asked.

The man spread his elegant hands. Ann glimpsed the silver watch and the finely etched cufflinks in the heavy cuffs of the silk shirt.

"Ann, how can a man live for four hundred years?" he said teasingly.

"Are you he?" Ann repeated.

"Would it make any difference if I were?" Segalla sipped from his glass of wine. "I'll answer any question," he added, "apart from that."

"But you make reference to it," Ann insisted.

Segalla shrugged. "I wrote a story for you. What the Americans call faction: a truth expressed in the form of a parable. I told the truth as I saw it. I write from the heart."

"Is it the truth?" Ann asked. "Did Nelson kill Darnley?"

"Yes, he did."

Segalla's face grew sombre and Ann had no more illusions: whatever the rest of the world might think, the man sitting opposite her had been present during those dark days of 1567.

"But," she protested, "the history books say different."

"Until five hundred years ago," Segalla replied, "most people thought the world was flat. Popular opinion, even the wisdom of the learned, does not necessarily constitute the truth."

"But all the accounts of Kirk o'Field," Ann persisted. "All the accounts, even scholarly works like Antonia Fraser's *Mary Queen of Scots,* maintain that Bothwell and his henchmen blew up Kirk o'Field." She took the package from the table and put it down beside her. "They do not necessarily blame him for Darnley's death. They even argue there were other gangs hiding in the darkness who caught Darnley as he fled."

Segalla leaned his elbows on the table and shook his head. "You have read my story, Ann. Look at the facts. Go to the Record Office in Chancery Lane: the drawing I made at Kirk o'Field." He smiled. "Now I have answered your first question; that drawing shows Darnley and Taylor lying in the orchard and, beside them, a robe, a chair, a dagger and a net."

"Yes, yes," Ann said. "I have seen a copy, but the net looks like a pile of cordage or rope."

"That's how I drew it," Segalla said. "From memory, but the mind plays tricks. Study that pile of rope carefully. Put it under a microscope. You will find, on closer examination, that the rope is really a pile of netting." He opened his briefcase and handed her a leather-bound book. "This is a study of Darnley's death written in 1930 by Major-General Mahon and published by Cambridge University Press. Now, turn to page one hundred ten."

Ann did so. On the page was a portion of the drawing of 1567 showing the personal effects that had been found near Darnley's corpse. This drawing, however, had been enlarged.

"What do you see?" Segalla asked.

"The dagger, the rope, the chair." Ann took out her glasses and put them on. She looked up in surprise. "What looks like a pile of rope in the original drawing is really netting."

Segalla put the book down. "Exactly. Mahon's book is probably one of the most scholarly studies of Darnley's death ever written, yet even he is baffled by Darnley's death and overlooks such evidence."

"The copy of the drawing in the Record Office," Ann said, "is the one you sent with Lindsay?"

Segalla nodded.

"What happened to them, her and Vartlett?"

Segalla's face remained impassive. "They disappeared as Nelson did."

"Now," Ann shook her head. "You claim Nelson was killed—"

"I know what you are going to say," Segalla interrupted. "Scotland did slide into civil war after Darnley's death. In May 1568, Mary was finally defeated at Langside. Bothwell had already fled abroad so Mary crossed the Solway into England, where she was taken into honourable captivity."

"Her death wish?" Ann intervened.

"At the time, yes. Mary was tired, depressed, sick of government and the politicking which flourished around her. Perhaps she was tired of ruling and thought Elizabeth might let her live in honourable retirement. Instead, Mary was moved from one prison to another. Now, Elizabeth held two investigations into Darnley's murder. The records of these so-called trials at York and Westminster are still with us, and Nelson's evidence at them plays a crucial role. But if you look at the documents carefully, they are described as the depositions of Thomas Nelson drawn up and endorsed by Elizabeth's Secretary of State, William Cecil."

"You mean—"

"Of course." Segalla half laughed. "Isn't it strange that, at

220

neither of these so-called trials at York or Westminster, Nelson and Symonds, the only two survivors of the explosion, were ever called in person? Nothing but depositions in Nelson's name." Segalla sighed. "Even then they tried to twist the truth: in these so-called depositions of Nelson, Mary is even accused of moving the beautiful bed she'd bought for Darnley out of Kirk o'Field before the explosion. Historians have shown this to be a lie."

"And the accepted story?" Ann asked. "In his book *Mary Queen of Scots,* the Duke of Hamilton lists fifteen murderers of Darnley." Ann opened her own bag, drew out the book and turned to an appendix. "All except two of them died violently."

Segalla took the book from her hands and stared at the list of names. "Aye." He closed the book and handed it back. "Bothwell was later accused of the murder. Some of his retinue were tortured. All of these confessed to a hand in the murder. But tell me, Ann, in any court in Europe would the confessions of men who had been tortured and then hanged hold much sway in a court of law?"

She shook her head.

"Of course not!" Segalla sipped his wine. "That was the beauty of the plot. Everything we know about Darnley's death comes either from the lips of tortured men who were given little time to recant or from letters supposedly written by Mary, the so-called Casket Letters. Isn't it strange that the originals of the Casket Letters have not survived? Moreover, apart from the confessions of tortured men, there is no other evidence either that Mary and Bothwell were lovers or that they plotted Darnley's death!" He leaned back in his chair and pointed at the book Ann was still holding. "Open it again. What happened to Patrick Wilson?"

"I don't have to open it," Ann said. "There's just a question mark beside his name, which indicates he disappeared."

"Of course he did," Segalla said. "Racked, tortured and

murdered. Wilson's body was probably tossed in some hole once Morton, Moray and Lethington had finished with him."

"And did you exact revenge?" Ann asked.

"Why do you ask that?"

Ann sipped her vodka to hide her nervousness. "It's just that . . ."

Segalla leaned across the table and grasped her by the hand.

"I am teasing you," he said. "Why should I make you ask what I already know? Remember, Ann, Segalla, in the manuscript you read, was given a commission directly by his Queen. Nelson was executed; in 1570 James Earl of Moray was shot by a secret assassin; the following year Darnley's father suffered the same fate; two years later Lethington committed suicide, drinking poison in Edinburgh Castle. Eight years afterwards Morton was sent to the 'Maiden,' the Scots' name for the new guillotine."

"And Sandy Durham?" Ann asked.

"Oh, read Miss Strickland's *Life of Mary Queen of Scots;* for a porter Durham received rapid promotion from my lord of Moray."

"But," Ann said, "late in the summer of 1567, Durham disappeared."

Segalla just stared at her.

"Were you behind their deaths?" Ann asked.

Segalla dropped his eyes. "God was!" he said.

"And Mary?"

Segalla rested his chin on his fist. "Oh, I had a hand in some of the many plots to free her, but it was impossible. Walsingham was intent on her death."

"And Bothwell?"

"He fled to Dragsholme in Denmark. There was little I could do for him: a good soldier but a bad counsellor."

"Did he feed Mary drugs?"

Segalla glanced up at her. "Yes, yes, I think he did. Even he used the Queen: loyal but wrongheaded."

"And Walsingham, surely," Ann said, "he should have been punished?"

"Oh, I watched him for years," Segalla said. "Do you know, he was personally involved in Mary's execution at Fotheringay. One of his agents hired a reprobate called Bull and promised him ten pounds to execute the Queen."

"That wasn't my question," Ann said. "I have read Lady Fraser's biography; Walsingham's spite and malice are more than apparent. Yet he died in his bed?"

Segalla's eyes became hard. "Read your books again, Ann," he said. "Some say Walsingham died of the dropsy, that his body became swollen and putrid. Some say it was the hand of God. Others say it was old age." His gaze shifted away again. "Walsingham managed to steal Mary's black pearls. Perhaps they brought him ill luck." Segalla looked fiercely at Ann. "A few," he whispered, "those who know such matters, say Walsingham died a cruel death, slowly poisoned." He leaned over and touched the brown package. "This is yours," he said. "Everything that is written in it is based on the truth. Publish it if you wish, and if people question you, ask them this question: How is it that the house of Kirk o'Field was blown to smithereens but, according to his own confession, Thomas Nelson, whom I knew as the Raven Master, managed to crawl out with a few cuts and grazes? Once you start with that, the mystery will unfold." He pointed to the window, towards Westminster Abbey. "You should go there," he said. "King James later brought his mother's corpse from Peterborough and buried it there in splendour. Mary, born to be Queen of England, now lies buried amongst the kingdom's other monarchs. Look at the spires, look at them, Ann!"

Ann looked over her shoulder and stared at the roof and towers of England's great mauseleum. She recalled Mary's own words, which she had embroidered whilst in captivity at Sheffield: "IN THE END IS MY BEGINNING." Ann found herself

223

whispering the words aloud: when she turned round, the seat opposite her was empty, the wine glass drained. Segalla had disappeared. Ann picked up the package and stared at the door.

"Madam?" The waiter came over. "Madam, the gentleman apologises but he said not to worry. You will surely meet him again."

Author's Note

I do not wish to rehearse what is written here: all the dramatis personae mentioned in this story once lived, breathed, loved and hated. Virtually ninety-five percent of what I have written is based on historical fact.

As for Nelson's being the killer:

1. In the spring of 1567, Drury at Berwick wrote to Cecil, "Darnley took a long time dying and did much pleading for his life." How did Drury know this? Nelson had arrived in Berwick just before that letter was written, yet was never seen alive again. All Nelson's later evidence was drawn up by Cecil and Walsingham.

2. On Monday, 10 February 1567, Mary wrote to Beaton in Paris that Kirk o'Field had been blown up "with such a vehemency, that of the whole lodging, walls and other, there is nothing remaining, no, not one stone upon another."

But how does this agree with Nelson's account published by Lang in 1819:

"He never knew of anything until the house wherein they lay was falling about them, out of which this deponer, (Nelson) escaped and stood upon the ruinous wall. . . ."

Finally, regarding the man who never dies: many people know about the Count of St. Germain who appeared in France in 1620, 1730, 1789 (Marie Antoinette wrote that she had not only met him but wished she had heeded his warnings). He met the Duc de Berri before the latter's murder in 1820: Emperor Napoleon III actually set up an Imperial Commission to investigate the phenomenon, but its reports were destroyed in a mysterious fire. In the U.S.A. he has also been seen: before the outbreak of World War II, both scientists and the Secret Service searched for a man who talked about plutonium long before that term was ever invented. Segalla may be he, or just one of a secret Cabal of people who never die.

Build yourself a library of paperback mysteries to die for—DEAD LETTER

NINE LIVES TO MURDER by Marian Babson
When actor Winstanley Fortescue takes a nasty fall—or was he pushed?—he finds himself trapped in the body of Monty, the backstage cat.
_____ 95580-4 ($4.99 U.S.)

THE BRIDLED GROOM by J. S. Borthwick
While planning their wedding, Sarah and Alex—a Nick and Nora Charles of the 90's—must solve a mystery at the High Hope horse farm.
_____ 95505-7 ($4.99 U.S./$5.99 Can.)

THE FAMOUS DAR MURDER MYSTERY
by Graham Landrum
The search for the grave of a Revolutionary War soldier takes a bizarre turn when the ladies of the DAR stumble on a modern-day corpse.
_____ 95568-5 ($4.50 U.S./$5.50 Can.)

COYOTE WIND by Peter Bowen
Gabriel Du Pré, a French-Indian fiddle player and part-time deputy, investigates a murder in the state of mind called Montana.
_____ 95601-0 ($4.50 U.S./$5.50 Can.)

As storm clouds gather over Europe and FDR receives such guests as Albert Einstein, Joe Kennedy and crime buster Eliot Ness, Eleanor is thrust into danger much closer to home. One of the President's staff has been found dead, poisoned by cyanide mixed in his evening bourbon. Even worse, the accused killer is another White house aide, diminutive beauty Thérèse Rolland.

Although the police are determined to pin the crime on Thérèse, Eleanor is immediately convinced she is innocent. Calmly, but firmly, the First Lady uncovers a web of lies and secrets swirling around the Louisiana political machine...until another shocking murder is discovered. Suddenly, the investigation is taking Eleanor Roosevelt places no proper First Lady would ever go—to the darkest underside of society, and toward a shattering truth that lies within the White House itself!

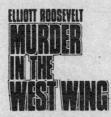

ELLIOTT ROOSEVELT
MURDER IN THE WEST WING

An Eleanor Roosevelt Mystery

"Compelling!" —*Kirkus*

MURDER IN THE WEST WING
Elliott Roosevelt
_____ 95144-2 $4.99 U.S./$5.99 Can.